Brim Over Boot

The Darling Brothers Book 2

Emmy Sanders

Beta Reading by Christie, Jen & Maxie of Smut Readers Society, and Willow

Editing by M.A. Hinkle

Proofreading by Lori Parks

Cover Design by Natasha Snow Designs

A special thank you to RJ Boerstler and Blair Wynters for your help with Remi

ISBN: 9781967130122

Content Warning: This book includes mention of past parental death.

For anyone who's ever watched a farrier get nibbled on...and was jealous of the horse.

Contents

Note to Readers

This series includes a character who's Deaf and several characters who use American Sign Language. Please note ASL and English do not share the same grammatical structure. However, for ease of reading, ASL conversations are written using English grammar.

Chapter 1

COLTON

Noah King.

The bane of my existence. The thorn in my boot. The man who's dedicated fifteen years of his life to thwarting me at every twist and turn.

Bet he wouldn't be so smug if my nippers could meet his balls.

I snort at the thought, and the mare I'm shoeing tries to tug her hoof away.

"Sorry, sorry," I tell her, reaching back to pat her leg. "You're doing good. Almost done, girl."

I finish clipping off the ends of the horseshoe nails before setting my nippers aside. It only takes another minute after that to crimp the nails down, clean the outside of her hoof, and let her go. I toss the rasp back in my bag, dusting my hands on my chaps as I look out over the misty morning on the Allens' farm.

It's damn cold for being the start of spring, dew still on the ground and a definite nip in the air that has me tugging my gloves back on quickly. Even so, my hometown of Darling, Montana is beautiful no matter the time of year. I've always thought so. Never really had a desire to leave, if I'm being honest.

Part of that probably has to do with my family, close as we are. But part of it, I'm sure, is because I've simply never felt the need to see what else is out there. Maybe I'm just a homebody. Or maybe I was born in the place that's right for me.

I don't much care when it comes down to it. I love Montana. I love the mountains, my job as a farrier, even our quaint downtown and the tourists we get throughout the year who stop here hoping to experience a little slice of life that's so foreign to them yet simply part of my everyday existence. I love Darling, period.

Even though I have to share my town with a certain infuriating King.

I pull out my phone, huffing a breath as I listen to the voicemail I've already heard a good dozen times.

"*Hey, Colton*," the voice of Henrietta Brooke says. "*I was hoping to catch you in person, but it seems a voicemail will have to do. There's no easy way to say this, but we've decided to switch our services to Noah. Times have been hard, and, well, he was able to cut us a deal. I hope you understand.*"

The recording ends, and I blow out an exhalation that whitens the air.

Another client. Stolen.

By Noah fucking King.

I shove my phone in my pocket and start collecting my gear, making sure I have all my tools packed and the area cleaned up before tugging off my chaps and plopping my hat back on my head. I cross paths with Tipper Allen on my way off his farm.

"Hey there, Colt. Any issues today?"

"Not a one," I tell him, knocking my hat up so I can see him better. "Miss Bonnie should be good for another six weeks, but just give me a holler if you have any issues in the meantime. She's a real sweet horse. Always love visiting her."

"She loves you, too," he says easily. "Wouldn't even let our last farrier near. I don't know what sort of magic you've got in that bag of yours, but don't lose it."

I huff a laugh. "It's not magic, Tipp. I just listen to what Bonnie's telling me. Don't hesitate to give me a call if you need to, all right?"

"Will do. Have a good day, Colt."

I bid farewell to Mr. Allen and get into my truck, the heavy-duty pickup in need of a good wash. Maybe I'll get to that later, assuming the sun sticks around.

Bonnie was my only client for the morning, so I head home, the wooden sign at the start of our gravel drive welcoming me. *Darling Ranch.* The place I was born, raised, and still live at thirty-seven years old. I could have moved out by now, maybe even built my own house on the property the way my brother Jackson did.

But I like staying close to my roots. My parents both live in their own cottages beside the main ranch house. Jackson is down a short quarter-mile-long drive. Remi, the youngest of us, is in the room next to mine, and even Lawson, our eldest brother, is back at home after separating from his soon-to-be ex-wife.

This ranch—it's ours. It's always been ours, back generations. Heck, back to when the town of Darling was founded by my great-great-great-something-grandfather.

This place? It's home. A damn good one.

Why would I want to leave?

I park in the busy lot in front of the house, a good couple dozen vehicles already occupying the space. The ranch hands are hard at work this time of day, some having started their shifts at an ungodly four in the morning.

Thank the heavens I was able to sleep in till eight.

I kick my boots against the mat at the front door before heading inside. When I reach the kitchen, I stop still and smirk.

"Necking where the biscuits are made? Really?"

My brother Jackson aims a glare my way as his boyfriend, and our ranch house cook, snorts. Ash is sitting atop the counter, looking nonplussed at being caught making out like a teenager, when he and my brother are far from it.

"Out," Jackson grunts.

Ash gives him a gentle shove, dropping down from the countertop. "It's fine. You need to get back to work anyway. Morning, Colton."

"Morning," I answer happily, heading for the fridge. "Don't suppose we have any bacon left from breakfast?"

Ash gives me a sympathetic look that answers my question. *Ah, well.* Guess that's what I get for missing the four o'clock meal.

"There might be some sausage links in the bottom drawer," he says, tucking his wavy blonde hair behind his ear. "You're back early. Done for the day?"

"Not in the least," I tell him, finding the sausages and letting out a triumphant, *"Aha."* Jackson rolls his eyes as I pull a link free and snap it in half with my teeth. "Got a busy afternoon. Just stopping back for a breather."

"Well, I'll be out on the porch if anyone needs me," Ash says, giving Jackson a pat on the chest as he passes. My brother watches him walk off, a lovesick expression on his face that never ceases to amuse me.

"You're so whipped," I mutter.

My brother smacks me on the shoulder hard enough that I almost fumble my second sausage link.

"Watch it!" I cry.

"You're such a shit," he grumbles. "Don't know why I even put up with you."

"Uh. Because we're family? It's what you do."

Jackson mutters a "Yeah, yeah" before grabbing his hat and heading out of the kitchen. I follow him into the large dining room at the back of the house as I finish my snack, the floor-to-ceiling windows letting in plenty of light and a rather sweeping view of the ranchland itself. Not to mention Ash, who's atop his yoga mat on the wraparound porch, running through some stretches.

"He doing okay?" I ask Jackson.

I had no clue Ash is living with chronic back pain until an incident last fall caused a major flare-up. He's doing better now, but still...

"He's all right," Jackson answers, voice a little gruffer than usual. "What're you following me for? Something on your mind?"

Shit. He knows me well.

I work my jaw for a second before spitting out three syllables I hate uttering, whether aloud or inside my own head. "Noah King."

"Ah," Jackson says, settling his hat back on his head. "What'd he do this time?"

"Took another client from me, Jackson. It's gotta stop."

My big brother by three years looks at me and sighs. His blue eyes, same as mine, radiate a stern sort of calm. "Is it really that big of a deal, Colt? You've got plenty of clients. I know you do. Your schedule is full, and you're not hurting financially. So what if Noah picks off a few?"

"So what?" I parrot. "It's the damn principle of the matter. He's always had it out for me, and I'm sick of it."

"Did you ever fix things with Marie Doherty?" he asks.

I cringe.

I *might* have implied to Mrs. Doherty that Noah was a less-than-skilled farrier, an honest mistake on my part that caused Marie to hire me and fire Noah. Noah was...not exactly thrilled to lose what amounted to thirty horses' worth of work.

"I tried to fix it," I tell my brother. "I did. I told her I was just in a bad mood that day and what I said was unfair and untrue, and I'd understand perfectly if she wanted to rehire Noah instead of keeping me on. She didn't. That's not my fault, Jackson. I don't know what else I could've done other than quit, and I wasn't gonna do that."

He grunts. "Colt, I know you won't wanna hear this, but I don't think he's the only one in the wrong here."

I sputter, but Jackson holds up a hand and goes on.

"You know I love you, and I *know* you'd never try to be underhanded on purpose. But you and Noah have let this animosity go on for far too long. Maybe if you just...stopped bristling every time the man's name is mentioned, the two of you could figure out how to coexist peacefully for once."

"I don't bristle," I defend.

"You bristle," he says flatly. "You're bristling right now."

I let my shoulders come down.

"Darling has more than enough horses for two farriers," Jackson says seriously. "Y'all are only rivals because you make it so. Why do you even hate the guy so much? What'd he ever do to you?"

"Other than try to steal all my clients?" I retort.

Jackson simply raises an eyebrow.

I throw my hands in the air with a huff. "I don't *know*, okay? He hated me on sight. He was an absolute asshole the first time I met him, and he hasn't stopped being one since. Maybe you should ask *him* why he hates *me* so much. I didn't do a goddamn thing to deserve it."

"Well," Jackson mumbles, pulling the door to outside open, a crisp breeze taking the opportunity to blow in. "I think you either needa sit down with Noah and talk this thing out or let it go. You let the man have too much of a hold over you, Colt. And that, whether or not you wanna admit it, is entirely your choice."

His piece spoken, my brother walks out the door, stopping only long enough to say a quick goodbye to Ash that involves locked lips and schmoopy expressions.

I don't *let* Noah have a hold over me, do I? Anyone would be justifiably indignant in my shoes. Noah King is a right asshole, and all of this—the fighting, the client stealing, the *rivalry* between us, as Jackson called it—is wholly his fault. It's been his fault since the start.

Well, there's one thing I know for certain. Sitting down with Noah isn't going to happen. Not ever.

But there ain't no way I'm letting it go.

Chapter 2

NOAH

"Morning, Noah."

"Jenna," I greet, plunking my handful of groceries onto the conveyor belt at the front of the store. "How're you?"

"Just fine, thanks. You see the buttercups blooming down the road? Spring is here."

"Sure is," I agree, pulling out my wallet as Jenna rings up a package of bacon, followed by a bag of all-purpose flour.

"Get your bike out yet?" she asks.

I give a brisk nod. With the snow having melted in town apart from a few parking lot drifts here and there, today was Daphne's first trip out. It always feels good, the first ride of the season. Like stretching my legs or, hell, a long-needed orgasm.

Speaking of...

"You still haven't taken *me* for a ride," Jenna says, tone switching from conversational to...decidedly not.

"I'm much too old for you, Jenna."

It's a point I've argued more than once, although it hasn't stopped Jenna's flirting.

She looks me up and down. Slowly. "You're kidding, right?"

"You're, what—twenty-five?"

"Twenty-six," she corrects.

"Which makes me twelve years your senior."

"Honey, there ain't nothing *senior* about you."

I shake my head, putting my wallet back in my pocket as the machine spits out a receipt. "The answer is no."

"Fine," she says breezily, handing my shopping bag over. "Enjoy your day."

I tip my head in a nod before exiting Plum's Grocers, bag in hand. It's not that I find Jenna unattractive, but my days of casually fooling around are long behind me. At thirty-eight, very little appeals to me about a romp in the sheets that results in the space next to me turning cold within minutes. And considering I *know* Jenna flirts with just about any age-appropriate—or possibly inappropriate—guy around, I highly doubt it's me she wants. Just a good time.

And I can appreciate that. Find it flattering, even.

Doesn't mean I'm interested.

Although I sure haven't put much effort into settling down, have I? I'm not even sure I want that. Not sure what I want, truth be told.

My thoughts come to an abrupt halt as I spot a face I'd recognize anywhere, the man himself strutting my way across the parking lot. Well, not directly my way, but walking toward the front of the grocery store I just left, smiling at the ground in that way he does. Always smiling. Always so damn *happy* for no conceivable reason.

Except...

Yep. There it is. Colton goddamn Darling lifts his dark head of hair, locks eyes with me, and scowls. Just like that.

I'd laugh if it wasn't so utterly maddening.

He doesn't say a word. Neither do I. The golden boy of Darling, Montana glares me down with ice-blue eyes until he's past, his boots plodding heavily against the asphalt.

I continue on toward Daphne, my motorcycle shining bright red in the midmorning light. With a little more force than necessary, I open up the saddlebags behind the seat and transfer my groceries inside.

Always found the name *saddlebags* a little ironic, considering my profession. Though I suppose Daphne does have plenty of horsepower of her own.

Zipping up the bags, I grab my helmet, mount my bike, and pull out of the parking lot. The house I share with my uncle isn't all that far from the center of town, just an eight-minute drive down paved roads. I spot the field of buttercups Jenna mentioned on my way, as well as a few other early season wildflowers starting to poke through the soil and still-brown grasses. The mountains, of course, sit high and wide in the distance, orange dancing off their peaks from the sun.

I slow as I turn onto the road where I live, pulling into my driveway not long after and cutting the engine. We have neighbors on both sides, but the houses aren't close together, affording privacy I appreciate. I'll need to do some upkeep on the property soon, now that the temperatures are on the upswing. But, for today, I grab the groceries and head inside to make a rather late breakfast.

I can hear my uncle getting a start on his day as I settle inside the kitchen, turning the burner on and placing a cast-iron skillet overtop. I lay down the strips of bacon I bought before pulling eggs out of the fridge.

"Morning," comes my uncle's voice less than a minute later.

"Smell of bacon get you moving?" I joke.

He snorts, using his walker to navigate over to the coffeemaker. The pot finishes spitting the last of the brew, and my uncle pours a cup into his favorite chipped mug. "If anything could get me moving, it'd be bacon, that's for sure."

He takes a seat at the kitchen table, maneuvering gingerly in a way that causes my chest to pinch. My uncle isn't a young man. Seventy-six now, although his scoliosis and arthritis are contributing factors to his lack of mobility. He likes to pretend it doesn't bother him, when I know it does. Even so, I give him a smile, not letting my own concern show.

"Didn't expect to see you here this morning," he goes on, smoothing out the newspaper I brought in on my way inside. "You should be out enjoying your weekend."

"That so?" I ask, flipping the bacon in the skillet to an accompanying sizzle. "And what sort of wild fun do you think I should be getting up to at eleven o'clock on a Saturday morning?"

He snorts, even as he shakes his head. "A date, how about? You haven't had one of those in a while."

I set down my tongs and turn to face my uncle. "Walter. Don't you tell me you're gonna start meddling in my love life now. You said you never would."

"I know, I know," he says, waving me off. "I'm not *meddling*. Just an observation."

"Mhm. Maybe next time, observe in silence."

He laughs, a hearty, booming thing. My uncle may be weaker than he once was, but his strength of spirit is as strong as ever. As is his sass. "With charm like that, I can't believe you don't have dates lined up down the block."

I shake my head and turn back to the stove, my lips twitching. "I'll have you know I got asked out just this morning."

Well...more like I got asked to take Jenna for a *ride*. But I don't think my uncle needs to hear those specifics.

"So what are you doing here?" he asks.

"Guess I just prefer your company more."

He mutters something about *charming, indeed*, but what I said isn't a lie. I love my uncle dearly. He's the closest thing I have to a parent, considering my own passed away when I was seventeen. Walter took me in all those years ago, no questions asked.

I don't know where I'd be without him. Certainly not here, in Darling, Montana.

"Wanna play some chess after breakfast?" I ask, dumping the bowl of whipped eggs into a pan to cook.

"When have I ever said no to chess?"

"Well, just last week," I remind him. "When I was on a winning streak, and you kept losing and losing and—"

"All right," he cuts in, slicing a hand through the air in a dismissive gesture. "No need to dredge up the past."

I snort, folding the eggs with a spatula before flipping the bacon again. I ready a plate with a paper towel to dry the grease off.

"Noah," my uncle says seriously, his tone of voice enough to have my focus shifting fully. "You don't have to be here."

"Walt..."

"I'm serious. You've got your own life to live, kiddo. You don't gotta stick around with my sorry ass out of some misguided sense of—"

"I'm not leaving," I tell him firmly. "This, right here, is where I wanna be. End of discussion."

"Stubborn boy," my uncle mutters, although he sounds fond.

"Learned from the best," I shoot back, pulling the bacon off the skillet and laying it on the paper towel, piece by piece.

"Yeah, well, my brother sure knew how to dig his heels in when he wanted something accomplished," Walter says. "Remember that shed he built for your ma? Thing was crooked as could be, but he finished it all by himself. Picked up the pieces by himself, too, when it fell down not a year later. Your father had many talents, but carpentry was not one of 'em."

Memories of that bright green garden shed ping around in my chest, both aching and sweetly familiar. I clear my throat before looking back at my uncle.

"I was talking about you, Walt."

"What?" he asks, jerking enough to unintentionally flip a page in his newspaper. "Kid, you were fully grown by the time you came here. Only thing I taught you was the right way to cook eggs. You're not burning those, by the way, are you?"

I shake my head, keeping my laughter to myself as I pull the pan of eggs off the heat. For all the ways in which Walter took up the mantle when I needed him most, he still can't fathom the effect he had on me.

Maybe one day I'll get it through his head.

"Oh boy," he says mildly, slapping his newspaper shut.

"What is it?"

"Nothing whatsoever," my uncle lies, taking a sip from his nearly empty coffee mug.

I set his plate down in front of him, steam wafting up from the eggs. "Mhm. Try again."

"Nothing you needa see."

I let out a sigh, retrieving the ketchup from the fridge for my uncle before snagging the paper from underneath his palm.

"I warned ya," he says.

Flipping the paper open, I find the local advertisements. Fucking knew it.

"New client special. First shoeing is free! You and your horse will appreciate the Darling touch. Call today."

"Colton goddamn Darling," I mutter, shoving the newspaper closed. "First shoeing for *free*. Fuck."

My uncle winces, not even needing to vocalize his thoughts. That's going to cost me clients.

"It's just business," he says, doing his best to soothe my rattled nerves.

I shake my head, tossing the paper in the recycling bin. "He's got plenty of business. This is personal. It's always personal with him."

My uncle holds his tongue until I've sat down beside him, my own plate in front of me. "You could always head back to Lincoln. There are plenty of farms and cattle ranches down there in need of a good farrier."

"We've got farms and cattle ranches here. I'm not leaving."

He shrugs, and I shovel a bite of eggs into my mouth, my thoughts stuck on the man who's gone out of his way to make sure I feel unwelcome here in Darling. Well, he should damn well know by now he's not going to run me off.

Colton Darling may have been born in this town. He may have the perfect *Darling* name backing his reputation. But I won't be coerced into leaving the only family I have left by a pompous man-child who wouldn't know a balanced shoe if it hit him upside the head.

I'll figure out a way to put Colton in his rightful place one of these days. To reveal the *golden boy* for the uncaring, selfish ass he is.

This town, it's my home.

And I'll fight to keep it.

Chapter 3

COLTON

'What about this one?' my brother signs before tapping the white hat on the rack in front of us. He's wearing his processor over the back of his ear, but I sign back without asking whether or not it's on.

I don't mind ASL over voice one bit, and Remi prefers the former.

'I'm not sure,' I tell him. *'I think I like brown better.'*

I'm also fairly certain Noah wears a white hat, and there's no way I want to match him, on purpose or incidentally.

Remi pulls one of the brown hats off the rack with a question in his eye. Now *that* one I like just fine. He passes it over, and I weigh it in my hands before trying it on.

'What happened to your other hat?' Remi asks, his motions loose and distracted as he eyes a few baseball caps nearby.

I groan, *really* not wanting to answer that.

Remi looks back at me with a raised brow.

'Heather,' I finally spell.

'The girl you...'

He doesn't finish his sentence, but he bounces his eyebrows in an obvious manner.

'The girl I used to,' I correct. *'This was just a...slip.'*

Heather and I dated briefly last year. We cut things off before it got too serious, a mutual decision. Guess I was just feeling a little lonely the other night when I ran into her at The Barrel, our town's one and only bar. Unfortunately for me, unless I want to go *back* to Heather's, my hat will remain forever lost.

Remi snorts. *'Get the brown one. Looks good.'*

I nod, plucking the hat off my head.

'Your hair's getting long,' my brother adds idly. *'Want me to cut it?'*

I consider that, fingers drifting through the strands curling now at my nape and around my ears, before I shake my head. *'I'll keep it for now.'*

He lifts his hands to say something else when a figure comes around the corner, bumping into me and sending me bumping into Remi. I help my brother catch his balance before turning to face...

Of course.

Noah fucking King.

"Oh, sorry. I—" The man cuts off abruptly, his eyes meeting mine before his teeth shut with an audible click.

"The fuck is your problem?" I say, my heart pounding fast, one hand still on Remi's shoulder to hold him steady or—I don't know—keep him away from Noah. My adrenaline is so high I barely even register Noah signing, *'Sorry,'* to my brother.

"Didn't see you," he adds gruffly in voice, making to step past.

"What deal did you cut with the Brookes?" I ask before he can walk away, the words practically gritted out. I haven't been able to stop wondering since I got Henrietta's call.

Noah stops, looking back at me, his hulking presence enough to ensure my adrenaline doesn't fade. The guy is big. Taller than me by an inch or so but bulkier by a good bit. The edgy cut to his dark brown hair—shaved at the sides but long on top—furthers the *tough guy* persona. As do the tattoos snaking out from under the collar of his shirt.

His eyes, a much lighter shade than his hair, narrow. "Why would I tell you?"

"'Cause I wanna know."

"Colt," my brother says softly, his hand on my arm squeezing once as he looks from Noah's lips to me.

"Listen to your brother, little Colt," Noah says with a sneer. "You won't like what I do if you don't let me go."

It's then I realize I have his arm in my grip. I drop him like a hot potato, and Noah huffs before walking off.

"Little Colt," I repeat to myself, practically shaking.

God, I hate him. I hate him so fucking much.

'Be right back,' I sign to Remi.

His voice follows me, "Colton" spoken with as much pleading as resignation, but I keep on. I catch up to Noah in the next aisle over, near the farrier supplies. The box of horseshoe nails in his hand lowers to his side as he turns to face me, his stupidly full lips set into a hard line.

"Don't," is all he says.

I get in his face, poking his chest with my finger. "What is your problem?"

"Me?" he asks, incredulous. "What's yours?"

"You," I answer. "Is that not obvious?"

"You couldn't make it any clearer," he says flatly, pushing my hand away. "Back. Up."

"Why?" I goad. "Feel like hitting me?"

His face runs through a myriad of emotions as my pulse beats a swift staccato in my ears. "Back up, Colton."

I don't know why I do it. I really don't.

"Make me," I spit out, shoving his chest.

The next second, there's a forearm pressing me into the shelves of neatly boxed nails at my back, Noah's presence looming over me and damn near suffocating.

"Jesus," I mutter, sucking in a breath as his eyes ping between my own, the copper-colored gaze hard and un-flinching.

He gives me another small shove before letting go, some of the boxes behind me rattling. Without a word, Noah King turns away, shaking his head as he walks off down the aisle.

Fuck.

My feet feel unsteady as I rejoin my brother. Remi's eyes sweep over me quickly, concern in his gaze. His hands move swiftly in question, the motions choppy and agitated. *'What the hell was that? You have a death wish all of a sudden?'*

My head shake is slow. *'Can't stand the guy.'*

He rolls his eyes in a *no shit* manner. *'Doesn't explain why you went after him.'*

"I don't know," I grumble aloud, hand rubbing down my face.

Remi flicks my shoulder before tapping his chin, a per-plexed frown on his face as he asks me what I said. And because I love my brother, I'll never, ever deny repeating anything he didn't catch the first time regardless of whether or not the words are ones I want to repeat.

'I don't know. I don't know what that was, okay? He...'

My hands wave around absently as I search for words before I let them fall at my sides with a groan. Remi pats my shoulder, as if he gets it.

I'm not even sure *I* get it.

Yes, Noah has always been a burr under my heel, but I'm not in the habit of purposefully antagonizing the man. I've never once tried to get him to—what? Snap right in front of me?

I shake out my arms, certain I don't want to find out what Noah might do to me under properly provoked circumstances. The guy is...not scary, exactly. But there's a threat there. One I should do my best to steer clear of.

'I don't know,' I sign again, shaking my head because I truly don't have an answer. *'Let's get out of here.'*

Remi nods, handing over the hat I'd dropped in my haste to chase after Noah. I tug the tag off after paying and plop the hat on my head, the wide brim doing its job of keeping the sun off my face as we head outside. Even so, I blink up at the sky for just a moment, the compulsion like pressing a bruise you know is going to ache.

Shaking my head once more, I face forward and put Noah fucking King firmly out of my mind.

I try. I really do.

On Monday, I head to the Morenos' farm for their horses' routine shoeings. Most of my work is exactly that: routine. A horse's hoof grows the same way as human fingernails. The horseshoe prevents it from wearing down naturally as it would in the wild. That's where the farrier comes in, among a good many other duties. We trim down the excess hoof, both the sole and the outer walls, and reaffix the metal shoe that strengthens and protects the workhorse's hooves. They'd wear far too quickly without it, causing more harm than good for the horse.

It's a painless process, assuming the horse has no hoof injuries that need tending to. The horseshoe can help with that, too.

What's not painless?

The fact that, no matter how hard I try, I can *not* get Noah King off my mind.

On Tuesday, I'm a county over, hitting a handful of single-horse clients in the area. As I pull shoes free, use my loop knife to scrape away overgrown frog on the underside of hooves, hammer in nails, crimp and rasp off the excess metal, and smooth down the surface of over a dozen hoof walls, Noah King is on my mind. As my back gets nibbled on by curious horses and the muscles in my arms and legs ache, I hope Noah King is aching just as badly. *More*. The man deserves it.

On Wednesday, when I'm pounding a new set of shoes into shape, sweat trickling down my temple, I wonder where Noah King even came from. The man just popped up in town fifteen years ago, a chip on his shoulder and hate in his eyes that seemed directed at me more than anyone. Where was he before? How did he learn to shoe? Was he self-taught, or did he go to school for farrier science, learn equine anatomy and physiology as I did, maybe even train in welding?

I don't know. And I shouldn't care.

On Thursday, I'm back at the ranch. Or, rather, I *stay* on the ranch. I wake up at my leisure, the sun drifting in through the window letting me know I succeeded in my plan to sleep in. I'm slow to get out of bed for no other reason than I can be.

I like that hazy morning feeling, where the sheets are warm and rumpled and it's oh so easy to drift in the space between asleep and awake. I laze there now, my hand sinking down my abdomen toward my crotch. Until Noah fucking King's face pops into my head.

With a scowl, I throw back my covers and swing out of bed. By the time I get downstairs, the ranchers are in the dining room, eating their eleven o'clock lunch. I pass Ash in the doorway, tossing him an upnod and a mumbled "Morning" he looks amused by.

The scraping of utensils against nearly two dozen plates and the many conversations floating down the exceptionally long dining table are part of every mealtime here at the Darling Ranch. Most of my family is present, apart from Lawson, who's at the school, teaching. Jackson is sitting across from an empty space that Ash likely vacated. Remi is having a conversation with Ira, one of the longtime ranch hands, Remi's head angled in Ira's direction and his eyes on the other man's lips to help catch his words amidst the various sounds in the room. Even my mom and dad are here, seemingly bickering over one thing or another, as they always do.

I plop down in an empty seat and grab a fancy-looking ham sandwich.

"Morning, Colton," my mom says lightly, her voice as amused as the look Ash threw me a minute ago.

I glance down at myself, checking that I'm dressed. I am.

"Morning," I reply, snagging a serving bowl that still has some pasta salad inside. I load a heaping spoonful on my plate as I chew my bite of sandwich. Ash is a damn good cook—I'll give him that.

"Late night?" my dad asks, his glasses perched down at the end of his nose.

I shrug. "Not really. Just needed the sleep."

Someone down the table snickers, and I look around.

"What?" I ask. "What is it?"

"Colton dear," my mom says, her brown eyes twinkling in a way I know means trouble. "You've got a little something..."

She taps her cheek in demonstration, and I scoot my chair hastily back, heading in the direction of the hallway bathroom. As soon as I see my reflection in the mirror, my eyes shoot wide.

"It wasn't like that!" I shout to a chorus of returned laughter, all good-natured enough I can't be upset by it. I wet a washcloth and scrub furiously at my cheek. Specifically, at the bright red imprint of lips. "It *wasn't.*"

"No shame in the game," my dad calls back.

Jesus Christ.

"It was Evelyn Jacobs," I yell.

There's more laughter at that, and someone wheezes.

"We didn't..."

I let my voice peter out, giving up on an explanation and shaking my head. Evelyn Jacobs is in her eighties, a terrifying woman on Darling's event planning committee. She caught me in town on my way home yesterday, verbally strong-arming me into attending this year's Blossom Bash—Darling's official springtime festival—with a demonstration on farriery. After procuring my resigned *yes*, she smacked a floral-scented kiss on my cheek and went on her way.

"It's cute," Remi says from the doorway, clearly battling his own laughter. "You two would make a fine couple."

"Get over here," I gripe, making a grab for him.

Remi deftly evades me, dancing away on lithe feet and disappearing up the stairs. I give up on trying to wipe away the red smudge and rejoin the lunch crowd. The food is good, even as my thoughts flit from Evelyn Jacobs—who I most certainly did *not* get with—to Heather and even the women I was with before her.

Every relationship I've been in—casual or not—has been fine. They've all been *fine*, but nothing much beyond that.

Is there a woman out there I'll want to spend my hazy mornings with? Someone who'll be more than *fine*. Maybe even someone capable of creating those fireworks I've heard other folks talking about?

If there is, I wish I knew where to find her.

Chapter 4

Noah

"See the hoof wall here?" Colton says, holding up a plastic model for the small crowd—mostly kids—gathered in front of him. "Every four to six weeks or so, this needs to be trimmed down."

"Doesn't that hurt the horse?" one small child in a bright pink tutu asks. A fuzzy coat sits above the skirt, considering the cool weather today.

"Not in the least," Colton says. "Does it hurt when you get your nails clipped?"

"No," the child answers.

"Same thing," Colton explains. "I trim their nails and clean up the soles of their hooves, same way folks exfoliate the dry skin off the bottom of their feet. I just do that part with a knife."

A couple kids gasp, and Colton chuckles, the sound raspy.

"I'm very careful," he says, holding up first a loop knife and then a slightly curved hoof knife with a pick at the end of the blade. It's left-handed. I had no idea he's left-handed. "These are the tools I use."

As Colton explains the process of trimming a hoof, I walk away from the large tree I'd been using as cover to watch him. Not that he would have noticed me anyway in the crowd, but still. No need to invite a repeat of the incident at the store, whatever the hell that was.

I tug the collar of my jacket up around my neck and stroll past the activities at the Blossom Bash. There's a rock painting station, a build-your-own paper sunflower craft, even a table where kids can plant flower seeds in small clay pots to bring home.

I barely see any of it.

Colton goddamn Darling.

It'd almost be better if he didn't know his stuff. Almost. Because while I'd never wish harm to the horses he tends to, I hate to admit the man is a fine farrier. Of course, I knew that already. Colton being bad at his job was never the issue.

It's the fact that he won't let me be. I don't know if he gets some sadistic pleasure out of needling me, but in all the years I've been here, he's never stopped. Just *poke, poke, poke* every time he steals another client or passes me in town, a glare aimed my way he never seems to direct toward anybody else.

There's a quickening of my heartbeat as I remember the way he stormed after me the other day. Now *that*, I wasn't expecting. For all Colton's inherent assholery, he's never come at me directly. Not like that.

I probably shouldn't have shoved him, but I can't find it in me to regret it.

I loop back around the kids' crafting stations, heading toward the food set up at the edge of the park. Trees are sprinkled throughout the grassy space, their bare branches starting to wake now that winter is over. Bundles of dark red buds cover the maple trees. Soon, the branches will be flush with bright green leaves.

Spotting a vendor selling tulip-shaped cookies and miniature pies, I head that way. My uncle never can resist a sugar cookie.

As I'm paying for my small bag of goods, I hear, "Well, hey there, Sierra. Doing all right?"

Sierra, the woman handing me my change, graces Colton with a wide smile. "Just fine, thanks. How's the ranch?"

Colton opens his mouth to answer when he realizes exactly who he's standing beside. As expected, his face transforms into a glower, but he recovers quickly, redirecting his attention Sierra's way and effectively dismissing me. I have the sudden urge to flick the man's cheek.

I thank Sierra and turn away, hearing Colton tell her about yoga classes at the petting farm that will be starting up again in a few weeks and some pony named Snickerdoodle. I've lived practically a stone's throw away from the man for well over a decade, yet there's so little I actually know about him. Because Colton won't let me know him. He never gave me the chance. He couldn't have made his preference for me to stay far, *far* away more clear if he tried.

Colton Darling, friend to everyone in town but me, with his pretty boy looks and windswept hair, the dark stubble, and those piercing blue eyes women like Sierra seem to love. I *hate* blue.

I pull a sugar cookie out of my bag, biting the tulip and its perfect baby blue frosting in half. It's strangely satisfying, and, admittedly, the cookie does taste good.

"I wanna know what you offered the Brookes."

Je-sus.

I turn slowly, regarding Colton, who followed me. *Again.* His jaw is set in a hard line, the squared muscles tense.

"Why?" I ask. "So you can undercut me?"

"Yes."

Well, fuck. At least he's honest. "I'm not gonna give my competitor tips."

He crosses his arms, even though he *had* to know I wasn't going to tell him. Truth be told, it wasn't just a cheaper cost I offered the Brookes. They'll be keeping me and my uncle stocked in goat cheese and soap for the next six months while they try to increase the revenue brought in by their farm. Well worth the trade of shoeing their horse, if you ask me.

"Is that all?" I ask Colton, who's standing less than ten feet away, still staring at me. "Need a kiss goodbye or something?"

He balks. "I don't want your mouth anywhere near me."

I huff what might be a laugh. "Makes two of us. You here to apologize then? For that shit you pulled last year?"

A muscle in his jaw tics, even as his expression turns distinctly guilty. "I didn't mean to do it," he grits out, the words so quiet they're hard to decipher.

"Still lost me thirty horses, little Colt. I only took back one. Doesn't seem like a fair trade to me."

Colton looks away, unable to hold my eye. What he pulled with Marie Doherty *was* downright shady. I've never sullied his name to get clients, only offered better deals.

"God," he spits. "You think you're so...*entitled.*"

"Sorry?" I say around a harsh laugh.

He waves a hand my way. "You. Big Noah King, all high and mighty, waiting for me to kneel in front of you."

Well, that's a fucking visual.

"This is one hell of an apology," I point out, voice flat.

He makes a frustrated sound close to a growl. "You steal clients from me *all* the damn time, Noah. All the time. I don't see why I should apologize. Maybe *you* should."

"It's called making a living," I say a little louder than intended. "You didn't make it easy to set down roots in this town. Everyone knows the precious goddamn Darlings who can do no wrong. What was I supposed to do? Not try to make a life for myself? Feed my family on one horse a month?"

He blinks, looking startled.

"If anyone here is entitled, it's *you*. Do you ever think of anyone but yourself?" I snap.

Colton looks taken aback, but it only lasts for a split second. He stalks closer, tension lining his frame. "You don't know anything about me."

"And you know nothing about *me*," I reply. "Run along, little Colt. Unless you're ready for that whole *drop to your knees* thing. I would so *love* to hear an apology coming out of your mouth."

"Fuck. Off," he says, only a few inches in front of me now. "And stop calling me that."

I smile. Slowly. "What? Little Colt?"

Colton shoves my shoulder, and I'm positive he'd come at me again if his brother Lawson didn't take that precise moment to approach.

"Jesus, Colt," the man says quietly, stepping in front of Colton, his back to me. "What are you doing?"

Lawson's teenage daughter—Wendy, I think her name is—is standing off to the side, watching us curiously.

"Nothing," Colton says, visibly shaking himself loose.

"That didn't look like nothing," Lawson says, taking a second to glance at me over his shoulder. Presumably seeing I'm not about to attack either of them, he walks Colton further away, but not far enough for me to miss his words. "It looks like you were about to sock him in public. What's going on?"

I don't wait to hear Colton's response. Pulse thundering and the bag of cookies crinkled slightly in my grip, I make my way to where my bike is parked on the other end of our town's one downtown street.

I wanted him to hit me, I realize. It would've given me an excuse to hit him back.

I store the cookies in my saddlebag before swinging my leg over my bike. Daphne purrs to life, the sound and vibration as familiar to me as that of the engine in my truck. Helmet on, I pull away from the bustling street and the still-busy Blossom Bash. I don't feel the cool air against my skin as I navigate toward home. My irritation is keeping me plenty hot.

After parking in my driveway, I head for the front of the house. It takes me a second to realize I'm stomping my way there. I slow my gait, frustrated with myself.

He's the only person who gets to me like this. The only person I'm painfully tempted to throttle, if only to feel the satisfaction of watching Colton Darling's eyes go wide in surprise. Anything would be better than that narrow-gazed hate he projects my way every time I'm within his sights.

Goddamn it.

I forcibly shove the man from my thoughts and unlock the front door.

"Walt?" I call.

"In the back."

I leave my boots on and head through the house, down the narrow hall toward the back room where the chessboard is set up in between a large bookshelf and a somewhat ratty couch we'll never get rid of because it was Walter's mother's. My grandmother's. The floral cushions are tufted, set atop vintage wooden legs that are curved in a decorative style and somewhat scuffed. It's where Walter reads. Me sometimes, too.

"Hey," I say, finding him sitting on the couch. He looks up at me through his reading glasses, eyes brightening when I toss the bag of sugar cookies his way.

"Bad for my health, you know," he says, pulling one delicate tulip free.

I huff a laugh, knowing my uncle never has and never will eat overly *healthy*. I just do my best to slip vegetables into his meals when I can.

"I'm gonna be out back for a bit," I tell him, heading for the door at the tail end of the house.

He raises an eyebrow, but he doesn't respond.

My gas forge is within the only barn on our property. I throw the doors wide for ventilation before turning on the burners. It'll take twenty or so minutes to heat, so I strip off my jacket, roll up my sleeves, and organize my workspace while I wait.

It's not often that I shape shoes from scratch. Some clients request it, and some horses need it, but most of the time, the folks I work for prefer for me to start with ready-made horseshoes. They require minimal shaping to fit a horse's hoof, making it more time and cost-effective for me, which in turn makes it a cheaper option for the client.

Doesn't mean I don't love taking a bar of steel and forcing it to be something else through a lot of heat and sheer determination. That's not what I'm doing today, though.

Once the forge is to temperature, I pull on my gloves and grab my scrap metal. The piece I'm working on is based loosely on a memory of my mother from when I was young. Seven or eight, maybe. We had gardens around our house in Lincoln, Wyoming, so big and sprawling you could get lost in them at the peak of summer. There wasn't anything unusual about that day. It was probably hot. The sun was surely shining. What I do remember is my mom, wearing a yellow gingham dress, sitting cross-legged in the grass and weaving flower crowns. She made three. One for me, one for herself, and one for my dad.

Maybe I shouldn't still miss them at almost forty, over twenty years after they passed. But I'm not sure grief has an expiration.

The metal crown isn't close to finished, not yet. I have to work slow with such thin pieces of steel. Bend them into twining patterns. Flatten out the leaves and carefully shape the petals.

But I'm in no rush.

It's the process I enjoy the most. The way it's almost meditative. How my mind can get lost in the work and there's no room for thinking about annoying Darling natives with their sharp blue eyes and unfriendly tongues.

Damn it.

I set aside the half-formed crown and turn off the forge. It glows orange as I put away my tools and store my gloves. The sun is still shining outside the barn, but a quick check of the time on my phone tells me I've been out here for several hours. Time to get dinner started.

As I'm closing the barn doors behind me, I realize the conversation I had with Colton at the spring festival—if you can even call it a *conversation*—was the longest we've ever spoken in a single stretch apart from the very first time we met.

Colton Darling and I will never be friends. That much is clear.

In fact, I'm not sure we'll ever be anything but enemies.

Chapter 5

COLTON

"Morning, Louise."

My mother's closest friend and owner of the sandwich shop in town raises an eyebrow and pointedly eyes the clock. "It's afternoon, hon."

"Afternoon, then," I quickly amend. "Can I get a roast beef panini, please?"

She hums, ringing me up before turning around to prepare my sandwich. I tap my card against the reader.

"Hey, Louise?"

"Yes?"

"You know, uh…" I look around and lower my voice, even though there are only a couple other customers inside the shop, eating their sandwiches. "Noah King?"

Louise pauses to look at me, and I silently curse. The woman is a gossip hound, and I think I just tossed her a morsel.

"I sure do," she says, layering cheese over the roast beef on my sandwich. "What about him?"

I lower my voice further and lean across the countertop. "He doesn't have, like, kids or something, does he?"

That eyebrow goes up again. "He does not. Why do you ask?"

"No reason," I say hastily. "Just curious."

Louise hums, putting my sandwich in the panini press. "Saw some of your demo at the Blossom Bash last weekend."

"Oh yeah?"

"So did Noah King."

I freeze, my gut nosediving in a way that has me wanting to grunt. I manage to keep the sound to myself. "Uh. Yeah?"

"Mhm. It was real good, your demonstration. You're a natural with those kids."

"Oh, uh...thanks," I reply.

Noah was watching me? Why?

Probably sizing up the competition.

I scowl.

"Here you are," Louise says, handing me my wrapped and bagged panini. "Enjoy your lunch."

"I will. Thanks."

I eat my sandwich on the drive back to the ranch, only managing to drip sauce once. I don't bother stopping inside the main house after I park. I just lug my things over to the horse barn. Remi, unsurprisingly, is inside, mucking stalls.

I flick the lights to announce my presence, and his sandy-brown head pops up. He looks in the opposite direction before locating me and pressing the button to turn his processor on.

"Hey," he says, glancing down at the bag in my hand as I head toward Clementine's stall. "You here to work?"

"Sure am," I tell him. "It's time to shoe my most favorite girl in the entire world."

Remi rolls his eyes, but there's a smile on his face as he goes back to raking horse shit and damp hay.

"Hey, girl," I coo to Clementine, opening her stall door. My horse greets me with an enthusiastic headbutt to my chest, nearly knocking me right out of the stall again. I snort, giving her plenty of good scratches as her nose comes up to huff against my face. She nips the brim of my hat between her teeth, tugging it off my head. "Hey, now. That's new."

Clementine doesn't protest as I take the hat back, setting it outside the stall. I give her a little wave forward, and she follows me out the door and into the hallway, where there's more space to work.

"Ready for some new shoes?" I ask her.

She doesn't answer with words, of course, but I see her eyeing the mini-fridge in the corner of the barn. I head that way, retrieving a carrot that I bring back for her. She snaps it up and crunches happily.

"Hey, Remi?" I ask loudly.

He makes an "mm" sound.

"Does, uh...Noah King have a wife?"

Remi is quiet for a moment, but then he steps into the hall. "A wife? I don't think so. Why?"

"Nothing. Just something he said that got me curious."

I can feel my brother's eyes on me as I pick up Clementine's front left hoof, tucking it between my knees and grabbing my tools. I take off the crimped nail ends before loosening the shoe itself and pulling it free with a few precision tugs. Clementine stands patiently, the most perfect horse there ever was.

"Far as I know," Remi says, "he dates some but hasn't had a real serious relationship. Just lives with his uncle."

My head shoots up. "Wait, what?"

"His uncle," my brother says again, peering at me. "You didn't know that?"

"No," I say, going back to Clementine's hoof. I use the hook on my knife to scrape the dirt away from her sole. "Why would I know that?"

"I dunno," Remi mumbles, almost too quietly for me to hear. "Maybe because you're obsessed with the guy?"

I sputter, nearly dropping Clementine's leg. "Am not."

Remi flashes me a quick letter R and the number two with his hand. *Are, too.* Cheeky little shit.

I grumble and grab my nippers. "I'm not *obsessed* with him. I just...can't escape him, you know? He's everywhere I look. In town. At the store. In the damn *newspaper.*"

"It's a small town," Remi points out. "You've met his uncle before, haven't you? Walter King?"

I think back. "Did he used to work at the post office?"

"Yep."

I nod idly, using the rasp to even out Clementine's hoof now that I've trimmed and tidied it. Heel to toe diagonally in one direction, toe to heel in the other.

I do remember Walter. He was a nice man, and it's only now I realize I haven't seen him in what—years? Why is that?

And why does Noah live with his uncle? Can he not afford his own place?

Guilt momentarily rears before I shake it off. I live at home, too. It's probably no big deal.

"Wanna go to The Barrel tonight?" I ask my brother. When he looks over, I can tell he missed part of that, so I add a signed, *'Drinks in town?'*

"Why not here?" he asks, cutting the strings off a fresh bale of hay. He uses a pitchfork to fling portions of it into the empty stalls he cleaned. I watch for a moment, impressed with his aim.

When Remi meets my eye, I shrug as best as I can from my position. "Dunno. Just wanna get out."

Truth be told, I'm feeling antsy. I like hanging out here, sitting around the bonfire behind Jackson's place, drinking whiskey and catching up with my brothers. But sometimes, like now, there's this restless urge beneath my skin that has me itching to move. To do something reckless. Maybe find a girl for the night and chase the high that seems so elusive and fleeting, gone by the time the morning sun comes up. It'd feel less meaningless, I'm sure, if I could find a woman I want to settle down with.

But Darling, Montana—like Remi said—is not a big place. And, with the exception of the occasional new townsperson like Ash, most of the fresh faces we get here are only passing through.

So a night is likely all I'll get.

I know I have Remi on board when he shakes his head with a look of fond exasperation on his face. "Yeah, all right. We'll head into town."

I hiss a "*Yes*," and Remi chuckles softly.

My brother leaves the barn before I'm done shoeing Clementine, likely to head over to the petting farm or take a break back at the house. I use my rasp to smooth down the outside of Clementine's hooves, having already hammered in and crimped the nails that keep her shoes on tight. I make sure each hoof is pristine and then hem the bottom edges with the rasp, creating a small groove against the metal that'll make the shoe easier to remove next time.

Done, I reward Clementine with a good brushing and some dates from Jackson's stash in the tack room.

"We'll go riding tomorrow," I promise her, since I still have a few of the other ranch horses on my schedule for today. She kicks her head up in acknowledgement. "In or out?"

In answer, Clementine whinnies and trots toward the barn door. With a chuckle, I follow her, double-checking that all the gates on the perimeter fence are shut before letting her loose and getting back to work.

Yeah. I have a good feeling about tonight.

The Barrel isn't a particularly large establishment. Wooden casks flank both sides of the front door, each filled with bright yellow flowers now that winter has sloughed off. Inside, conversation flows and glasses clink, the noise loud to even my ears. Remi pulls out his phone, adjusting the volume settings on his processor.

Luckily, two stools open up at the bar as soon as we arrive. We snag them before anyone else can.

"Hello, gentlemen," Virginia says, setting a couple napkins down on the bar top in front of us. "Just you two tonight?"

Virginia, in addition to being The Barrel's primary bartender, is Ash's closest friend from way back when. I have a feeling I know who she's really asking after.

"Considering your friend was eyefucking my brother all dinner long, I didn't bother asking them to tag along," I tell her, signing the words as I speak for Remi's benefit.

He snorts softly, and Virginia's lips twitch.

"Sounds about right," she allows. "And Lawson?"

"Declined," I reply.

Truth is Lawson has been pretty down lately, ever since his wife Laura asked for a divorce. I hate seeing him so upset, but he doesn't seem to want me—or anyone—to cheer him up right now.

"Well, what can I get for two of my favorite Darlings?" Virginia asks.

Remi and I both order beer. As Virginia fills our pint glasses, I swivel on my stool and take in the crowded bar.

Remi taps my arm, having noticed my wandering gaze. *'Don't tell me you brought me here to be your wingman,'* he signs.

I shake my head quickly. *'No, of course not,'* I answer, even though I *was* thinking about the possibility of picking someone up if the opportunity presented itself.

My brother merely snorts. *'Don't lose your hat this time.'*

I pat it more firmly onto my head, turning back around to thank Virginia as she drops off our drinks.

A prickling at my back has me glancing over my shoulder again. Licking the beer foam from my lip, I set eyes on the very last person I wanted to see tonight.

"Oh, you've got to be kidding me," I mutter under my breath.

Remi turns in my periphery, likely having caught my reaction, but my focus is on Noah King as the door shuts behind him. His eyes sweep over the interior of the bar quickly, his broad form covered in jeans and a simple black t-shirt topped by his usual leather jacket. He brushes his hair back, mussed maybe from his motorcycle helmet, although it always looks a little tousled. I don't know why he keeps it shaved so close on the sides, like he thinks he's some sort of hotshot instead of a small-town farrier with a superiority complex.

The man's eyes lock with mine, and I turn away, facing my beer.

"Colt," Remi says to get my attention, raising his hands once I look his way. *'Tell me you're not going to start something.'*

'I'm not,' I sign back quickly. *'Why would I?'*

He lifts an eyebrow, and *yeah*, I guess I get it. He knows secondhand about the festival and firsthand about me following Noah at the farm supply store. Both stupid mistakes—snap decisions—I won't be making again.

In fact, I've decided my new goal in life will be staying as far away from Noah as possible.

"Little Colt," the man himself says, his presence heavy at my side. I suck in a breath as he seats himself at the stool next to me.

"Really?" I ask. "You're gonna sit there?"

"No other seats," he replies easily, but I swear the fucker delights in toying with me. I'm sure he'd get a lot of satisfaction out of pressing charges if I finally give in to my temptation to slug him in his stupid fucking face.

"You're a dick," I answer, keeping myself faced forward.

He huffs a laugh and orders a stout from Virginia.

Remi prods my arm again and raises an eyebrow in question. It's a *do you want to get out of here* look. I shake my head, assuring him everything is fine.

It is.

I'll be damned if I let Noah King get to me. The man means nothing, and it's about time he got the memo.

Chapter 6

Noah

Colton Darling is doing his absolute best to pretend I'm invisible.

And failing spectacularly.

Honestly, it's so amusing I'm having a hard time not laughing. But he might actually punch me if I do that, so I pretend I can't see the glares he throws my way every so often, followed by his head whipping quickly away.

If I liked the guy, I'd worry for the safety of his neck.

Colton and Remington are having a conversation I can't understand, not that I'm making a point of intruding on what is clearly private and meant for just the two of them. But even if I did try, I'm pretty sure I wouldn't be able to keep up with the speed of their ASL. I only know a few words and phrases, enough to communicate with Remington in a pinch, not that I've ever needed to.

I'm not entirely sure why I'm sitting here, nursing my stout. My plan was to stop in, pick up a growler to take home, and enjoy an evening in front of the TV.

Instead, I'm planted next to the person who likes me least in all of Darling, getting some sort of sick thrill out of making him uncomfortable.

Christ. I really am an asshole.

"Another?" Virginia asks, stopping in front of me on the other side of the bar.

"Why not?" I answer.

She looks somewhat amused as she slides a second pint my way. Colton, noticing the new beer, sends me another glare.

I flash him a smile and take a sip.

His "*argh*" is audible, even over the din of the bar. He's wearing his hat inside, but that isn't all that uncommon. Even so, I want to pluck it off his head just to see what he'd do. I don't give in to the impulse. Instead, I watch as Colton spins back toward Remington, signing something that looks angry and terse, based on his body language.

Remington, for his part, looks far less concerned. His response appears placating or perhaps soothing.

Deciding I'm far too invested in the two, I look away. Only to spot someone approaching in the reflection of the mirror behind the bar.

Crap.

"Hey, Noah," Jenna says, stopping beside me on the opposite side of where Colton is sitting.

I give her a polite nod. "Jenna."

"I don't usually run into you outside the grocery store," she says, leaning her weight against the bar top, her elbow on the surface.

I inch the tiniest bit away to give her more room. "Guess I don't get out much," I tell her, which is the truth.

She hums. "Wanna come sit over with me and my friends? There's an extra chair."

I glance at where she's indicating, seeing a table with four other women around Jenna's age. That is to say *young*. "I'm good."

She does that thing where she sticks her lips out, like a pout. "Fine. You know where to find me if you change your mind."

"Yep."

As Jenna walks off, Colton utters a dry, "Wow."

"What?" I ask.

He shrugs a shoulder. "Nothing. I'm just surprised you have an admirer, is all. What with that sunny attitude of yours."

Remington groans, Colton having signed his words as he spoke. It's a habit I'm fairly sure is ingrained in the man.

I wish I could say I don't admire that, but it'd be a lie.

"I have no problem finding interested parties," I tell him, enjoying the twitch at the corner of his eye.

"Mhm. Sure. Well, there's an open seat now. So why don't you just..." He shoos me with his hand.

"I'm good," I assure him.

He nearly growls.

"Noah," Remington says, startling me somewhat. I meet his eye, and he holds mine, signing something I have no hope of catching.

Colton groans, likely pained by our extended conversation. "He says, 'How's your uncle?'"

"Oh. Good, all things considered. Thanks for asking."

Colton is the one to reply to that, even as he sounds surly about it. "What does that mean? 'All things considered.'"

I debate answering him, positive he doesn't care. But Remington is watching for my response, too, and I don't want to be rude to the guy just because his brother is a superb pain in my ass.

"He has scoliosis that's progressed enough to cause some pain, and his arthritis makes it difficult to walk. But he's otherwise fine."

Colton frowns, but then he interprets for his brother. "Remi says, 'I'm sorry to hear that.'"

'Thanks,' I tell Remington directly, my hand moving from my chin.

He gives me a small smile, but Colton simply grunts, turning away enough that I know our little moment of semi-peace is shattered. That's fine. Not like I want to get friendly with the guy anyways. The chance for that has long passed.

I sip my stout, no longer enjoying it. Deciding to call it a night, I drop a tip on the bar and push my half-full glass away. Colton catches the movement, another frown marring his face.

I can't quite help myself. "Sweet dreams, little Colt."

The man grits his teeth, and I smile, heading for the door.

Sound cuts off almost immediately when I step outside, the air crisp with an underlying hint of dirt I associate with this time of year, like the earth is waking up from its hibernation.

I like this region any time of year, but spring might be my favorite. Temperatures are warming but aren't as sweltering as we get in the height of summer. Flowers come out to play, reminding me of new life and my mother's gardens from so many years ago. Plus, springtime is when we get the most new foals born on the farms and ranches around town.

I dare anybody to be upset when there are baby horses running around.

Since the streetside parking was full when I arrived at The Barrel, I head to where I parked my bike in the lot behind the building. My boots crunch over the occasional small rock on the pavement, my thoughts a scattered mess of seasonal changes, my uncle back at home, and the man inside the bar who boils my blood without even trying. *Especially* when he's trying.

And try he does.

Fuck. Why won't he just...go away? Why does he have to be so—

"Noah."

"Oh my *God*," I groan aloud, turning in place. "What now?"

Colton emerges from the narrow alley beside the bar. He strides my way, his hat obscuring his face with the shadows cast by the streetlights.

"What?" I repeat, my ire up.

"You know ASL," he says, almost like an accusation. Actually, definitely an accusation. He comes to a stop in front of me, crossing his arms and waiting for my answer.

"Very little," I tell him.

"Why?" he spits.

I throw my hands in the air. "Why? Maybe because there's a Deaf individual in my community who I'd like to be able to talk to?"

Colton looks gobsmacked. "But you hate me," he says vehemently, no question in his tone.

"Not everything is about you."

There goes his scowl again.

"Is that why you came out here?" I ask. "To see if I—what? Was spying on your conversation?"

"Well, were you?"

"Why? What were you saying about me that you don't want me to know?"

"Not everything is about you," he parrots, lips twisting wryly.

"Jesus Christ, Colt. Leave me be."

I turn toward my bike, but he follows after me. I spin again, not about to be caught unawares with this man at my back.

"I challenge you," he says unprompted, his voice low.

"I'm sorry, what?" I say around a hoarse laugh. "What are we, Hamilton and Burr?"

"Not to a duel, jackass. I challenge you to a Shoein'."

"Oh, Jesus. No."

"No?"

"Do people even do that anymore?" I ask. "Gather in the town square to watch the local farriers go head to head in a friendly horseshoeing competition?"

"I don't see why not," he says easily.

"The last Shoein' had to have been decades ago. No," I repeat. "Not doing it."

He works his jaw for a moment, shadows cutting a sharp line across his face. "You don't think you'll win."

I laugh. *Hard.* Hard enough I have to clutch my knees as Colton stares at me with lethal venom in his gaze. "Oh, fuck you. I'd win."

"Prove it."

"Oh my God. What are we, twelve?"

"If you're so sure you can beat me," Colton says slowly, taking a step forward, "then prove it. But if *I* beat you..."

Suddenly, my pulse is hammering so heavily I can barely hear my own breath. "What? I give you my clients?"

"No," he says at once. I ease out a breath, even though I'm not doing it. I'm not accepting Colton's...*challenge*. Finally, he proposes, "Bragging rights."

I shake my head, but Colton takes another step forward.

"C'mon, King. Where's the cocky assurance now? What happened to *'King Farrier Service, best in town,'* huh? Why don't you back up that claim already?"

I grit my teeth at Colton's mention of one of my many newspaper ads. "I'm not fighting you, Colt."

He scoffs. "It's a friendly competition. No fighting involved."

Right. Friendly.

"When *I* win," I say, hardly able to believe the words coming out of my mouth, "I want something else. Something more than bragging rights."

Colton waves his hand in the air as if to say *go on.*

My grin is a slow thing. "I want my name tattooed on your ass."

His eyes widen, and he sputters, "No way."

"Afraid you'll lose?"

"No. Way," he says again, the meaning entirely different.

I shrug. "Your choice. Those are my terms. Winner gets proof they're the best farrier. Loser gets some fresh ink."

Colton makes a sound of superb frustration, and I nearly laugh.

"Hey, you started this," I point out. "I just upped the ante."

"You're insufferable," he grits out, pacing in a tight circle, his steps taking him away from me and then closer again. "God, I just—"

He cuts off, signing something I'm almost positive is an inventive insult, based on the tight, jerky movements of his hands and arms.

I grunt. "Say it to my face, Colt."

He stops his circle abruptly, shifting to come my way. The next second, he's in my space, shoving me backwards. "God, I can't stand you."

"Feeling's mutual," I assure him, bracing myself for him to come at me again. If he does, I might just sock him in that perfect nose of his.

"You're an ass. Pompous. Infuriating," he says, apparently having decided to list my faults after all. "You think you're so much better than me, and why? Because I'm...smaller than you? Because you like feeling like the bigger man?"

"That has nothing to do with it," I shoot back, my frustration returning tenfold. "I never claimed to be better than you as a person. If anything, it's the other way around."

Colton swats my hand away, making me realize I'd been pressing a finger into his chest. "What the fuck is that supposed to mean? I've never done *anything* to you without good reason."

I laugh harshly.

"Stop treating this like a joke," he practically shouts. "Jesus, you arrogant, self-centered prick of a human being."

"Get out of my face," I tell him, the man toe to toe with me now.

"Does anyone else get to see this side of you, huh?" he asks, not moving a muscle except to get closer. "Or am I just so special that—"

Colton makes to shove my shoulder again, so I spin him into the truck at our sides. One second, there's Colton's shocked expression mixed with a small wince of pain, and then my mouth is shutting the man up.

I feel triumphant. Giddy even, to have found a way to render Colton absolutely speechless. There's no talking with my lips pressed so firmly against his, the force of my attack bruising. His hand on my chest flexes, his entire body jolting almost, as I bite his lip. I do it again, as hard as I dare without drawing blood, my soul singing in smug satisfaction and—

The return of my senses has me stepping swiftly back and releasing Colton. He blinks his eyes open, bright blue staring at me in that wide-eyed surprise I was so desperate to get a glimpse of only a handful of days ago. But my smugness at having elicited such a reaction quickly turns to something else entirely.

Because *fuck*.

I have never, not once, been interested in a man. Never kissed one or even wanted to.

And of all the men in the world I could have chosen to kiss, hate-fueled or otherwise, it just had to be Colton goddamn Darling.

Chapter 7

COLTON

I'm too shocked to move as Noah spins away from me, all but stomping to his motorcycle. The engine revs to life, and he takes off, not once looking back.

What. The fuck. Was that?

I wipe my mouth and look down at my semi.

"What the actual fuck," I hiss.

I did not just get a hate-boner over Noah King.

Did I?

No. No fucking way.

Fuuuck.

"Colt?" my brother calls.

"What?" I shout much too loudly, pushing off from the truck behind me. I swipe my hat off the ground and head toward the alleyway.

Remi appears a moment later, his eyes sweeping the area, confusion and concern in his gaze. "You were gone when I got back from the bathroom," he says. "Don't tell me you went after Noah again?"

"No," I lie, immediately wincing. "Maybe. It's nothing."

My brother groans. "Colt, you're gonna get yourself into trouble."

I think I already have.

"Home?" I ask tightly.

Remi nods, and we head toward the truck. We're both quiet on the way back to the ranch, me driving, Remi looking out the passenger window. When I pull into a spot in front of the house, we exit the vehicle without a word.

I'm so in my own head—my thoughts a jumbled mess I don't even know how to start unraveling—that I miss the fact that Remi is talking to me. He snaps his fingers in front of my face, and I startle, blinking at him inside the entryway of the house.

"Sorry," I say quickly. "What?"

Remi looks at me for a long moment, his eyes seemingly trying to pick me apart. Remi and I don't look all that similar, apart from our blue eyes. His cheekbones are a little sharper, like Jackson's. And he's always had a leaner build, though he's strong as hell.

"I said be careful," my brother says, those eyes still boring into me.

For a second, I wonder if he knows what happened. But how could he?

I don't even know what happened.

"I will be," I tell him.

He sighs like he doesn't quite believe me, but then he leaves me be, heading further into the house. I kick off my boots and set my hat on the coatrack inside the door. It's late, nearly midnight, but I still detour into the kitchen to find a quick snack.

I know I hit jackpot when I spot the foil marked in pen with my name. I unwrap the bundle quickly, groaning happily when I see four strips of bacon.

"Fuck, yes," I mutter, biting cleanly through two. I send a quick thank-you to Ash and kick the fridge door shut.

Once upstairs, I take care of business and wash up before heading for my bedroom. Mine is right next to Remi's, across the hallway from where Lawson is temporarily staying. Remi's door is shut, no sound coming from within.

Truth be told, I think my younger brother is a big part of why I've never left this place. Not that I've *wanted* to, per se. And Remi would kick my ass if he thought I saw him as anything other than strong.

He *is* strong. He's one of the strongest people I know, utterly unafraid to be himself, kind but not self-sacrificing when it comes to his own comfort, especially where it pertains to being Deaf. I know my brother doesn't need me to coddle him. He doesn't need that from anybody.

But there are times when he has a rough go of it. When his migraines flare up, and it's all he can do to ride out the storm, hunkered down in his room as he waits for it to pass. Those are the times I want to be near, to help him however I can.

I know it's not my job. But he's my brother. So, in a way, it's something bigger than that.

Once inside my room, I peel off my jeans and toss my shirt haphazardly into my hamper before flopping on my bed. Almost immediately, I'm back up again, pulling an old shoebox out from my closet. I bring it over to my mattress and lift the lid.

It's mostly papers. Old clippings from the town newspaper. Some printouts. I rifle through them, my frustration an immediate thing as I look at the attempts of my archnemesis to beat me at my own game.

"Custom-fit or ready-made shoes, King Farrier Service has you covered."

"Royal service and fair costs. If you want the best, go King."

"We know your horse is part of your family. Treat them to the finest care with King Farrier Service."

I growl, slapping the papers down and shutting the box.

See? I clearly hate the guy. That hasn't changed. Won't *ever* change.

So what in the absolute fuck was the deal with that...that *kiss*? And my reaction to it?

Actually, no. I'm not calling it that. Kisses are tender and sweet. That was an attack. A *mauling*. It was all brute force and angry grappling and goddamn *biting* and—

My gut tightens, and I let out an involuntary sound I wish I could take back.

No. Nope. Nuh-uh.

We do *not* like Noah fucking King.

Maybe it had nothing to do with the man, I rationalize not twelve hours later. Maybe it was simply...circumstance.

Exhibit one.

I've never been into guys. And I've *tried*. Kinda. Jackson is gay. Remi is pan. The idea of liking someone other than a woman has never been a problem for me in theory. But I simply *haven't*. Haven't wanted to bone any guys, haven't wanted to kiss them.

So it's not that. I don't think.

Exhibit two.

If I were going to test-drive dick for the first time, it would not be with Noah fucking King. Of all the men in Darling or any-goddamn-where, he would be my absolute last choice. Literal bottom of the barrel. Last two men on Earth? Hard pass.

So it's *definitely* not that.

Exhibit three.

I've never been with a woman who...threw me around like that before. None have even tried. A couple have been a little more wild in bed, but even then, it was them wanting me to toss *them* around. Not the reverse.

And I think I liked it. It was kind of...a thrill.

So, there. It has to be that, right? The circumstances.

"Do you think it's possible to have latent masochistic tendencies?"

Jackson looks at me slowly, the laptop in front of him all but forgotten. We're sitting in the dining room, the late morning sun brightening the space. "I don't wanna ask. I really, really don't."

"The thing is," I go on, keeping my voice low, even though no one else is in the ranch house right now, as far as I'm aware, "I kinda got roughed up a bit the other night? And I...liked it?"

Jackson lets out a sigh that sounds endlessly weary. "First, are you all right?"

"What? Yeah, of course."

He nods. "The partner that roughed you up... Do I know her?"

I nearly balk. That's Jackson's polite way of asking if it was someone from town—maybe even an ex of mine—or one of the tourists passing through. But how in the hell do I answer him when it wasn't even a *her* to begin with? Saying that will make it sound like a big deal. Like Noah and I had a *thing*. We most definitely do not have a *thing*.

"You've met," I say, skirting the topic best as I can.

He looks contemplative. "If you liked it and she liked it, then, well, I don't think it's something you should worry about. As for it being…masochism. Was it the pain you enjoyed?"

I think that over. "Actually, don't think so. It was just…"

What? The roughness? Being almost helpless?

No way am I saying that out loud.

"I'll figure it out," I tell my brother, standing quickly. "Thanks, Jackson."

He lets out a dubious, "Mhm," and goes back to the spreadsheets on his laptop.

I'm working at Marie Doherty's place today. I have a couple days set aside every four weeks for the thirty-some horses on her farm-slash-equestrian clinic. Marie is the only person in a good hundred-mile radius who teaches dressage and show jumping. There are usually a handful of teens or young adults there on any given day, running horses through their complicated routines.

Aside from that, she also keeps chickens. A whole *lot* of them. Her eggs are the best you can get at Plum's Grocers.

When I arrive on her property, I head inside the massive indoor arena, making my way up the stairs to her perch overlooking three separate training rings. As expected, Marie is there, giving instructions from on high to her students.

"Marie," I say quietly, although I'm sure she heard me coming.

"Morning, Colton."

"Anything I need to know before I set to work?"

"Watch your timing, Andrea!" Marie calls to one of the riders. "Nearly nicked the board on the way down. You're jumping early and pulling your punches. Try again, and this time don't slow as you near the board." Turning, she says at a much softer volume, "Yes, in fact. I've got a horse in stall nineteen without a shoe."

"How'd that happen?"

"Hit a block just right," she answers. "Enough to pull the shoe away from his hoof on one side. I would've called you in, but it only happened an hour ago. We removed it the rest of the way and set him up in his stall."

"Any damage from the nails that broke free?" I ask.

An almost-smile touches the corner of Marie's lips. "Not that I could tell. They snapped cleanly. Almost like someone knew what they were doing when they set them."

I hold back my scoff. "It's certainly not my first rodeo."

Truth is it's not uncommon for a nail to cause a little damage on the way out if they're pulled wrong. We crimp the ends to keep the nails—and thus the shoe—in place, like tiny hooks. Then we rasp the metal even with the outside of the hoof so the surface is nice and smooth. That also ensures the bent edge of the nail is thin enough to snap if enough pressure is applied to it.

They're meant to break cleanly so the nail can pull straight out, but that doesn't always happen under duress. Especially if a farrier doesn't crimp right.

It's a good thing I know what I'm doing.

"I'll head to stall nineteen first," I tell Marie, knowing she'll want me to start with that horse.

"Appreciate it," she says. I'm halfway to the exit when she adds, "Oh, Colton? I've got another fifteen horses arriving in less than two weeks. They'll be staying here through the summer for some workshops I've got going on. Can you shoe them when they arrive?"

I chew on the inside of my cheek, mentally running over my schedule that I *know* is full. "You need 'em done right away?"

"Would prefer it. I want them ready to ride and on the same routine as the rest."

"Let me see what I can do," I tell her.

Marie gives me a nod and turns back to her work. Once on ground level, I check my phone only to confirm that *yep*. My calendar for the next few weeks is booked solid. Slipping a single horse in wouldn't be a big deal, but fifteen? I could rearrange things some, I'm sure. Work a handful of twelve-hour days in a row. *Or...*

I dismiss the thought before it can fully take shape and carry my things over to stall nineteen. The horse inside is a handsome brown Westphalian I recognize instantly.

"Well, hey there, Ludo. I hear you lost a shoe?"

The horse snuffles my palm when I open the door, letting me rub over his muzzle and along his neck. After a good minute of petting, I give his halter a gentle tug, and he dutifully follows me out of the stall.

It doesn't take long to outfit Ludo with a new set of shoes. And Marie was right. There's not a single bit of damage to his hoof wall from the nails pulling through.

With a small sigh, my mind returns to my busy schedule and the fact that I wouldn't be taking care of Ludo here in the first place if it wasn't for me running my damn mouth last year and losing Noah this job.

Fuck.

I could rearrange my entire schedule. *Or...* I could tell Marie to grab Noah for the influx of horses.

I wait until I'm done with Ludo to return up to Marie's perch. She gives me a quick look before her focus returns to her students. "Yes?"

"I think you should hire Noah for the extra horses," I tell her. "It'll be difficult for me to fit them into my schedule on such short notice."

Not a lie, even though I know I could manage it.

"This isn't the first time you've suggested I take him back," she says, a hint of curiosity in her tone.

I try not to groan. "He really is a damn fine farrier, Marie. I've seen some of his work firsthand. His craftsmanship is excellent, his attention to sole depth shows a keen under-standing of equine husbandry as it relates to hoof care and posture, and I've never heard a single complaint about his handling."

She mulls it over, her fingers tapping the railing in front of her.

"I appreciate that you've known me and my family for longer," I go on. "And that you trust me with your horses. But you can trust me with this, too. I wouldn't suggest pulling Noah in if I didn't think he could more than handle it. You never had problems when he was here before, did you?"

"Suppose not," she agrees. I wait, and, after a tense silence, Marie says, "I'll give him a call."

My breath whooshes out of me.

There. See?

I can be civil.

I can be *nice* to Noah King.

He'll take these horses off my plate, and then I can wipe my hands of the arrogant farrier for good. Debt paid. No reason to see or even talk to him ever again. No reason to see his stupid face or wonder why he mauled my lips with his own.

Nope.
No reason at all.

Chapter 8

NOAH

I'm not doing a very good job of ignoring my Colton problem.

I kissed the man.

On the mouth.

Looking back, I can honestly say I have no clue what I was thinking, except... I *wasn't* thinking. Only reacting. I wanted to shut Colton up. To rattle him. To wipe that look of frustrated animosity off his face and replace it with... I don't know.

He hasn't said a word about it. Not to me. Hasn't sought me out. Hasn't punched me or asked what the hell I was doing.

I don't know if that makes it better or worse.

I finish raking the dead leaves and pine needles out behind the house into a neat pile. Next will be cleaning up the flower beds. It's warm enough that I don't need a jacket, yet the breeze keeps me from sweating under the sun.

"Gonna vacuum the woods when you're done with that?" my uncle calls.

I squint against the sunlight, finding him standing at the back door. "What now?"

"You've been fussing. Finding excuses to keep busy for days. Wanna talk about it?"

Jesus.

I almost wish the man didn't know me so well.

"Nothing to talk about," I call back.

He lets out a loud *harrumph* just as my phone starts to ring from inside my pocket. I pull it free as my uncle walks back into the house, my brows shooting up when I see the name onscreen. I quickly answer.

"Afternoon, Mrs. Doherty."

"Noah," she replies.

"What can I do for you?"

There's a brief pause before Marie Doherty says, "I've got fifteen new horses coming to stay with me soon. Can you take them on?"

This time, it's me pausing. "You don't want Colton to handle them?"

"His schedule is full. He recommended you."

I nearly bark a laugh entirely devoid of humor. What in the hell is he up to?

"I can take 'em," I tell her, not about to pass up the chance, even if I don't trust Colton Darling one fucking bit.

"Good," Marie says simply. "They'll be here in twelve days. Can you be here in thirteen?"

"I sure can. I'll see you then."

With a quick goodbye, Marie ends the call, and I stand there, wondering what the fuck Colton is playing at. There's no way the man I know wouldn't have moved heaven and earth to fit those horses into his schedule if for no other reason than to keep me from getting the business. So what is this? What's the goddamn catch?

I store my rake and head inside, done with yard work for the day. My uncle is seated in the back room now, his reading glasses on and a book in his hand.

"I'm here if you wanna talk," he says.

My upper body deflates with my breath. "Love you, Walt."

"You, too, kiddo."

I continue on my way, hopping in the shower once upstairs and scrubbing the dirt off my hands and forearms. I use a brush to get underneath my fingernails, the same one I use each and every day after shoeing horses.

No one ever said farriery was tidy work.

By the time I'm done, I've made up my mind.

I need to pay Colton Darling a visit.

The Darling Ranch is a sprawling property not that far south of where I live. I wait until the evening is well underway to drive over, knowing I'll have a better chance of catching Colton after work hours, even on the weekend.

The place isn't busy when I pull up. I'm guessing most of the ranch hands are gone by five. The lights in the house are on, as well as in the two small cottage-style homes I'm fairly certain belong to Colton's parents.

I don't know if the sound of my bike alerted Colton to my presence, but he comes out the front door before I've even set both feet on the ground.

"What are you doing here?" he calls, storming over with his jeans crumpled up around the tops of his boots like he shoved the footwear on hastily.

"Needa talk with you," I answer, setting my helmet on my bike seat.

After a couple seconds of staring as if he's calculating whether or not I'm serious, Colton waves me toward the side of the house. Away from prying eyes maybe?

I follow him off the gravel and onto grass, my heart thumping viciously now that I'm here.

"Talk," Colton says, spinning toward me and crossing his arms.

"Fuck," I mutter, already feeling the beginnings of a headache coming on. "Do you have to be so…"

I wave a hand his way, not even knowing how to finish my sentence.

So infuriating?

So frustrating?

So goddamn annoying I want to level something? Preferably him?

"Oh, I'm sorry," Colton retorts icily. "Was I supposed to welcome you with open arms?"

"Christ, Colt. I'm trying to be an adult here."

"By all means, please do try."

Groaning, I scrub my hands through my hair and exhale a breath. "Why the fuck did you let me have Marie's new horses?"

"I was being *nice*," he grits out.

I don't believe that for one goddamn second. "I wanted them fair and square, Colt. Not because you…*pity* me or something."

He throws his hands in the air, eyes wide. "I can't win! You want her horses back. You don't want them. Which is it?"

"I want them because I *earned* them. Not because you stole them and then decided to toss a few back my way as a consolation prize."

"Jesus Christ," he groans, looking heavenward. "I can't with you."

"You never could."

"The fuck does that mean?"

I shake my head, not wanting to get into history that's so far behind us it's not even worth dredging up.

"I accepted the job," I tell him. "Because I know I'll do right by those horses. But if this is some ploy to make me look bad or trick me or—"

"Trick you?" he cuts in, incredulous. "How?"

"I don't *know*. But I don't trust you."

And that's the crux of it, isn't it? Colton Darling has proven he's someone I can't trust.

"Well that's *fine*," he shoots back. "Not like I was planning on inviting you in to make friendship bracelets or anything."

I huff, realizing, at some point, we moved closer to one another. I take a big step back, debating whether or not I even want to bring up the other thing. The topic that's been weighing on me for days.

But if I don't, I'll keep wondering. Keep waiting for Colton to use it against me somehow.

"I didn't mean to do it," I tell him. "Behind the bar."

He looks confused for all of a split second before his expression blanks, becoming surprisingly unreadable.

"I don't like you," I go on, wanting to make that absolutely clear.

Colton crosses his arms again, the lines of his face and body tense. "Are you..."

"Am I what?" I ask when the silence becomes too much.

"Nothing," he says quickly. "Doesn't matter. You kiss me again, and I'll knee you in the balls."

"I won't be kissing you again," I say firmly, my skin prickling in irritation. "Got it?"

"Good. I'd hate to have to file a restraining order."

I shake my head, beyond done with this conversation, and turn to go.

"I'm not trying to trick you," Colton says at my back. "I'm trying to make things right. I know you don't believe me, Noah, but I never meant to lose you that job."

"And yet I still haven't heard an apology come out of your mouth," I point out, not bothering to turn around.

Colton doesn't offer one now, and I walk away.

Unbelievable.

Of all the people in this town to be at odds with, it has to be the one—the *only* one—who's a direct threat to my livelihood. I can't get away from it. From *him.*

Why does he have to be so goddamn—

I come up short, registering someone standing beside my bike.

"Pretty," the man I recognize as Hank Darling says. Colton's father.

I give him a nod. "Thanks, sir."

He snorts. "*Sir.* Just Hank is fine. You know, my son has never been the best at turning his feelings into words."

I don't say a word myself, not sure what he's getting at. He must have seen us talking, though, to know that's why I'm here.

Or he simply assumed as much.

"I remember when Colton was, oh, ten or so," he says, bending down to inspect my motorcycle. "He snuck an entire strawberry cream pie up into his room because he was afraid there wouldn't be any left for him to eat. It was his birthday party, so his worry wasn't unfounded considering all the guests. But..." Hank stands upright, rounding my bike to look at it from another angle. "Instead of asking me or his mom to make sure there was a piece set aside just for him, he hid the whole pie away and got so sick the next day from gorging himself, he hasn't touched one since."

I wince, something unwelcome, like sympathy, pinging around in my chest.

"My point is," Hank says almost lazily, hands in his pockets as he rocks back on his heels, "Colton doesn't handle his emotions in the most obvious of ways. He grew up with three brothers. And they all liked strawberry cream pie."

"So, what?" I ask, keeping my tone as even as possible. "He learned to simply take what he wants?"

Like my clients.

Hank rolls his eyes. "Good Lord. *No.* My son," he stresses, "is so used to putting others first that when there's something he really wants, he doesn't know how to ask for it. He's scared if he does, he'll end up without a piece at all." With that, Mr. Darling pats my helmet, like a punctuation mark at the end of his story. "Evening, Noah."

"Evening," I mumble, watching the man walk off.

When I glance back at the house, I don't see Colton. Not inside or out. The lights are still on, but there's no movement beyond the windows.

I swing my leg over my bike and head down the gravel drive.

I could move a ways out of Darling and find plenty of work. Farriers are in high demand around these parts with so many ranches and farms claiming massive swaths of land. I could relocate elsewhere in Montana or even move back to Wyoming like my uncle suggested.

But there's more than enough work here in Darling, too. And it's my *home*. It has been since the very moment Walter took me in. I've carved out a life for myself here. A good one. Yes, losing thirty horses in one sweep was a blow, but I have enough business to ensure Walter and I are comfortable. I'm doing *fine*. We're doing fine.

The only hiccup in my otherwise peaceful life is Colton goddamn Darling.

I can't give him the satisfaction of winning. I won't leave. Won't accept defeat.

Our war started long ago.

And fuck if I can't see the end of it, no matter how hard I try.

Chapter 9

COLTON

I can't believe I didn't think to question it before.

Is Noah King bi?

I hadn't stopped to wonder, too caught up in my own reaction to that...*kiss* to even consider Noah.

He didn't say as much. Didn't even imply that kissing guys might be commonplace for him.

Surely I would've heard if that were the case, wouldn't I? Secrets don't keep in this town.

Not that any of it explains why he kissed *me*.

Fuck, I don't know what to think. I've been trying not to, if I'm being honest with myself. I don't want to think about Noah King or why that mauling behind The Barrel made me feel so...

I throw down my rasp with a little more force than necessary. The metal clangs against the other tools in my bag, and I wince, apologizing to both my tools and the horse I just finished shoeing. I untie her lead and walk her back into her stall before cleaning up my workspace.

I need to head back to Marie Doherty's this afternoon, and there's a good chance I'll see Noah there. The new horses have arrived, and although I'm not in charge of them, one of the horses I *am* in charge of started walking funny this morning. Marie asked—demanded, more like—for me to come check it over before bothering with a vet visit. Could be an easy fix.

I take my time, returning to the ranch for lunch first. Not because I'm avoiding Noah. Everybody's gotta eat.

The dining room is bustling when I arrive. I find an empty chair and grab a roll before the platter can be picked clean. As I'm ladling homemade chicken noodle soup into my bowl, I catch part of a conversation a couple of the ranch hands are having.

"Hear the town is holding a treasure hunt this year?"

That was Colleen.

"You serious?" Marty asks.

Colleen nods. "It's supposed to be some sort of fundraiser for the accessible playground the board approved. I guess you buy a ticket to enter and then follow the clues throughout town. Not sure what the prize is gonna be."

Marty hums. "Maybe cash?"

"Or a crate of Darling Whiskey?" Colleen proposes.

"Heck, if that's it, I'm definitely entering. How much are tickets?"

"Flyer said fifty bucks," Colleen answers.

A nudge against my arm draws my attention away from talk of the treasure hunt. "Pass the butter?" my dad asks.

I hand it over and dig back into my soup, wondering if Noah might buy a ticket or if he'd think such a thing too childish and fun. I'm *positive* Noah doesn't know the meaning of the word fun, stick in the mud that he is.

Ugh.

I wipe my thoughts of the man. Again.

As the ranchers head off to finish their day of work, I linger in the dining room. Ash gives me a pointed look as I start collecting silverware alongside him, figuring I might as well lend a hand. He doesn't say anything. Not until he finds me at the sink, rinsing dishes.

"Okay, spit it out," he demands, cocking a hip against the counter.

"Spit what out?"

"Whatever it is that has you cleaning after lunch when you know that's my job."

"What, a guy can't help out around here?" I mutter.

Ash raises an eyebrow in a way that reminds me distinctly of my brother Jackson.

I groan and hastily dry my hands. An inquisition is the last thing I need right now. I wouldn't even know what to say. "It's nothing. I got work to do."

I can feel Ash's gaze following me out the doorway, but I pay it no mind.

When I arrive at Mrs. Doherty's, a familiar blue pickup is parked out front. I curse a good dozen times, but it doesn't stop me from grabbing my things and heading toward the stables attached to the arena. I gird myself as I walk through the doors, looking around, hoping if I spot the man, I can take a route to avoid him.

No such luck.

Noah is set up in the center aisle, dust-covered chaps over his dark jeans, the white hat on his head blocking my view of his face but not the tattoos visible on his forearms. Or what looks like an inked horseshoe peeking out near his collarbone.

I heave an internal sigh and walk his way.

He must hear me approaching because his head lifts, his movements stilling for all of a second before he goes back to his work.

Good. We're ignoring each other. That I can do. And happily.

I trudge past toward stall five on the right. Peanut, the horse I need to check, is inside as expected. I greet him, voice low, and open the stall door. Peanut doesn't seem overly bothered as I urge him to lift his hoof, used to that sort of thing from me. It takes me a good minute to spot the problem, but, finally, I see a small object embedded into his sole right along the edge of his shoe.

"Well, dang," I say, letting his hoof down. "Let's get that outta there, huh?"

Peanut doesn't argue.

I step back into the hall, rummaging through my bag for the thin-tipped pliers I know are there. Noah is still hard at work, his ass aimed my way. I flip him off while he can't see it.

Back in Peanut's stall, I hunker low, letting the horse's front leg rest on my thigh as I take a better look at the underside of his hoof. I use the end of the pliers to scrape away the excess dirt, avoiding the object itself. Looks like metal.

From outside the stall, I can hear Noah talking to his charge. "Nah, nah, none of that," he says. The horse is probably nibbling on him, as they like to do. "There you go. Yep. That's a good boy."

My head whips up so fast I nail it on the metal hay feeder attached to the wall. I grunt, closing my eyes tight against the sting.

"All right over there?" Noah asks.

"Yep," I manage. "Fine."

Fuck, that smarts.

I rub gingerly over my head as Noah goes back to soothing his horse with gently spoken words. I forcibly tune it out, setting to work on getting the object free from Peanut's hoof. It doesn't take long to realize I need to remove the shoe to avoid hurting him. Whatever it is—a fence nail, maybe?—is embedded at such an angle I can't get a good grip.

I go through the process of removing his shoe and try again. But the moment I get a good grip on the metal, Peanut tugs his leg away.

I mutter a quiet apology to the horse and try again. And *again*, Peanut isn't having it.

"Need help?"

"*Christ*," I growl, nearly bashing my head for a second time as I look up at Noah in the doorway. "Warn a guy, would ya?"

Noah pointedly clears his throat before saying, once more, "Need help?"

"No," I spit out, immediately amending it to, "Maybe."

He steps into the stall, making the space feel much too cramped. Heavy boots pass by as Noah situates himself on the other side of me, one hand on the horse's halter, the other rubbing over his neck. I pick up Peanut's hoof again, and when he tries to look back at me, Noah clicks in a soothing manner and talks to the horse.

The distraction is enough to give me a chance to get ahold of the object with the pliers and give an experimental tug. Peanut tries to pull free, but I hold on, anticipating the move, and Noah distracts him again. The embedded nail moves enough that, this time, I don't hesitate to give it a swift and decisive pull. It comes clean out, and I let Peanut drop his hoof back to the ground.

"Gonna need to clean that out," Noah says, referring to the horse's hoof.

"Oh, really?" I ask, looking up at him. "I had no *clue* I might want to clean a flesh wound to, y'know, prevent infection or an abscess. Thank *God* you were here to tell me."

Noah huffs, giving Peanut another pat before stepping over my still-bent leg. "You're a dick," he says plainly.

"Takes one to know one," I shoot back.

"God, do you have to be contrary every damn time we speak?" Noah asks, stopping in the doorway and turning back around, his irritation evident in every line of his body and the set of his jaw.

"Do you have to assume I'm bad at my job? I know how to take care of a hoof, Noah."

"So glad to hear it, little Colt," he says dryly. "I can rest easy at night knowing you're aware of what an abscess is."

"Jesus fuck, what is your problem?" I spit, standing up.

"You," he says, sounding at a loss. "The answer to that is always you."

"Well, don't I feel special."

Silence stretches following my words, and my heart pounds. Noah's jaw is tense, his eyes boring into me, and I hate it. I want him to *do* something. To go already or...

Noah turns with a shake of his head, and I pull in a breath, the force of the inhale surprising me.

"Fine," I find myself calling. Noah stops. "I accept your terms."

"My terms," he says, looking back at me.

"The...ink."

His eyebrow pops up, and he turns fully, crossing his arms and regarding me. "Really? But you're a virgin."

I huff. "I am *not*—"

"Your skin," he says, seeming *amused*. "Unless you have a tattoo I'm unaware of?"

"No. And I won't be getting one. Because I'll win the Shoein'."

He scoffs, taking a step closer. "I'm *really* going to enjoy seeing my name tattooed across your ass."

"Why the *fuck* would you be seeing it?" I ask, alarmed.

He comes up short, his eyes widening as if he hadn't thought of that, but a voice from down the hall has both of our heads whipping to the side.

"Well? What's the verdict?" Marie asks, looking from me to Noah and back again.

Noah leaves us to it, heading to his makeshift station, and I give Marie the news.

"Peanut had a small nail in his sole. It didn't appear to have caused much of an issue and came out just fine. I'll soak his hoof, clean the wound, and wrap him up. But you'll want to check with your vet to make sure his tetanus is up to date."

"Jesus," Marie says, pinching the bridge of her nose. "A nail? Who the hell is leaving nails out in my yard?"

It's a rhetorical question I don't bother answering, knowing Marie isn't actually accusing anyone of planting it.

"I'll pay you for your time and supplies," she says, sounding tired. "Thanks, Colton."

"Not a problem," I assure her.

Marie heads off, going out the front door instead of back the way she came. Probably to check on the other half of her business: her chickens.

I glance at where Noah is leading a new horse out into the aisle. The ink on his left forearm snakes around him like a vine, disappearing up under his shirt. The design is distinctly floral, except it's not actually vines at the center, I realize. It's rope.

I'm not sure what the flowers are.

Noah catches me looking, and I quickly turn around, focusing on Peanut instead of my archenemy. The one who, apparently, has colorful flowers tattooed on his skin.

I find a bucket in the tack room to soak Peanut's hoof, and the next forty minutes is spent tending to his minor wound. Once he's wrapped up and reshod, I add a fabric boot to help keep the bandages clean. Marie can take it off as she sees fit.

Closing the door to Peanut's stall, I hesitate.

Maybe noticing the sudden stillness in the air, Noah turns his head, his hat set aside now and his hair falling messily over his forehead. His eyes narrow as I step his way.

"Don't, Colton," he says stiffly, refocusing on the hoof held between his knees. "I'm just trying to do my work."

I clear my throat. "The Shoein'."

Noah sighs heavily, but he doesn't look my way. "You issued the challenge. Name a time."

My heart is racing again, and I'm not quite sure why. I know I'll win.

"Next weekend," I tell him.

"Fine."

"It's customary to put an advert in the paper. So folks can attend."

He shakes his head slightly. "Fine."

"Fine?" I ask, his easy acquiescence seeming too...*easy.*

"Fine," he says again, pointedly.

For a moment, the only sound is the soft scrape of his hoof knife.

"You just gonna stand there and stare at my ass?" Noah asks. "Or do you actually have work to get back to?"

I huff, backpedaling to grab my supplies off the ground. "I wasn't staring at your ass," I bite out, heading past the man. "I don't *like* your ass."

"Mhm."

"Fucking dick," I mutter, heading through the door.

If Noah utters a reply, I don't hear it.

It's only once I'm safely within the confines of my truck that a thought strikes...

Did he *want* me to be staring at his ass?

Fucking Noah King.

I turn the ignition and get the hell away from the man, not once looking back.

Chapter 10

NOAH

I can't believe I agreed to this.

Colton is standing not far off, talking to one of the judges that was pulled together for the town's first Shoein' in over twenty-six years. According to custom, five judges have been assigned from the board after Colton notified them of the...*friendly* competition we agreed to and got permission to hold the event in the town center. Also custom.

And the judges aren't the only ones here.

It looks as if half of Darling showed up for this spectacle, many having brought camp chairs, others set up on picnic blankets or sitting in the grass. Someone apparently got a permit to sell popcorn because bags of it are making the rounds. Salted popcorn, caramel corn, even flavors like apple pie and peanut brittle.

Why the *fuck* did I agree to this?

My uncle looks more amused than anything as I help him into his own foldable chair that we brought from home. "Big crowd," he comments, shifting to adjust his position.

I grunt my acknowledgement.

"Nervous?" he asks.

"Please."

He snorts. "You know this is just for fun, right? No one takes these things all that seriously."

Tell that to Colton Darling.

I glance back at the man, who's bouncing on the soles of his feet now, looking as if he's getting a pep talk from the entire Darling family. All of his brothers are here. His parents, too.

If I ever needed more proof of our differences, I'd only need set foot inside the Darling Ranch to see it for myself.

Before I can turn away, Remington meets my eye from across the park. He gives me a smile and a nod.

I nod back before checking in with my uncle. "Comfortable enough?"

"It'll do," he says, which is the best I can hope for. *Comfortable* doesn't come easy for him these days.

"This shouldn't take long," I assure him.

He chuckles. "Get me a bag of caramel corn?"

I nod and head off to find the vendor. I'm paying for the bag when I hear the last person I want to talk to right now. Or anytime, really.

"Ready to lose?" Colton asks, stepping up beside me.

I glance over at him. At the cocky assurance in his blue eyes and the rough stubble covering his jaw. Against my permission, my memory dredges up the feeling of that stubble against my lips, and I quickly avert my gaze, not needing the reminder of that mistake.

"The only thing I'll be losing is the chance to book more ink," I say, voice tight.

Colton scoffs. "Dream on, King."

"Oh, I'm sure my dreams will be sweet tonight. I'll have your defeated face to recall as I'm drifting off to sleep."

"Look at that," he says wryly. "You have a sense of humor after all. Who knew?"

I turn away before the impulse to smack the man becomes too strong to ignore.

"Judges need to go over the rules with us," Colton says before I can get far.

"Be there in a minute," I grit out.

I hand off the caramel corn to my uncle and take a moment to collect myself. It's not that I'm worried about losing this competition. I have it in the bag.

It's the fact that Colton goddamn Darling has the singular ability to make me unreasonably angry anytime he opens his mouth. Hell, all he has to do is look at me, and I want to clock him.

I'm not a violent guy. Not usually.

But *fuck*, he brings it out in me.

Once I'm fairly confident I won't give the man a black eye, I head over to the judges' table. Colton is already there, waiting. He gives me a smirk I ignore.

"Gentlemen," Kamal Yadav says, a man in his sixties who's been on the board as long as I can remember. Pretty sure he stopped by my uncle's with a cranberry tart when I first got to town, although that time right after my parents passed is somewhat muddled in my mind. "I'll be going over scoring so we're all clear on the parameters of today's competition."

Colton and I both nod, and he goes on.

"Timeliness only accounts for a quarter of your total. So getting done first shouldn't be your main objective. Another quarter goes to cleanliness and evenness of the trim. Another quarter to proper shoe shaping. And the final quarter for over-all aesthetics. Got it?"

We nod again.

"We have two horses offered up by a local for today's Shoein'. Neither horse has been worked on by either of you in the past, so we're on neutral ground here. Both are five weeks from their last shod, so again, even turf. You remove their shoes. Trim and outfit them with a new set from the ready-made stock provided. Once you're done, we'll judge your work. Any questions?"

Colton meets my eye briefly before shaking his head. "Nope."

"All good," I say.

Mr. Yadav nods. "All right then. Let's get this Shoein' started. Take your places and we'll bring out the horses. Oh, and boys?" He pauses, gracing us with a smile. "Have fun."

Colton and I turn in tandem, heading over to the area set up for us. I can feel the man's glare on the side of my head, and when I continue to ignore it, Colton huffs.

As Colton checks the tools in his bag—we each brought our own—I tug off my jacket. I toss it aside before turning back, finding Colton's gaze wandering down my exposed arms before he quickly looks away.

The creak of the horse trailer door pulls our attention. The animals are led out one at a time, both Quarter Horses, both seeming nonplussed by the crowd and the steady stream of noise and chatter. I eye the one brought my way, holding out my hand as soon as she's close enough. She gives me a huffing sniff as the attendant ties her lead to a pole.

"Hey, girl," I say softly, running my hand up her nose. "You and me today, all right?"

Her big eyes watch me calmly.

Testing the waters, I glide my hand over her flank and down her leg, giving it a tug. She lifts her foot easily—a great sign—and I let her go, rubbing her neck.

We're given just a minute to get acquainted with our horses, and then Mr. Yadav introduces us to the crowd with a short speech about the history of the Darling Shoein'. It's warming up enough that I'm grateful I put on a t-shirt today and not something heavier. The folks gathered listen raptly, the excitement in the air palpable.

It's been a long time since our townsfolk have seen this. Many of them, myself included, never have.

When Mr. Yadav draws to a close, he waves Colton and me in.

"All right, gentlemen. Let's shake on it, and then we'll begin."

Colton's grip is tight when my hand meets his. He tries his best to crush the bones in my fingers. And, honestly, I do the same. Our eyes hold. Neither of us gives ground. Icy, icy blue stares back at me.

The word is given, and we let go. It's on.

I don't hear the crowd as I race to my horse. Don't even notice Colton. I focus on my work, settling into the familiar rhythm with a single-minded focus. Luckily, my horse doesn't put up a single fuss as I make quick work of pulling off her shoes, but I position myself carefully each time nonetheless should she decide to twist away. Before tossing the shoes to the side, I check the shape of each, committing the unique curves to memory.

Trimming her hooves is a swift process. They're in good condition, just needing the sort of routine clip I could do in my sleep. I'm careful not to take too much dead sole off, since the depth is already shallower than I'd prefer. Once her hooves are as clean and even as they'll get, I rush to the box of ready-made horseshoes.

An anvil is set up for shaping, and I make quick work of it. A handful of hammer strikes to each curve of metal creates the shape I need. I grab a box of nails afterward and head back. After checking each shoe against her hoof, I hammer them into place, only needing to go back to the anvil once for a correction. I'm feeling rather proud of myself when I hear a swell from the crowd.

I glance over, finding Colton's horse nearly finished. He's down to rasping the outsides of her hooves.

Fuck.

It's a race against time—and the man beside me—to crimp my nails and finish. My pulse is galloping away, the cheering from the crowd muddled in with the sound of my own breaths.

I'm so close. *So* close.

I don't make it in time.

From the corner of my eye, I see Colton set down his rasp and stand. He steps away from his horse, hands in the air as he calls out, "Done."

There's enthusiastic clapping and hooting from the crowd, and I curse inside my own head, slowing right the fuck down. I wanted to finish first, of course, but now that Colton won in speed, I need to be strategic. I can't gain those points back, but I can still beat him in overall aesthetics.

I take my time smoothing the outside of each hoof and adding a perfect hem along the edge of the shoes. My pulse steadies as I work, and I tune out the noise of the crowd.

As well as the eyes of my competition.

Knowing I've done all I can with brute force, I pull out the only thing that might put me ahead. The polish.

"What the fuck?" Colton says in shock. "What are you do-ing? That's not...that's not necessary."

"No interference," one of the judges calls as Colton takes a step my way.

He steps right back, growling low in his throat.

I look over and give the man a slow wink, rather enjoying the way he bristles in response. "All's fair in war, little Colt."

Colton's face settles into that scowl I'm so familiar with, his blue eyes promising retribution. With a muttered profanity, he starts to pace, his hands raking through his too-long hair.

I put the man out of my mind, proceeding to polish my horse's hooves until they're gleaming and show-ready.

Once done, I stand up and set down my things. "Done," I announce.

There's renewed clapping from the crowd, some shouted encouragement. Colton and I wait on the sidelines as the judges get out of their seats and approach.

"That was fucking dirty," he hisses to me, his arms crossed in front of him, his gaze not on me but the judges.

"It was perfectly within the rules," I say calmly. "You're just jealous you didn't think of it."

He scoffs. "Bet your shoe work is shoddy."

"It's not," I assure him.

"God, I hate you so much."

I nearly snort. What's new?

The judges head back to their table to mark their scores, and Colton starts pacing again. Remington catches up to him before long, slowing his brother down and giving his arm a squeeze. They exchange a few words, Colton's movements jerky and agitated, Remington's calm, before Colton nods.

I go wait by Walter.

"Nice job, kid," he says as I approach.

I shrug. "He was quicker."

"Eh," my uncle says, waving his hand through the air. "Slow and steady wins the race."

I don't know about that, but I do know I did everything I could to present a perfect shoeing. Losing a quarter of the available points to Colton's quick handling is going to hurt, but there's nothing I can do about that now.

When the judges wave us over to stand in front of our horses, the gathered crowd hushes.

"Timeliness," Mr. Yadav calls out.

The judges hold up their indicators, a blue card for me, a red for Colton.

There are five red.

I hold in my groan, having known it was coming. Even so, it doesn't feel good watching a tally of five added to the board below Colton's name.

"Yes, Colt!" someone shouts. One of his brothers, I think.

Colton rubs his hands together, rocking on the balls of his feet as Mr. Yadav caps his marker. The crowd quiets again.

"Hoof trim," the head judge calls out.

Another round of cards are held in the air. My eyes sweep over them quickly. Three blue and two red. *Three blue.*

I ease out a breath as Mr. Yadav adjusts our totals. Colton at seven. Me at three.

"God, I'm gonna throw up," Colton mutters.

I know the feeling.

Mr. Yadav holds his hand for quiet again. "Shoe technique."

Five more cards rise in the air. Three blue again and two red. *Holy shit.* Colton is at nine. I'm at six.

I could win this. If I get all five for aesthetics, I'll win this.

Colton seems to have come to the same conclusion as me, his hands on his knees as he mutters words too quietly for me to hear.

"Overall aesthetic," Mr. Yadav calls.

I swear you could hear a pin drop in the silence that follows. The judges grab their cards and hold them up. There's a beat where it feels like time stalls.

And then I see it.

Five blue.

A roar goes up in the crowd, the sound a match for the beat of my heart. I glance over at Colton, unable to help myself. He looks...shocked. Absolutely stunned. And for the briefest of moments, I feel...*sympathy*.

I hear my uncle whistling as a few people come over, slapping my shoulder, congratulating me. But I can't look away from my rival. From that expression plastered on his face.

I thought victory would taste oh so sweet after all these years with this man at my throat, trying his best to dig in. I *wanted* to put him in his place. Wanted to prove I was the better farrier.

Instead?

All I feel in lieu of the victory I was expecting is a sting I wasn't prepared for in the least.

Fuck.

Chapter 11

Colton

It feels as if I'm submerged in water as I walk Noah's way, everything around me dampened and hazy, moving slower than it should be.

He looks wary. Maybe. It's hard to tell.

I hold out my hand, and Noah takes it.

"Congratulations," I tell him, the word tasting flat and hollow on my tongue.

Lips pressed into a flat line, Noah nods once. If he says anything in response as I turn to go, I don't hear it.

My family comes over while I'm collecting my things.

"Damn fine effort," my dad says, slapping me on the shoulder.

I shrug, and my mom gives me a hug. "You did good."

Did I, though? Not good enough, apparently.

I mutter a response, and my mom lets me go. There are more words—conciliatory and kind—but they don't feel like much of anything, passing me by like smoke.

Noah is standing next to the man I recognize as his uncle, smiling. My breath stutters in my lungs at the sight.

I don't think I've ever seen that smile before now.

My movements feel stiff as I pick up my bag. Someone tails me—Remi, I think—as I head over to the judges to see if they need help disassembling anything. They assure me it's all taken care of, and when I look back, I realize that's the case. The horses are already back in their trailer, the temporary setup for the Shoein' being taken apart as I watch.

I field a few more half-hearted comments from townsfolk as I head toward my truck. It's blessedly silent once I shut myself inside. Remi rides with me, quiet on our way back to the ranch. He keeps looking over, but my gaze is locked out the window.

When I park in front of the ranch house, I fully intend to head up to my room to sulk, but Remi snags my arm before I can.

"Come on," he says, tugging me in the direction of Jackson's house.

I sigh but follow along.

Jackson and Ash are already home when we arrive. The bonfire out back flickers to life, a tiny orange flame working through the wood in the pit as Jackson stokes it. It's not dark yet, but it doesn't matter.

I slump into an Adirondack chair, and a minute later, Ash passes me a whiskey tin.

"Thanks," I mutter, taking a sip. The liquor burns, and I welcome it.

"Doing all right?" Jackson asks, settling into his chair across the fire. Ash follows him, all but sitting on my brother's lap. Lawson is seated and silent to my right, his feet crossed at his ankles. Remi is a pretzel in the chair to my left.

"Fine," I mumble.

"You did real good," Remi says, to which the others nod or murmur their agreement.

"I lost."

"Barely," Lawson puts in.

"I feel like an idiot," I admit, sucking in a breath. "I was *so sure* I was gonna win. So sure."

"It doesn't make you any less of a farrier," Jackson says. "No one's gonna think that."

I shake my head. "It's not even..."

It's not even about that, is it? Not really. I *know* I'm a good farrier. I'm damn fucking good at my job.

It was just about—*fuck*. Getting one over on Noah King for once? Proving to him I'm worth more than whatever it is he sees when he looks at me?

"Folks had fun today, Colt," Lawson says, pulling me out of my thoughts. "They loved watching you and Noah compete. You should be proud of what you accomplished."

My chest burns, and I can't even chalk it up to the whiskey. "I don't feel proud."

There's a long silence that follows my words, the fire crackling.

When Ash slaps the tops of his thigh, I nearly jump. "All right," he says, all chipper. "How about that Noah fucking King?"

Jackson snorts, and I huff my own laugh, unable to help it.

"The worst," Remi says, his lips twitching.

"Seems pretty surly," Jackson puts in.

"Really?" Ash asks, looking back at him. "This coming from you?"

Jackson scowls, and Ash laughs, reaching up to pull my brother down into a quick kiss. It's so cute I want to fling myself into the fire.

"You know I like you that way," Ash replies, patting Jackson's cheek.

"Oh God," I groan. "It's end days, isn't it? Jackson is smiling, and Noah fucking King is beating me at my own game. What's next? Fire raining from the sky? Lawson getting laid again?"

"Wait, what?" my oldest brother says, a frown on his face.

"You probably would've won if it weren't for that polish," Remi says, my most favorite person ever.

"See? Yes," I cry, sitting forward in my seat. "I would've. Because I'm a damn expert at my craft. And Noah King is...is *sneaky*. And I don't like him. And what the fuck is up with that last name? King? As if. The man doesn't deserve a crown, and there ain't no way I'll ever kneel before him."

I sit back with a huff, my skin feeling hot, adrenaline coursing through me. I prefer it to the numbness I felt before at hearing Noah declared the winner of the Shoein'. I'd rather be pissed at the guy than sad for myself.

Being pissed is easier.

"Um," Remi starts, "why would you be kneel—"

"Boys," our mom calls, startling all of us. She strides toward the bonfire, a few foil-covered plates stacked in her hands. Our dad pops into view next, even more plates balanced in his arms. "I knew I'd find y'all out here. Since apparently my *sons*, all of whom are grown-ass men and should know better, decided the smart course of action would be to get into the damned whiskey before filling their stomachs with dinner. Come on now—take a plate. And a thank-you would be nice for walking all this way."

"It's five minutes down the road," Jackson mutters under his breath.

Our mom passes the plate she was about to hand to Jackson over to Ash and then walks the next one to Remi.

"Oh, c'mon now," Jackson grumbles.

"Here you go," my dad says, handing me a plate from his pile. "So what are we doing? Stewing or cheering up?"

A slow smile spreads across my face as my parents join us in front of the fire. We eat our dinner with our fingers, seeing as they didn't bother bringing forks. No one seems to mind. The sky slowly turns dark as we exchange stories and the occasional attempt is made at making me feel better. It doesn't work. Not fully. But I'm ever so grateful for my family for trying.

It's late when Remi, Lawson, and I head back to the ranch house, my parents having left long ago. Lawson ruffles my hair like I'm still a kid before heading to his room, but Remi doesn't go quite so quickly. He follows after me, peering at me in that way he does. He's always been able to read me better than most.

"Will you be okay?" he asks. I appreciate that he understands, right now, I'm not.

I nod. "It was just a stupid competition."

He raises an eyebrow. "We both know it wasn't stupid. Not to you."

I let out a sigh and plunk down on the corner of my bed, my hands feeling heavy as I lift them to speak for me. It feels easier, somehow, to air my feelings in silence. *'I can't stand the guy, Remi. He's always made me feel like I'm not good enough. Like he doesn't think I'm good enough. Why? What did I ever do to him?'*

'You mean other than compete with the man for the same business for the past fifteen years?'

Remi's expression is full of sass, but I hold his gaze. *'The first time I met the guy, he barely gave me the time of day. He couldn't have made it clearer he thought I was gum under his shoe.'*

'I don't know then.' My brother huffs as he joins me at the edge of the bed. *'Not everyone gets along.'*

'I know that. I just wish...'

I don't finish my sentence, and Remi's softly spoken, "Hey," pulls my gaze. He pats my chest before his hands move slowly and assuredly. *'I know your heart inside and out. If Noah can't see it, that's on him. Not you.'*

I'm embarrassed to feel tears prickling at the corners of my eyes. I blink rapidly to dispel them. "Yeah," I say, all I can manage.

Remi lets out a soft sigh before giving me a hug. When he goes, I walk to my window, looking out over our land and the cows resting in the dairy field under the light of the moon.

Noah fucking King.

Why can't I get over the guy?

I try to go to sleep. I do. But all I succeed in is tossing and turning, my thoughts a whirlwind that won't settle. With a huff, I swing my feet out of bed and grab my phone.

It takes a few texts to folks around town to find out Noah's address. I shove my clothes back on, step into my boots, and head out the door.

I don't know what I'm doing. Not really. Have no clue what I hope to accomplish.

I just can't get past this day without some sort of...*closure.* I'm sure, deep in my gut, if I confront Noah, I'll feel better. Somehow. Some way.

I follow my GPS to his place, a house set back from the road with privacy on both sides. It's quiet when I turn off my truck, and I sit in the driver's seat for a minute, looking at the darkened house, second-guessing my being here. What if I wake Noah's uncle instead of him?

But then I see a flicker of light coming from a barn set out back behind the house and open my door.

No backing out now.

A clang rings out as I walk across the grass toward the barn. It's open, light spilling out from inside. I take a deep breath before rounding the corner.

And then I stop still.

The barn is filled with metal sculptures. *Art.* A western saddle sits on a narrow wooden pedestal, every inch of it crafted from various kinds and colors of metal, every detail precise. There's a horse head, the eyes eerily lifelike, the mane flowing like waves over the side of its neck. Smaller pieces sit along tables. A bird with a seed in its mouth. A bundle of flowers. What looks like triangles perched precariously one over top of the other.

"What the fuck?" I mutter, taking it all in.

Noah whips around, practically jumping a foot in the air. "Colton?" he says in shock. "The hell are you doing here?"

His tone isn't welcoming. If anything, there's an edge of threat to it I should probably heed.

Instead, I step further into the barn and wave my hand through the air. "What is this?"

Noah doesn't answer me. He turns back around, shutting off his forge before tugging his gloves off one at the time. The man is wearing a t-shirt, a fine layer of sweat covering his skin from the heat of the fire. He swipes his hair back and all but slaps his gloves onto the table in front of me. "Get the fuck out."

"Did you...*make* these? Holy shit, Noah, I—"

"Did you hear what I said?" he cuts in. "You're not welcome here, little Colt."

I suck in a breath, tension ratcheting my shoulders tight. "*Jesus*, why do you gotta be such a dick? I just…"

"You just what?" he asks, coming around the table toward me.

I hold my ground, even as I feel the urge to fight or flee pulling at my skin. "You know what? I just came here to talk. To settle some things. But you're being all…" Struggling for the right word, I indicate the man before me. "*You.*"

"I thought we already settled things," he says coolly, crossing his sizable arms. "Isn't that what today was about?"

I bristle, the reminder of my loss far too fresh a wound to brush off. "You know what? Fuck you."

Noah shakes his head, looking upward. "My *God*. Thank you so much for coming into my home and telling me to fuck off. So glad you're here. You can be going now."

"That's not why…" I let out a snarl of frustration, taking a step closer, my very bones feeling as if they're rattling. "Can you just…"

"Just what, Colt? What do you want from me?"

I don't fucking know.

"If this is about the tattoo, I'm not going to make you—"

"It's not about the tattoo," I all but yell. "It's *you*. It's always fucking you."

To my surprise, my hand makes contact with the man's chest, shoving him back a step. His eyes darken, body tensing.

"Colt," he says in warning.

"I want to know why you're stuck in my head. In my life," I growl, shoving the man again. "I want—"

Noah grabs my arm and spins me bodily into his workbench. I scramble to grab ahold of it, catching my weight, the wooden edge digging into my ass as Noah's hand grips the front of my throat. He wedges his knee between my legs and drives it upwards, forcing me harder against the table.

"I'm going to ask you one more time," he says, voice dangerously low, his eyes dark in the limited light of the barn. "What do you *want* from me, Colt?"

I pull in a shuddering breath, and Noah stills, his attention snapping downwards as—to my utter and profound mortification—my dick starts to swell.

Oh, fuck. Holy fuck.

Chapter 12

NOAH

It takes me a prolonged second to register what's happening.

I'd been feeling bad about the hurt I saw on Colton's face when I won the Shoein'. When he looked as if I'd personally kicked his puppy right in front of him.

But all that lingering concern I was holding on to? Shattered to dust the moment Colton goddamn Darling barged into my sanctuary without warning or invitation.

And now my hand is around his neck, and Colton—this man who's made no secret of despising my very existence—is getting hard against my thigh.

He's hard.

Turned on, undeniably.

And he looks scared to death of it.

Colton shoves me, and I quickly let go, taking a step back. My hand burns where it was touching his skin, and I shake it out, only to stutter a step in surprise when Colton comes at me again.

"Don't," I say, trying to brush off his advance. "Walk out the door, Colt."

He doesn't. He tries to grab me, and I twist his arm, pinning it between us as I tug his back to my chest. He inhales sharply, going still, the scent of leather and citrus washing over me with his proximity. His breathing is labored, and my own starts to match.

"Is this what you want?" I ask at a rumble. "To fight?"

He doesn't say a word, so I let him go again, only to grunt when the heel of Colton's boot lands on my foot. I shove him forward against the table, his palms slapping the surface and my own quickly following to keep him down. An involuntary noise leaves his mouth, and my body flashes hot in an instant.

We both freeze, our breaths the only sound in the barn.

I shift my hips, an unconscious action that has me rubbing against Colton's ass, and he *moans*, his head dropping forward.

"Is *this* what you want?" I ask in disbelief. We're so close his hair is tickling my face, the waves spilling forward to hide his features. "You want me to keep you pinned?"

"No," he says halfheartedly, the word barely audible.

I look down over Colton's shoulder. "Your dick says otherwise."

He bucks back against me, but I grip him harder. Colton makes another sound, wounded almost, like surrender. His back heaves beneath my chest, the man shaking. "And yours doesn't?" he grinds out.

Oh, my dick likes this a hell of a lot, apparently. Colton Darling, at my mercy, trembling beneath me like a lamb waiting for slaughter.

"Do you want me to touch you?" I whisper against his ear.

He grunts, not a no, and I pull one of his hands off the table, pressing it over his crotch with my own. Colton's breath shudders out of him.

"Beg me for it, little Colt."

"Fuck you."

I let out a contemplative hum. "Not this time."

Colton stills, but it only lasts until I press his palm harder against his dick. He moans, his body sagging.

"I want to hear you beg," I tell him, running my nose through the hair near his ear. "Tell me to touch you."

"Hate you," he mutters.

"So you say," I soothe, rubbing his hand up and down over the denim of his jeans. Up and down. "But I'm still not going to touch you unless you beg for it."

"*God*," he spits, some of that fire returning. "You're insuffer-able. I don't..."

He cuts off, and I still the motion of our hands, waiting for more words that don't come.

"Do you want me to stop?" I ask, entirely serious.

"Fuck. *Fuck*," he nearly shouts. "Put your hand on my dick already."

"The magic word?"

"*Please*, you fucker."

My smile is a slow thing. "There we go. Was that so difficult?"

Colton groans as I let go of his hand, his sound not one of pleasure. But then I'm popping the button on his jeans and sliding down the zipper, and his breathing picks up. He plants his palm back on the table, and I draw my lips down his neck, satisfied when he shivers.

I don't stop to think about the fact that I've never touched a dick other than my own. I slide my hand along the fabric of his underwear, over the unmistakable hardness of his shaft, and squeeze. Colton lets out a stuttered moan, and I grin into the curve of his neck.

"So hard for me," I whisper.

He sounds as if he wants to argue, but I slip my fingers inside his briefs, and the sound promptly chokes out.

"Oh, fuck," he gasps. "Fuck, fuck."

He tries to hitch into my grip, but with the way the tops of his thighs are pressed into the table, he can't manage it. I run my fingers down the underside of his cock slowly, his skin incredibly warm, the length of him nearly spanning my entire hand.

"Not so little," I murmur, sinking my teeth into his neck as I wrap my fist around him.

Colton grunts, his entire body jerking, his cock throbbing against my palm. I swear I can feel his pulse. Against my fingers. On my tongue.

I release his neck and press my face into his hair again. Colton's scent hits me. It doesn't surprise me that he smells like leather, like tack and all the equipment we work with on a daily basis. The citrus must be his body wash.

"I like the way you're shaking," I tell him, stroking his shaft slowly. So slowly I'm surprised he hasn't complained about it yet.

"Shut up," he mutters.

"Mm. No thanks. Do you want me to go faster?"

"I want you to stop talking."

"Why? So you can pretend I'm a girl? Doesn't work like that, Colt."

He shakes his head, the movement minute. "So I can pretend it's not *you*."

I huff a harsh laugh. "You like that it's me. Otherwise you would have stormed out that door the first chance you got."

He whimpers when I smooth his precum down his shaft.

"Oh, you love it, all right," I murmur, finding his earlobe and drawing it between my teeth.

"You're like a fucking...horse," he says between breathes. "Nibbling me."

He swats my hip, as if to tell me off, but then his hand goes right back to the table, supporting his weight. I squeeze the other to remind him he's not going anywhere, not that I think he'll try. His answering moan is like poetry to my ears.

"You know what I think?" I ask him, my hand gliding over his cock smoothly now. He's leaking like a faucet. "I think it has to be me. Because who else wouldn't be afraid to hold you down? Wouldn't care if it hurt a little? Who else could overpower you. Every. Single. Time?"

His breathing kicks up.

"Does that scare you?" I ask.

He shakes his head in a little jerk.

"It excites you."

He doesn't answer.

"Well," I say lowly, squeezing his dick in a way that has him groaning, "you know what *I* like?"

"Don't...care."

"Manners, little Colt."

I nip the tender spot at his neck before letting his hand go to tug his head to the side. Colton stills once more, the line of his neck exposed, the side of his face finally bared to me, all blinking blue eyes and rough stubble.

Guess that long hair is useful after all.

"I like feeling you squirm beneath me," I tell him, palming the head of his cock before stroking again, a little faster, my knuckles brushing against the fabric of his briefs. "I like how eager you are for my hand on your cock. I like the sound you make when I do this."

Colton lets out a breathy moan as I rub myself against his ass, his body bowing further over the table. He has to feel how hard I am. Has to know this isn't one-sided.

"But you know what I like best?" I ask, rubbing my nose along that stubbled jaw.

He screws his eyes shut, his cock so hard in my fist he has to be close.

"I like the sound of that *please* on your lips. Say it again."

"Fuck off," he moans.

"Do you wanna come?"

He lets out a stuttered cry when I stop stroking him, instead rubbing my thumb along the top of his dick. He licks his lips, eyes still shut.

"Say it, Colt."

"You're an ass," he says with feeling.

"Funny. That didn't sound like 'please.'"

"God," he pants. "I already begged once. What do you want from me? You really need me to humiliate myself further?"

"No," I say firmly, giving his cock a single, smooth stroke. "I want you to know that all you have to do is ask and it's yours."

He pulls in a breath, his eyes flying open, even as they stare straight ahead at the inside of my barn.

"Please," he finally says. "Make me come. Please, goddamn it. *Please.*"

My own eyes slip shut, my breath leaving me as I find Colton's neck. I press my lips there, jerking him off with intention, the same way I would myself. His body stiffens, breaths coming out in little fits and bursts as he edges closer to orgasm. When he inhales on a gasp, I fit my teeth to his skin and twist my wrist.

Colton spills in a flash, coating my fingers, as well as the inside of his briefs. He moans through it, the sound unabashed and surprised in a way I understand. My own cock throbs, *wanting* in the face of its neglect, and I allow myself a single rut against Colton's backside before easing off. I slow my hand, stopping only when he has nothing left to give, and then I remove it entirely.

I don't let go of the man. Not right away. I wipe my palm over my shirt before grabbing his hip to hold him steady, watching what I can of the expressions that flit over his face.

"Okay?" I check.

He draws his head around, dislodging my grip from his hair. Colton doesn't answer, only clears his throat and gives me a decisive shove backwards. I let go and watch as he zips up his jeans, not meeting my gaze. His cheeks are red, that scowl I'm so used to seeing absent.

I'm not sure I like this better.

"Colt..."

He shoves past me, disappearing through the barn doors without a single word. I let him run. Of course I do.

I mutter a curse as I put my things to rights. The gloves that got knocked to the ground. The table that skidded a good several inches over. The forge is cooling now, the fire long since dead.

With a sigh, I look down at my hand and the remnants of what just happened. There's no doubt in my mind I got off on pushing Colton goddamn Darling over the edge, even though I didn't *get off* at all. Does that make me bi? Does it matter?

A single shared orgasm certainly doesn't turn us into friends. Doesn't even make me like the guy.

I've been enemies with Colton Darling since nearly the moment I stepped foot in this town. Back when we were barely men at all. Kids, really. Both of us stupid, maybe. But him crueler than I ever expected.

It should be water under the bridge by now. I shouldn't care how Colton is feeling after letting me jerk him off in my barn.

But when the fuck do feelings ever truly make sense?

Chapter 13

COLTON

I pace. Not sleep. Pace.

I already showered off the...mess from whatever the fuck that was in Noah's barn. Now I'm dressed in fresh clothes, the sky above me dark as my feet carry me along the river running through our property. The moon reflects brightly off the surface of the still water, my boots leaving treads in the soft ground. I kick at a tall weed, feeling none the better.

What the *fuck* was that?

One minute, Noah and I were fighting. And then...

I groan, the memories assaulting me against my will, not all of them unpleasant.

I *liked* that. Liked Noah shoving me against the table. Liked him holding me down and—*fuck*—jerking me off, his hand callused and so fucking big there was no way to mistake him for anything other than a man.

A man.

I just had...sex? Can I even call it that? With a man.

But it was *Noah*. And that's the one piece of the equation I did not like. The asshole made me *beg*.

Jesus Christ, how am I ever going to face him again?

I spin and walk in the other direction, realizing I'm a good couple miles away from the house now. It's quiet out, not even the cows in the fields next to where I'm walking making any noise.

It had to be the manhandling. I simply discovered—through sheer accident—some sort of kink I didn't know I had because none of the women I've been with have ever tried pushing me around.

The question is...

Is that all? Or did I also like the fact that it was a man doing it?

I certainly didn't hate Noah's size. Didn't hate the smell of him or how roughly he held me. Didn't even hate the feel of his cock pressed against my ass.

If he were any other guy, I would have been curious enough to touch him back and—

Well, shit.

I think that answers my question, doesn't it?

Does it?

Fuck. Why does this have to be so damn complicated? Why can't I just *know*? Who realizes at thirty-seven fucking years old that they might have a little untriggered thing for dudes?

And *why* did it have to be Noah? Of all the people in the goddamn world to wake up this side of me, why did it have to be *him*?

"Fuck!"

My shout rings in the air for a moment before an owl hoots an answering call.

Exhausted, buzzing, and more confused than ever, I head back to the ranch house and try my best to sleep.

I don't sleep.

Despite my best efforts, I can't shut off my brain, which is why I find myself out of bed before the ass crack of dawn, shoving perfectly crispy strips of bacon into my mouth. The dining room is bustling, the first-shift ranchers eating their breakfast as usual to fuel up before the start of their busy day. Some will head off to milk the dairy cows after this. Others will saddle up horses and ride west, overseeing the many acres of land over which our beef cattle roam.

Jackson will make sure everything is running smoothly, as he does every day. Ash will keep us all happily fed. Remi will take care of the horses and the animals at the petting farm. Lawson will head into town to the school to teach bright young minds the genius of William Shakespeare or Harper Lee. My mom will probably work on her vegetable gardens, getting beds ready for planting and putting up trellises. My dad will...I dunno. Tend to the honey bees he got last year, maybe?

And me?

I'll be shoeing horses as if my life didn't just irrevocably change last night. As if I'm the same person I was a couple days ago, when I know, for a fact, that isn't true. I *am* changed.

I just don't know if it's for the better.

My morning passes in a fog. Changing shoes. Trimming hooves. Trying—and failing—to banish thoughts of Noah every time a horse nibbles on my back or neck.

"I want you to know that all you have to do is ask and it's yours."

Fuck.

I drive to my appointments, keeping my eyes peeled each time I'm on the road, like I might see Noah's bike or his blue pickup. I eat lunch at home, not daring to venture into town. And I repeat the process all over again in the afternoon.

Shoes. Hooves. Tiny bites on my arms and attempts to grab my hair. Noah.

"Beg me for it, little Colt."

Nope, nope, nope.

More driving. Dinner at the ranch. A few looks thrown my way from my family that I ignore.

By the time my day is well and truly done, so am I. I take a shower, my legs feeling like lead, and fall onto my mattress.

A soft knock comes a moment later. "Colt?"

"Come in," I tell my brother.

Remi eases the door open, concern obvious on his face. "Hey. You doing okay?"

I'm not surprised he noticed something off with me, but I don't know what the fuck to say to him. How to explain I'm having a sexual crisis because I begged my longstanding rival to make me come and busted a nut so intense I thought, for a second, I might pass out.

"Do you think," I say slowly, "you could bring me to a gay club this weekend?"

Remi's eyebrows fly up. "Did you say a gay club?"

I nod, turning my face more fully his way so he can read me better. "I'm kind of freaking out over here."

Remi closes the door and comes over quickly, slapping my legs out of the way so he can take a seat. I ease into a sitting position against the headboard, my chest feeling tight.

"Explain," my brother says.

"Fuck, Remi. I let Noah..." I stop and hastily spell out, *jerk me off*, before continuing in voice. "And I didn't hate it, even though you *know* I hate him. So now I needa...test it? Figure myself out, I guess? Because what the fuck? Like, what the actual fuck?"

"Okay," Remi says slowly, easing out a breath I replicate on instinct. "Noah?"

I nod.

"As in Noah King?"

"Do we know any others?" I groan before rubbing my eyes.

"Just checking," he says mildly, sounding borderline amused. "How did it happen? Do I even wanna know?"

I shake my head furiously.

"But you think you might be into guys?" he asks.

I let my hands drop from my face and nod. "How'd you know?"

Remi tilts his head back and forth. "I guess, for me, it was more a matter of realizing I like *people*. Not genders."

"But you...like dick?" I ask, cringing.

Remi's lips twitch, evil spawn that he is. "Oh, yes."

"God," I groan out, rubbing my face again. "Forget I asked. I do *not* need to hear details of your sex life. Not a single goddamn one."

Remi flicks me in the chest, and I drop my hands, realizing I'd been covering my mouth.

"Sorry," I say more clearly. "I said I don't need any more details, little bro. I'd have to bleach my brain."

He snorts. "Yet you want me to take you to a gay club. I've only been once, you know."

"But will you?" I ask, pulling out the face that was most successful in scoring me extra cookies as a child.

Remi rolls his eyes. "Of course I will. Wanna invite Jackson and Ash?"

"Could we maybe just...keep this between us for now?"

He locks his lips. "Done. It'll be okay, you know. Any which way."

"I know," I say on a sigh.

It's not the thought of being bisexual that's scary. Not really.

It's learning something so fundamental to my being that I never realized before. It's the fear of wondering why now?

Why him?

"Get some sleep," my brother says, patting my leg as he stands. "You look like a raccoon."

"Do not," I protest hotly. "Take it back."

My brother shoots me a one-handed, *'I love you,'* as he walks out the door. I let out a sigh, knocking my head back against the wall.

This will be good. I'll go to a club, check out some guys, and then I should know, right? If I'm attracted to any of them, that answers my question. And, if not...

I don't want to think about *if not.*

I'm just settling down in bed, lights off, when my phone dings. With a grumble, I snatch the device off my nightstand, only to come up short.

Unknown: Are you okay?

Nooo. No, it's not. Is it?

My response is four incredulous letters.

Me: King?

My phone pings again, and I nearly drop it.

Unknown: Your detective work is superb, little Colt.

"Oh, fuck you, you fucking..."

My fingers fly across the keyboard, blood pumping hot.

Me: How'd you get my number?

Unknown: Christ. Let me ask again. Are. You. Okay?
Me: What's it to you?

My chest heaves as I wait for his response, having no clue what I want him to say. Why is he even texting? He doesn't actually *care*, does he? No fucking way.

For a split second, I debate blocking his number. Instead, I save the contact.

Noah: Fuck, Colton. I want to make sure I didn't force myself on you.

I freeze, everything around me stilling before I exhale in a whoosh.

He's been worrying he—what? Took advantage of me? While I've been freaking out over my sexuality, Noah King has been thinking...

Me: You didn't. I wouldn't have let you.

A long pause.

Noah: You're okay?

"Jesus," I groan, my voice low.

Me: We're not doing this. We're not friends, Noah. Won't ever be.

Noah: I'm well aware.

Me: So how I am is none of your concern.

Noah: Do you have to be such a stubborn ass all the time?

Before I can fire off a comeback, my phone rings.

"The fuck?"

I don't answer, blinking at Noah's name on my screen. The call goes to voicemail, and another text comes through.

Noah: Pick up your phone, Colt.

Noah: Or I'm coming over.

I hit call, and Noah answers not one ring later.

"The fuck is your problem?" I demand.

"Really? You wonder why I might be a little concerned after last night? Neither of us was expecting that—"

"No shit."

"—and you left like your ass was on fire. Excuse me for wanting to make sure you weren't going off the deep end."

"I'm not that fragile, Noah. Believe it or not, you didn't manage to break me."

He practically growls. "Oh, fuck you, Colt. I know you think I'm this terrible person, but I would never intentionally hurt you. Not like you hurt me."

"What's that supposed to mean?" I ask, my mind flitting rapidly through the events of last night. Is he talking about me stomping on his foot?

"All I wanted to know is if you're all right," he grits out. "But clearly, you're the same Colton Darling as ever."

Except I'm not the same as I was before. But I won't give Noah the satisfaction of admitting he's the reason why.

"I'm fine," I tell him, forcing myself to believe the words. "So leave me be."

"Fine," he spits.

"*Fine*."

Noah hangs up, and I puff out a breath, nearly slamming my phone back onto my nightstand. I hope no one can hear me screaming into my pillow.

After I punch the fluffy rectangle back into shape, I plop my head down and stare up at the moonlit ceiling above, trying not to remember the feel of Noah's hand wrapped around my cock. Trying not to recall the sound of his voice or the sheer relief I felt when he trapped me against that table, taking away my option to flee.

I try my best to put Noah fucking King out of my mind.

And I hate that I fail.

Chapter 14

NOAH

My arm burns as I hammer the last of the horseshoes into shape, the ringing of metal on metal feeling appropriately jarring considering the back and forth of my thoughts.

Colton Darling.

The man I've hated for years.

The look on his face when he came.

How exasperating he is. Always.

The way he went pliant when I tugged his hair and palmed his cock.

How fast he ran away.

The sounds he made when I sank my teeth into his neck. Did I leave a mark?

Shit.

I wince at the glancing blow to my thumb and refocus my attention, checking the shape of the shoe to make sure it's level. Hefting a sigh that's more mental than physical, I grab the rest of the set and head back to Brownie, the sweet-as-can-be mare I'm shoeing.

"Needed new ones?" a voice asks off to my right.

I glance that way and give Henrietta Brooke a nod. "She did. Her old shoes were worn enough I thought it best to do a full replacement."

She purses her lips slightly, although she doesn't look surprised nor upset. "I'll add some goat butter to your basket. Made fresh just yesterday."

"You don't have to—"

"Let me add the butter, Noah," Henrietta says firmly. "You're doing us a favor here. At least let me make sure you're paid your due."

"Fair enough," I concede. "Thank you."

"Mhm. I'll leave you to it. Come on up to the house when you're done."

Henrietta walks off, her light cardigan pulled tight around her shoulders, and I get back to outfitting Brownie with a fresh set of shoes. Although the Brookes are new clients, Brownie has quickly become one of my favorite horses. She's incredibly gentle and far more intuitive than most humans.

For a split second, I wonder if Colton misses working with her. But I dismiss the thought immediately.

Brownie's muzzle rests against my shoulder as I finish rasping the outside of her final hoof, her breathing like a comfortable metronome in my ear.

"All set," I tell her, letting her hoof down and standing upright.

Brownie hooks her head over my shoulder and tugs. I chuckle, stepping in close and rubbing along both sides of her body. The hug is welcome, and I let myself lean my weight against the sturdy mare, wishing everything in life was this easy and uncomplicated.

"If I had a horse, I'd want one just like you," I tell her.

She ruffles a soft breath against my back.

After gathering some much-needed strength from the horse, I give her a final pat, clean up my things, and head up to the Brookes' house. Even though my basket of goods is waiting on the porch, I still knock on the door, knowing Henrietta will want to say goodbye.

As expected, she gives me a smile as she steps out onto the porch in front of me. "Thanks again, Noah. I can't tell you how much I appreciate this."

"I'm happy to be here," I tell her honestly. "Six weeks again?"

"Please," she says.

I give a nod as I pick up the wicker basket stuffed full of goat cheese, soap, and the fresh butter Henrietta promised. "If I don't see you around town, I hope you have a good start to your spring."

"Same to you," she replies. "And say hello to your uncle for me."

I tell her I will and leave the Brookes' farm, heading toward Plum's to grab a few things for dinner. I promised my uncle steak tonight if he agreed to eat a salad. He grumbled about it, but I won in the end.

Being that it's Friday, the grocery store is suitably busy when I arrive, plenty of folks making their weekly runs or picking up something special for the weekend. I say hello to my neighbor as we pass one another in the produce section, amused that I see her more frequently here than I do on the road we share.

I'm just adding some early season tomatoes to my cart—which won't taste nearly as good as the local ones we'll get in a few months' time—when I catch sight of a familiar face.

A familiar, scowling face.

Colton must have spotted me first, considering that patented scowl of his is already set in stone, the man's blue eyes flinty beneath the brim of his hat, his hair curling around his nape in a way I find distracting. Any other day, I'd simply ignore the man. Just ignore him and head on my way.

Not today.

Maybe it's because of what happened between us. Or maybe I'm sick of being Colton Darling's target practice. Either way, I let my mouth curl into a smile I know is far from kind, and Colton's eyes flicker. Surprise. Trepidation. Anger.

He doesn't stop to talk to me, not that I thought he would. He storms silently past, a waft of his scent hitting me as he goes. Why I never noticed the way the man smells—or, maybe more appropriately, why I *am* noticing now—I try not to think about.

My eyes drop to Colton's ass as he walks away. Can't quite help it. There's a simmer of...something in my gut. Something I'd half hoped was only a fluke.

Seems not.

I head up to the register to pay for my groceries, grateful to find a lane open without Jenna at the helm, which makes me feel guilty in turn. Jenna's a perfectly nice person. Just a little *too* nice at times.

I'm not really in the mood to deal with *too nice* right now.

As the last of my items are making their way from the conveyor belt into bags, someone steps into the lane behind me. Figures. Colton, upon seeing me, spins right back around and walks away. I bark a laugh.

"Something funny?" the employee at the register—Margie—asks as she bags my tomatoes.

I shake my head, giving her a smile. "Nah. Nothing at all."

Colton's black truck is nowhere to be seen when I get out to the parking lot. Probably for the best.

Definitely for the best.

Once I arrive home, I find my uncle in the kitchen, doing the crossword on the tablet I got him a couple years ago. He doesn't look up to say, "Get the steak?"

"I got it," I assure him, setting the bags and the basket from Henrietta on the counter to unload. "Plus some fresh greens."

He grumbles at that, finally looking over, his glasses slipped halfway down his nose. "What you got there?"

"Goat butter," I tell him. "From the Brookes. Henrietta says hello, by the way."

He hums. "You gonna—"

"Yes, I'll cook the steak in the butter."

"Good," he grunts.

I chuckle. "Wanna head into town this weekend?"

"What for?" my uncle asks.

I shrug, setting the wrapped steaks on the cutting board. "Just to get out of the house for a bit. We could hit the farmer's market or see if Bob has any new antiques. Maybe even grab some lunch."

He hums, considering. "It has been a long time since I've been to the antiques market."

"See? We'll go visit Bob, then."

"Fine," he says, not managing to sound nearly as surly as he's trying to pull off. "You should get out for yourself, too, Noah. Go have some fun. Do you even remember how?"

"I have fun," I defend.

He raises an eyebrow. "Yeah? Name the last time."

I huff. "Earlier today. I hung out with Miss Brownie. That was fun."

My uncle shakes his head, eyes back on his crossword. "That's work. It ain't the same thing."

"Is for me."

"Psh."

I roll my eyes, but apparently, he's not done.

"How about this? You can drag me to the antiques market tomorrow so long as you go out tonight."

"What is this?" I ask, amused despite myself. "Some sort of reverse curfew you're trying to impose? You realize I'm nearly forty years old, right?"

"Forty years going on sixty," my uncle retorts. "Live a little, Noah. Don't end up like...well, like me."

I frown, closing the fridge door and grabbing the empty grocery bags off the counter to put away. "What's wrong with being like you?"

He sighs. "I've lived a very solitary life. You know that. Heck, you've been around for a good deal of it. And I don't regret *you* one bit. That's not what I'm saying, so don't go getting any ideas." He gives me a stern look, waiting until I nod to go on. "It's just that sometimes I wonder what my life would be like now if I'd tried a little harder back then to find somebody to share it all with. Might've been better. For both of us."

"Walter," I say, pulling out a chair to sit down beside my uncle. "You are the best thing that could've possibly happened to me. When I lost my home, you opened yours. Do you realize you've been a parent to me for longer than my own father ever was?"

He looks shocked by that, but it's the truth. So much time has passed, even though it barely feels it.

"You did everything right," I tell him seriously. "I couldn't have asked for better, not then and not now. And frankly, I'd be proud to end up like you. But...if you're lonely, it's not too late to find someone to share your life with. A partner. Friends, even. You *can* still have that."

He shakes his head as if the notion is ridiculous, and I don't push, recognizing the reticence on his face for what it is and knowing I won't get anywhere tonight if I try. Instead, I give his shoulder a squeeze and let him think about what I said.

"I'm gonna shower, and then I'll get those steaks on the heat."

"And tonight?" my uncle says, typing an answer into his crossword. "You'll go out?"

I sigh, even as a smile quirks my lips. "I'll think about it. How about that?"

He gives a firm nod, and I head upstairs to my bedroom. My shoulders feel tight as I tug off my shirt, my pants quickly following. I take a moment to stretch my arms up high, my fingertips brushing one of the stationary blades of the ceiling fan. There's a soft pop in my spine that has me sighing in relief, and I drop my arms.

Hunkering over horse hooves all day doesn't make for the happiest back.

After shucking off my briefs and wrapping a towel around my waist, I head across the narrow hallway to the bathroom. As the shower heats, I contemplate, once again, my Colton problem.

The man clearly despises me. Always has, and I'm pretty sure he always will. Nothing has changed just because of a single moment of weakness on his part. And my own. I didn't even expect it to.

But *fuck*, seeing that scowl aimed my way earlier had me itching to wipe the look off his face and replace it with the sweet surrender he fought so hard against the other night. *That* look is one I won't forget for a long, long time.

Colton Darling, brought to heel. Because of me.

If only I could get him down on his knees, too.

The thought has a shiver coursing through my body, even as I step into the heat of the shower. Considering the probability of Colton begging me to touch him again is damn near nil, I don't see that scenario playing out apart from within my own ill-advised fantasies. Heck, the man will likely do his best to stay as far away from me as possible. Nothing new there.

But it doesn't change the fact that something shifted for me the moment I touched Colton Darling. Before then, even. The kiss?

I always assumed I was straight. I had no reason to think otherwise.

Not until him.

I can't shove that newfound knowledge back down again. Don't even want to. I won't ignore that part of myself, even if I've yet to understand it.

Well, if my phone call with Colton taught me one thing, it's that revisiting the subject with him isn't an option. I'm on my own. And it's for the best, really.

Because let's face it.

Fucking around with my bitter enemy would lead to nothing but absolute disaster.

Chapter 15

COLTON

My heart thumps as I turn off my truck. The club waits up ahead, looking innocuous enough, its façade not giving much away.

It could be any club or bar. Just a normal night out.

But it's not. The fact that it took nearly an hour to get here is evidence enough. Add onto that what's waiting inside...

"Ready?" Remi asks, his voice startling me.

"Jesus," I groan. "I don't know. How do I know if I'm ready? How do I...*flirt* with men, Remi? I don't know what the fuck I'm doing."

My brother looks more amused than anything. "You flirt with them the same way you'd flirt with women. Don't try too hard. Just...relax and see what happens."

"Relax," I mutter. "Sure. I'm plenty relaxed."

He snorts. "I'm gonna turn off my CI. Don't...sign your attempts at flirting, please? I really don't need to see that."

Despite my nerves, I stifle a laugh and nod, unsurprised Remi doesn't want to listen to the blaring music inside the club.

"All right," I say, shoring myself up as he holds down the on/off button on his processor. With my best smile in place, I move my hands in a decisive, *'Let's do this.'*

There's no wait at the door. We walk right in, the thump of the music so heavy I can feel it in the soles of my shoes. There's a bouncer just inside who checks our IDs, and then we're waved forward. Remi grabs my arm and directs me toward the bar.

I can't help but let my eyes wander as we move through the crowd. I'm no stranger to seeing men cuddle up close or kiss, and it's never once bothered me. No more than seeing any two people be all lovey-dovey over one another in public. But I've never looked at a man and wondered, *Do I want to kiss him?* Not before.

Now? Every man I set eyes on, it's all I can ask myself.

I can thank—or blame—Noah for that.

Remi gets my attention as we reach the bar. *'Jack and coke,'* he signs. *'Just one.'*

I nod and wait for the bartender to notice us, which takes a minute. He's a big guy, nearly the size of the bouncer. Rugged-looking. Tattoos over his arms, like Noah.

Fuck Noah.

Even though the bartender is subjectively handsome, there's no...spark. No desire to kiss him as he comes our way, hitching his head up in a nod. "What'll you have?" he asks over the music.

"Jack and coke and just Jack," I tell the guy.

He knocks the bar top and walks off.

Remi pulls my attention. *'See anyone?'*

I pinch my fingers in a quick *'no'* before looking around again. *'I don't know what my type is. I'm so confused.'*

Remi gives my arm a squeeze, his expression telling me *you'll figure it out.* I huff and turn back to the bar just in time to accept our drinks. After paying, Remi and I work our way toward the edge of the room, standing in a small open pocket of space beside the dance floor. We sip our whiskeys, eyes roaming, me doing my damndest to find *attraction* lurking somewhere in this mess.

A punch to my shoulder has me looking over at my brother. *'You're trying too hard,'* he signs pointedly, moving his body to the beat of the music. *'Stop thinking. Just...feel.'*

Just feel. I can do that. I nod, loosening my shoulders and downing the rest of my drink. I look out over the busy club again, not seeking out faces this time. Instead, I watch the way people dance. The bodies moving together, hands grabbing, the imitation of sex. I let myself look freely at the men grinding against one another, remembering the feel of Noah's hands pressing me down, his body blanketing mine like a furnace, his teeth nipping at my neck and the feel of his crotch pressed to my ass.

Fuck.

I wipe my thoughts and try again. Men dancing. Grinding. Groping. Hands slipping over denim. Noah guiding me to get myself off.

God fucking—

"Hey," some guy all but shouts, giving Remi a once-over that has me grimacing because, *Jesus*, that's my baby brother. "Wanna dance?"

Remi leans closer to him to both say and sign, "I'm Deaf."

It's a challenge, whether or not the guy knows it.

The newcomer blinks once before doing a couple stilted dance moves and then opening his hands wide in a questioning gesture. Remi snorts and nods, the stranger having passed his test. He checks in with me, an eyebrow raised.

I flick my hands in a reassuring, *'Go. Dance. Have fun. I'll find you later.'*

Remi nods, following the guy out onto the dance floor. I watch only long enough to decide I don't need to see that, thank you very much, and then I set out through the crowd, determined to find someone who revs my engine. *Stop thinking. Feel.*

I get approached by several men as I wander, their hands grabbing me in question. I stop only long enough to suss out how I'm feeling. Which is...lackluster.

I don't fucking get it. I *know* I liked what happened with Noah. So why the hell doesn't the thought of doing that with any of these men thrill me? Why doesn't it get my blood pumping? Why doesn't it make my cock ache? Why did it have to be—

Holy Jesus.

Noah fucking King.

Standing at the edge of the room.

With some guy's *hand* underneath his shirt.

I'm storming over before I've even registered the movement of my feet. My blood sure is pumping now, righteous indignation coursing through me.

Because how *dare* he. How fucking dare he!

"Hey," I shout, tugging the unknown guy off Noah, only barely clocking the widening of both men's eyes before I'm in Noah's face. "Are you fucking kidding me right now?"

"Colton?" he asks, shocked.

"Hey, asshole," the other guy says, trying to pull me back. I don't let him.

"Tell him to go," I grit out, not breaking Noah's gaze.

His eyes ping between my own several times before he looks over my shoulder and shakes his head just a little. The guy lets out a sound of frustration and kicks the back of my boot before presumably trudging off. I don't turn to check.

"What are you doing here?" Noah asks, a frown marring his face.

"Seriously?" I retort, a frantic edge leaking into my tone. "What're *you* doing? You make me goddamn *question* things, Noah, and then I find you here—what? Getting your kicks with somebody else? Is it all just a fucking game to you? Huh? Was *I* just a game?"

Noah's frown is deeper now, the coppery brown of his eyes looking dark in the club. He leans close, and my pulse jumps, breath stuttering as his hand grips my hip hard enough for me to feel the indentation of each fingertip.

"Did you ever stop to think I'm trying to figure myself out, too?" he asks slowly, his voice nearly disappearing amidst the throb of the music.

I come up short. Because no. That hadn't once crossed my mind. I figured, after what happened, he had to be *not straight* and aware of it. The way he acted...so confident and in control. I thought, surely...

Noah dips his head, lips near my ear as I try to control my breathing. "I've never touched a man before you, little Colt."

A shiver runs down my spine. One I'm quick to slough off.

I step back, meeting Noah's gaze. "Guess that makes two of us."

His eyes move between my own again, as if he's trying to read me. I hate it. I don't want Noah King inside my head.

I turn to go, my brain just now catching up to the rashness of my decision to race over here. And what for? What good did I possibly think it would do?

But Noah doesn't let me go. His grip on my hip tightens, and he turns me into the wall at his back, putting it at mine. I let out a curse, knocking his hand away, only to get pinned in by his massive arms on both sides of me. My heart pounds heavily in my chest, and I do my damndest not to feel the stirring below my belt.

Because *no*. He doesn't get to have that. Noah fucking King doesn't get to be the one damn man I'm attracted to. I'm *not*. I can't be. Not him.

Not him.

"Were you jealous, little Colt?"

"Knock it off," I tell him, pushing against his arm. He moves his hand to my chest, planting it firmly, his thumb at the hollow of my throat.

"Tell me," he persists, his eyes half-lidded as he crowds me into the wall.

My pulse is beating so fast I'm more than positive he can feel it.

"Fuck. You," I say instead.

Noah's chuckle is dark, something I can't even hear. I can sense it, though. Feel it reverberating from him to me. "Would you like that?" he asks, shocking me into silence. Noah presses his advantage, his hand slipping up to my throat, cradling me almost, except for the distinct edge of threat I can feel from his person. "Do you want me?"

"In your dreams," I fire back, praying he doesn't move any closer. If he does, there will be no hiding how turned on I am.

I'm fucked up. This is so fucked up.

"I have had very nice dreams about you," he says, almost taunting.

I huff out a breath. "Oh yeah? What were we doing? Braiding each other's hair? 'Cause I hate to break it to you, King. But I don't see that happening in our lifetime."

His chuckle is short-lived. "No," he says, moving closer, his thumb pressing up on my jaw, the flower-laden rope vining darkly over his skin keeping me caged in. He waits until I meet his eye before saying, "You were on your knees for me. If I asked nicely, would you bow before me now?"

"Fuck. You," I say again, with feeling.

My eyes slip shut when Noah's body presses to mine, the weight of him impossible to ignore, the way he *grinds* slowly against me proof I'm not fooling anyone. Least of all him.

"I think you were jealous," he says at my ear, his hand slipping from the front of my throat to the back of my neck. He holds me tightly. Possessively. "I think I like you jealous."

"Why?" I huff out, willing my erection a swift death. Instead of going down, it throbs against Noah's hip, liking the rough handling far too much.

Noah hums, the vibration of it traveling from his chest to mine. His lips are still pressed close to my ear, and I wonder what we look like to anyone bothering to pay us any mind. Two men in an intimate embrace, no different than anyone else inside this club?

"Because," he says, stopping long enough to nip the shell of my ear, "I like having your reins in my hand, little Colt. Tell me. If I tug, will you come to heel?"

My breath stutters out of me, my immediate refusal getting caught on the way out of my throat. I want to scream *no*. No fucking way will I let Noah King lead me around by the balls. But I already have, haven't I? I let him once. And my conviction of it never happening again is weakening the longer Noah's hand remains wrapped around my neck.

"I don't like you," I remind him.

"You don't have to. Not for this."

Ah, fuck.

My hips hitch against Noah before I can stop myself. He feels it. Of course he does. His hand tightens almost painfully against my nape before fingers sift up into my hair. He tugs my head to the side, his lips at my neck.

I need to push him away. I need...

A moan works its way out of my throat as Noah's mouth clamps down on my skin, sucking harshly, the flit of his tongue driving an electric current from my spine to my balls. I blink rapidly, trying to get my head on straight, trying to remember why this is a bad fucking idea.

It is, isn't it? The worst.

Noah's lips slide upwards, sucking again, and my head thunks against the wall. His fingers massage the back of my head—an apology?—before he's tugging me back around, meeting my eye. He's so close, his lashes looking dark, his eyes asking a question I don't know the answer to.

Hate him. Hate this man.

So why I lean forward to catch his stupidly full lips with my own, I have no fucking clue. Noah crowds me into the wall, both hands in my hair now, and when the hell did I grab his shirt? I don't have a single brain cell left to make sense of this.

Because Noah's lips are on mine. Ruthless. Powerful. All-consuming.

He's kissing me. I'm kissing *him*.

And it's so much more than lackluster.

Fuck.

Fuck.

I have a hate-on for Noah fucking King.

Chapter 16

NOAH

If he pulls away, I might just die.

Luckily, Colton doesn't seem to be going anywhere, pinned as he is to the wall like a bug, his hand in my shirt shifting to my lower back, tugging me closer. I try to corral the groan that wants to break free, but I don't quite manage it.

This man makes me unhinged. He brings me undone.

And I'm past caring about the repercussions. At least for now.

Colton tastes like whiskey, and somehow the harshness of it matches this man, who's biting at my mouth as if he wants to make sure I know damn well I'm on his shit list.

I'm well aware.

I tighten my grip in his hair and slide my other hand down to grab his crotch none too gently. He stills, breath puffing out. *Much better.* I reclaim his mouth, not caring to dissect why his submission feels like far more than victory. It doesn't matter. This won't ever be anything more than exactly what it is now.

Blowing off steam. A chance, even, to have this man under my thumb.

I break from Colton's lips as I rub his crotch, the hitch of his breath more visible than audible. "Do you want to give everyone here a show?" I ask, sliding my thumb along the length of his cock, tightly confined by his jeans. "Or will you be good and come with me out back?"

"Fuck," Colton mouths, refusing to meet my eye, his gaze pinging from my lips down to my chest. I can see him trying to reconstruct his walls, and that won't do.

"Let me rephrase that," I say at a rumble, bringing my lips close to his ear. "Come out back with me. Because I'm dying to make you keen, little Colt, and I won't do it with an audience."

"Why?" he huffs out, his hips rolling against my hand, even as his voice sounds harsh. "Are you embarrassed?"

I pull my head back and raise an eyebrow. "Do I look like a man embarrassed to have a dick in his hand?"

"It's not in your hand yet," he shoots back, the contrary fuck.

"And whose fault is that?"

He doesn't seem to have a response. His eyes flit around, as if he's just now remembering where we are. Not that anyone is paying us much mind. We're certainly not the only ones copping a feel inside the darkly lit club.

"Colton," I nearly growl. His gaze snaps back to me. *Finally.* "Do I needa throw you over my shoulder? Would that make this easier?"

Easier for him to accept. To let himself have what he so clearly wants.

He doesn't answer, his wide eyes and uptick in breath the only giveaway to how he's feeling. I wait him out. Five seconds. Ten.

"Last chance to walk," I tell him, letting my hands drop, giving him an easy exit.

His grip tightens on my shirt, but he doesn't make a single move to go. Not one.

"All right," I mutter, grabbing Colton's arm and bending down. I maneuver him over my shoulder, much to his verbal shock.

"The fuck," he croaks. "Noah. What the ever-loving *fuck?*"

"I warned you," I answer, weaving through the dense crowd at the edge of the room, folks stepping aside easily with amused eyes as I haul Colton toward the back hall. A couple hoots are thrown our way. One suggestive *get it.*

There are a smattering of people in the hallway. Some hidden away in dark corners doing who knows what. Several waiting on the bathrooms. I find the back door, breathing a sigh of relief to see it propped open already. Won't be setting off any fire alarms.

Colton stops his squirming as I shove the door open with my hip, walking him through. The heavy metal clunks behind us as it hits the brick blocking it from shutting. We're only a few steps outside when Colton makes his desire to be put down known.

The second his feet hit the ground, he's coming at me, hair ruffled and cheeks red.

"You've got some nerve, you know that?" he barks, pushing against my chest.

I let him shove me backwards, around the edge of the building where it's darker, the din of the club quieting the further away we get.

"You're such a goddamn *asshole*," he persists, eyes darkly blue out here, the flush on his cheeks getting harder to make out. He shoves me again and again, his brow furrowing when

I start to smile. "You think this is funny? It's not funny, Noah. None of this is fucking *funny*. It's messed up is what it is. You and me? In what fucking world does that make any goddamn sense?"

"It doesn't," I agree.

"Then what the fuck are you smiling about?" he asks, nearly frantic. "What are we *doing*, King?"

"I don't know," I tell him honestly, grabbing his arm when he tries to shove me again and pulling him close. His breath stutters out, his chest colliding into mine as I grip his ass to hold him steady. I use the purchase to grind him against me, my hold rough, and Colton's eyes shutter. "Feels fucking good, though, doesn't it?"

"God fucking *damn* it," he hisses, head dropping forward, his hair brushing the side of my face. His hold on my arm is tight, as if he doesn't know whether to pull me closer or push me away.

"You tell me to stop, and I will," I make sure he knows, *needing* him to know. "But you wanna fight this a little? I'm all for it, Colt. I have no problem making you mine."

"I'm not yours," he grits out. "Will never be yours."

"We'll see about that."

Colton tries to tug away, but all he succeeds in doing is rubbing himself against me, the moan that follows surely not meant to be heard by my ears. "Fucking touch me already."

I click my tongue. "Try again."

He uses his shoulder to shove me backwards, but I tug him with me, spinning at the last second so he's the one who ends up against the side of the building. He grunts, eyes flashing.

"Pinned again," I tell him with a grin.

"Fucking. Touch me," he repeats, fire and gravel in his voice. "*Please*."

"Such a quick learner," I praise, tugging his waistband away from his skin, the backs of my fingers skimming heated flesh. I pop the button open. "Are you gonna be good, or should I hold you down like last time?"

In answer, he growls and tries to hook my foot with his own, but I block the move and press him back into the wall.

My chuckle is hoarse. "You got it," I tell him, slowly wrapping my hand around his throat, the curve a perfect match for my palm. Colton's eyes slip shut, his hands shaking where he's holding me. "You could just ask for it, y'know."

"Fuck you," he says, although it lacks any real venom.

I let out a sigh, slipping my other hand beneath his underwear to curl around his dick. "Like I said, maybe if you ask nicely. Now open my jeans."

His eyes pop wide, surprise there. Curiosity, definitely. A little trepidation.

"Don't make me ask again," I say slowly, figuring the edge of demand will help him past his nerves.

It seems to do the trick. He grits his jaw, eyes on me as he fumbles for my waistband. He gets ahold of it, easing down the zipper as I rub my thumb over the head of his cock. His breath comes in short pants through his nose as I toy with him.

"Now pull me out, little Colt. And *be nice.*"

"Hate your hair," he mumbles, sliding his dominant hand—the left—inside my pants.

"That so?" I ask, my stomach tightening as Colton's fingers wrap around me. He maneuvers my dick out of my briefs, managing to look like a disgruntled cat every step of the way.

"And your fucking voice," he adds. "Grating."

I hum, grabbing Colton's hand off my dick and bringing it up to his mouth. "Spit," I tell him.

He looks affronted.

"It's either a dry rub or spit, little Colt. Unless you brought lube with you?"

He shakes his head, eyes pinging down to his waiting palm. I loosen my grip on his neck just so and raise an eyebrow. Finally, Colton works his jaw and spits into his hand.

"There you go," I say, wrapping his palm back around my dick. "You *can* listen to direction." I ignore his answering scowl and squeeze his hand, running his fist down and back up again. "*Fuck.*"

His expression turns to one of subtle smugness, as if he's proud to have caused my composure to crack just a little. And while I like that look on Colton Darling a hell of a lot more than I thought I would, it's not the surrender I'm aching for.

Letting his hand go, I pull his cock out from his underwear and step in close. Colton sucks in a breath when I swat his hand off my dick, replacing it with my own to wrap both of us in my grip. He tries to look down, but my hold on his neck doesn't allow for it.

"Do you like that, little Colt? The feel of my dick on yours?"

He looks as if he wants to say no but can't. I give us a couple jerks before flexing my hips, causing my cock to slide alongside his.

"Fuck," Colton says on a gasp.

"Do you wanna see what it looks like?"

"Why're you doing this?" he croaks out, his eyes going hazy as his dick starts to leak. I swipe my thumb through the precum.

"Getting you off?" I question.

"Tormenting me."

I still for just a second before resuming the slow up-and-down glide of my fist. Running my nose up Colton's stubbled jaw and cheek, I stop at his ear. "It's not torment, and we both fucking know it. Look down."

I release Colton's neck, and he does, his hand gripping my arm tight as I lean against the wall. His chest bounces a few times, quick breaths in and out, his cock jerking against my hold.

"Nice, isn't it?" I say, knowing the word isn't enough. It looks obscene. Our cocks pressed together, his with a gentle curve, mine straight, our cockheads the only thing peeking out above my partially closed fist before my hand glides down again.

A groan is his only answer.

"If I'd known all it would take to render you speechless was this, I'd have tried it ages ago," I tell him.

"Liar," he pants out, exhaling heavily when I return my grip to his throat. He meets my eye, unable to hide the force of his *want*.

And there it is. Exactly what I was aching for.

Colton's surrender.

My chest feels hot as I start stroking us in earnest, angling Colton's head to the side. I run my lips over his cheek, the sharpness of his jaw, smelling leather and citrus. When I bring Colton's face back around, he doesn't hesitate. He meets my lips, all fire and whiskey and a sharp edge of desperation that's a match for my own. His breath stutters when I buck against him, the added friction of our dicks rubbing together feeling too fucking good to keep up for long.

I kiss him hard—once, twice—before pulling back. "Come on, little Colt," I urge, my hand taking us closer to the edge. "Let me hear you keen."

"Fuck off," he mumbles, panting hard now.

I nip his ear. "Whinny for me, baby."

Colton lets out a laugh, and it's so unexpected I rear back and stare at him in shock.

But then his eyes are rolling up, and his body is tensing. "Ah fuck, *fuck*," he mutters, his cock swelling in my fist. I have just enough time to move my hand from his throat to the top of our dicks before Colton is shooting against my palm.

He does moan, a beautiful, pained sound that grabs me by the balls. I don't know if I truly do like his torment or it's simply the satisfaction of seeing Colton Darling brought to pieces, but I follow him over the edge immediately, catching my release before it can coat our shirts. I bury my face against Colton's neck as my body is wracked in spasms, imagining I can taste the bruise I left against his skin. It's enough to have a final throb passing through my dick, my hand unmoving now, my other cradling most of the mess.

"Fuck," Colton says. And then again. "Fuck."

His eyes meet mine blearily when I pull my face from his neck. He looks wrecked. And *that*. That has a smirk tugging at my lips.

I hold up my hand like an offering. "Take care of this for me?"

"Oh, fuck off," Colton says, shoving my arm away.

I huff a laugh, not having expected him to actually swallow down our cum, and fling it unceremoniously onto the ground. I wipe my hand on the side of the building as Colton balks.

"What? Did you have a better idea?"

"No," he admits, taking my cue and shoving his softening dick back in his pants. His eyes flick up to mine before dropping back down again.

I zip up my jeans. "Don't freak out."

"I'm not freaking out," he bites back.

"It's just orgasms."

"I know," he says haughtily, brushing his hair off his face.

I groan a little, unable to help but step forward again, wrapping my hand in the strands. "Say thank you," I tell him softly, mapping the way his scowl draws his brows together and the pinch at the corners of his mouth.

The expected "Fuck you" comes swiftly.

It takes concerted effort not to laugh. *Fuck*. Since when do I find Colton goddamn Darling *amusing?*

"Fine," I mutter, drawing him forward. Colton tenses when I bite his lip, but then he's melting into my touch, a heady fucking thing a guy could get addicted to. I draw back, enjoying the slow blink of his eyes as they reopen. "You're welcome."

Colton elbows me off of him, and, this time, I do laugh. He shakes his head, looking around as if trying to figure out where he is or what he's supposed to do now.

"Door's that way," I tell him.

He flips me the bird before heading off, grumbling all the while.

"See you at home," I call.

He doesn't deign to give me a response, but his frustrated yell is music to my ears.

Chapter 17

COLTON

'Come on,' I sign quickly to Remi, finding him still out on the dance floor. *'We have to leave.'*

He looks concerned but nods immediately. "Gotta go," he appears to call to the guy he's dancing with. He pats him on the chest before heading my way. Remi doesn't notice the guy's confused questioning at his back.

My brother's hands cut swiftly through the air as he approaches. *'What's going on?'*

I just shake my head, waving him toward the door, needing to escape as quickly as humanly possible and praying we don't pass Noah in the parking lot.

The air outside is like a shock to my overheated system, even though I'd only been back inside for a couple minutes at most. I scan the area quickly, ridiculously relieved when I don't spot a certain small-town farrier I can't *believe* I ran into all the way out here.

Except—it's not that preposterous, is it? This is the closest gay club to Darling unless, maybe, you cross up into Canada.

If Noah was looking to test out his attraction, same as me, it makes sense that he'd come here.

A stone fills my gut.

Was he attracted to other men? Did he...*like* that guy touching him before I came along?

I dismiss the hypothetical outright, not willing to entertain notions of Noah fucking King and the men he might be attracted to.

He's attracted to you, a little voice inside my head pipes cheerfully.

I swat the thought away.

Remi catches up to me as we reach the truck. He turns his processor back on, blinking a couple times as he acclimates before asking, "What's wrong?"

I tug the driver's side door open, and Remi gets in opposite me. "I just... I needa go."

"Okay," Remi says slowly, the word nearly swallowed by the turn of the engine. "Care to share why?"

I bite my lip, looking behind us and easing out of the parking spot. I startle when Remi's fingertip touches my neck.

"Holy shit," he says, tone shifting from concern to bemusement. "Were you making out with someone?"

"What?" I nearly screech, rubbing the spot on my neck before putting my hand back on the wheel. I get us safely out onto the road. "No, I..."

"You have a hickey," he states plainly. "Who was he?"

"It's nothing," I answer. "It was no one."

When I glance over, Remi's wearing an incredulous expression. "Really? 'Cause you didn't have that when we went inside the club. So unless you're going to convince me a ghost was snacking on your neck, try again."

I groan. "Really, it was no one. Just...some guy I met."

I nearly wince at the blatant lie, hating that I'm being dishonest with Remi of all people. But what would I possibly say? How the *fuck* would I explain I ran into Noah King outside of Darling and that *he* was the one snacking on my neck?

It doesn't make sense. Not even to me. How am I supposed to make it make sense to him?

"Colt," Remi says softly. "If you're freaking out about kissing a guy, it's okay. I know it probably feels like this big thing, and in some ways, it is. But none of it changes who you are at your core. You're still *you*."

I shake my head, trying to figure out what to say to my younger brother. "It's not that," I tell him truthfully. "It doesn't bother me that it was a man, it's just... This was the *wrong* man, Remi. Just trust me on that. But he was the only one in that club I even..." *Fuck*. "He was the only one I wanted to kiss. So what does that say about me? What the *fuck* does that mean?"

Remi is silent for a moment, the headlights from oncoming cars my only distraction before he speaks again. "Being bi isn't always a fifty-fifty split. It doesn't mean you automatically like as many men as you do women, or vice versa. Attraction is different for everyone. So if it's only a guy here or there..."

He lets the sentiment hang, but I fill in the blank. "That doesn't make me less bi."

When I glance Remi's way again, he has a calm, almost proud look on his face. Which, coming from my baby brother, is just plain weird. Sweet, but weird. "You think you are?" he asks, tone devoid of judgement. "Bi, I mean?"

"Yeah," I say, letting out a breath as I signal to turn onto the highway. "I guess I am."

But why the fuck does the man I'm attracted to have to be the one who's worst for me in every single way?

"Will you tell our brothers?" Remi asks, his voice again lacking judgement. "And our parents?"

"Nah," I say nonchalantly. "Figure I'll just wait until the wedding invites go out and let them clue in for themselves."

"Ass," Remi says lightly, punching my leg.

"Jesus. You been moving hay bales? That fucking hurt."

"Did not," he says.

Kinda did.

After another sigh, I add, "Yes, I'll tell 'em. Just have to figure out what to say."

"You will," Remi says. "You'll figure it all out."

I sure fucking hope he's right.

When we get home, the hour late, Remi heads to bed. I find my feet carrying me toward one of my most trusted companions.

The horse barn is closed up and dark when I arrive. I flick on an interior light, the dimmest one in the hallway that won't wake the horses. Clementine's ears twitch when I lift the latch to her stall, but she doesn't get up.

"Sorry, Clem," I say as softly as I can, easing her door open enough to step through. "Didn't mean to wake you."

I find a clear area near her head to sit down, the straw crunching under me, and Clementine shifts enough to bump me with her nose. I dutifully rub along her head and behind her ears, the swell and ebb of her ribcage as she breathes soothing.

"So, uh, turns out I'm kinda messed up," I tell my confidant. "Apparently I have a thing for my archnemesis jacking me off? I don't get it, Clem. I don't like the guy. Never have. He's rude and clearly thinks he's better than me. *Little Colt.* Pft."

I ignore the way my chest heats at the memory of that nickname falling from Noah's lips, the phantom of his voice, his touch, his *everything* searing. Like fire.

Dangerous, is what it is.

"He's a dick," I mutter, voice rough.

Clementine huffs softly as if in agreement.

"And he *has* a dick, which is just…"

Different, I decide on. It's really fucking different than what I'm used to. And I *touched* it. I spat in my hand and stroked the moisture down Noah's cock. And I didn't hate it? Not like I hate the guy, at least. His dick was really fucking pretty, actually, which is not something I've ever thought about a penis before. But his…

It was straight. Thick in my grip. Hot. And the head…it was almost intimidating, like the man himself. Demanding my attention.

Christ, even the guy's *cock* is cocky.

"Fucking Noah King," I mumble. "It's not gonna happen again, Clem. I never needed dick before. I certainly don't need it now."

I nod swiftly, lowering my hat over my face as I sink down into the straw.

Before I fall asleep, the image of me down on my knees flits hazily through my head, Noah standing in front of me, his hand curling in my hair and *little Colt* falling like a whisper from his lips.

Only in the safety of my mind can I admit to the thrill I get from imagining him putting me there.

Messed up, indeed.

The sharp clang of a bell has me jackknifing into a sitting position, my hat falling to the ground beside me as light assaults my eyes. Clementine is already standing, fully awake. It takes me a moment of blinking heavily to locate the source of the ungodly noise.

My mother, positioned in the doorway of the stall, sets down her cowbell. "Oh good. You're up."

"The fuck?" I mutter, looking around, trying to get my bearings. "What time is it?"

"Eight-thirty," she tells me, passing over a thermos of what I assume to be coffee. "Better get a move on. You've already missed breakfast."

"It's the weekend," I groan, closing my eyes again.

Something thwacks me lightly on the head. I glare at my mom, who's smiling much too cheerfully. "Don't know how you slept through the morning crew saddling up, Colton dear. But you best get yourself in gear. Unless... Don't tell me you forgot about the trail ride you agreed to lead?"

Yes.

"No," I answer, groaning as I pull myself more upright. "That's today?"

"Mhm. Here."

My mom passes me a covered plate. I peel the corner of the foil back, mouth pooling with saliva when I see the sausage links next to a rolled-up omelet and a couple dry pancakes.

"Thanks," I mumble, snapping a link off in my mouth.

She hums again before clearing her throat. "You, uh, see Evelyn Jacobs again last night?"

It takes me a second—a *long* second—to figure out what she's talking about. I cough around my bite of sausage, slapping a hand over the goddamn *hickey* Noah left on my neck. "What? No! It wasn't..."

My mom's lips twitch, and I heave a defeated breath.

"You know what? Nuh-uh," I tell her. "I'm not discussing this with you. My *business* is my own."

"And every sighted individual's within twenty feet of you," my mom shoots back.

"You're a mean person," I say evenly. "Very, very mean."

"Sure, dear. Lemme know if you wanna borrow some of my coverup," she says, already walking away, *laughing* as she goes.

I shove another sausage link in my mouth with a grumble.

It doesn't take long to finish my breakfast, and then I head to the ranch house to wash up. I manage to avoid my family as I go, which I appreciate greatly.

Not that I don't love them.

I just don't need their teasing right now.

Once I'm dressed and ready, my shirt collar hiding my bruised neck, I head back to the stables. I get the horses prepared for today's riding tour, something we do only on the weekends. It's rare for me to cover the trail rides, but I'm grateful for the distraction today. It leaves me less time to think about a certain dark-eyed farrier with stupid tattoos and even stupider lips.

Fuck.

I find my trail ride group waiting near the petting farm and lead them back to the horses, giving the usual spiel about our ranch and how long my family has lived here—which is precisely since the time the town was founded. I talk a bit about my grandparents and how the ranch ran differently a couple generations back, both the beef side of things and the dairy operation.

The parents seem more interested in our history, whereas the kids are just excited to see the horses.

I can't blame them.

After making sure everyone is on a suitable riding companion, stirrups are sitting in comfortable positions, and folks know how to hold the reins, I lead them off. Being an advanced rider isn't a necessity for this. The horses follow one another, and with me at the helm, our visitors can sit back and simply enjoy the ride.

We head across open land until we reach the trees, settling into a slow pace along the well-trodden paths in the woods. And it's...nice. Really nice. To ride with Clementine, pointing out some landmarks along the way and describing a few of the tree species and other plant and animal life we encounter. It forces me to slow down for a minute. To clear my head and let my pulse meld with the steady cadence of hoofbeats.

Nothing is ever going to come of this...*thing* with Noah. We're both clearly just releasing some tension. And maybe the way we've found to do it is better than the alternative, like a black eye for either of us. Preferably him.

Like Remi said, finding out I like Noah's infuriating smirk when it's accompanied with his hand on my dick doesn't change who I am underneath it all. It just means I'm discovering something I didn't know about myself before.

Maybe I'm not a masochist. Not really.

I'm just *curious*. And Noah happens to be curious, too. Something we finally have in common, apart from our jobs.

I'll just have to find somebody else I can shift this curiosity onto. Because no way in hell will I give Noah King the satisfaction of pulling my reins.

Chapter 18

NOAH

I watch Colton for a moment without his knowing. He's talking to Louise Harper at the front counter of her sandwich shop, a smile on his face. The same smile he wears anytime he's talking to anyone and everyone who's not me.

A flicker of something hot and tight curls in my chest, but I force the sensation away.

I'm long past letting Colton Darling hurt me in any fashion.

Pushing the door open, I step inside the shop. Colton's gaze flicks in my direction, his smile slipping immediately. The expression that takes over his face isn't the scowl I'm so used to seeing but something more...hesitant. Fearful, almost.

Does he think I'd share our little...*secret* around town? I'd never out him like that. But, of course, Colton doesn't know the first thing about me.

"Louise," I greet, giving the owner of the shop a smile as I step up to the counter beside Colton. She's bagging up his sandwich.

"Well, hey there, Noah. How've you been?"

"Just fine, thanks. August and Benson doing all right?"

"My boys are healthy as horses," Louise answers. She raises her voice to add, "Of course, it'd be nice if my oldest called every once in a while."

I'm fairly certain Benson can't hear his mother from across state lines, but I offer a sympathetic nod regardless.

"Auggie working today?" Colton asks.

The door to the back swings open, and August himself steps through, his hair, like Louise's, unmistakably ginger. "I am," he says, shooting Colton a quick smile before aiming a glare his mother's way. "And we talked about shouting our family business inside the shop, remember?"

Louise *pshts* her son. "Colton and Noah are practically family."

I raise a brow. I know Louise and her sons have always been close with the Darlings, and Remington and August are good friends. But me? I certainly don't fit into the equation. Not the way Colton does.

"Uh-huh," August says mildly, transferring some baguettes onto the sandwich-assembly counter. "Well, if it were your choice, you'd have everyone in town officially adopted, and then we'd be out of business."

Louise cocks her head. "August, honey, what makes you think I wouldn't charge family?"

August looks as if he's trying not to roll his eyes, an indulgent smile on his face as he disappears through the swinging door at the back of the shop.

Louise passes Colton his sandwich. "That boy," she says, sounding both fond and exasperated. "Such a pessimistic type. Now, you enjoy your lunch, Colton. Noah, what can I get for ya?"

Colton walks out of the shop without so much as a glance in my direction, and I relay my lunch order to Louise, my mind already on the rest of my afternoon. My schedule is packed, but I'm glad for it. It means business is good.

Idly, I wonder about Colton's appointments for the day before dismissing the man outright. No need to be thinking about my competitor's workload. Probably time I run another ad in the paper, though.

When I step outside, ready to get a move on, I come to a dead stop. Colton is standing a dozen feet away on the sidewalk, looking as if he's waiting. For *me*.

"Yes?" I ask cautiously.

His eyes dart around, and I nearly laugh. If he's going for sneaky, he's failing rather spectacularly. I take a few steps closer as Colton licks his lips.

"Were you following me?" he asks, voice low.

My head rocks back, my incredulity surely showing on my face. "Really, Colt? You think I have nothing better to do than wait around until I spot you and—what?—trail in your wake so I can find out what your sandwich order is?"

Not that I need to. I already know it's roast beef.

The man is criminally predictable.

Colton scowls, looking down at the ground, his hat hiding his face. If I didn't know better, I'd almost think that answer upset him.

Except hold up... Did it?

Did Colton...*want* me to be stalking him?

"Colt," I say, taking another step closer. He bristles. I can see it in the way his shoulders tighten, even before his eyes flash back up to mine, defiance there.

"Don't," he says, tone hard. "I don't want you around, King."

"That so?" I say flatly, crossing my arms, my sandwich bag dangling from one hand. "Never would've guessed."

If we were any younger, I'm positive Colton would stick out his tongue. As is, his lips purse, but he looks...off. Not his usual angry self where I'm concerned. And he's still not leaving.

I take another step closer.

"Are you mad that I didn't check in...after?" I ask, keeping my question vague for Colton's benefit. No doubt he wouldn't want me saying anything more revealing here, even with the sidewalk empty apart from us.

"What?" he sputters, blinking rapidly. "No, that's not... *No*. I don't want...that."

"'Kay," I say slowly.

He peers at me, cheeks flushed. "We're not..." He flicks his hand through the air, not finishing his sentence, but he doesn't need to.

No, we're not anything.

"In that case," I say evenly, "I have work to get to. Nice talking to you, as always."

Colton doesn't say anything as I turn to go. No snappy retort. No final word or parting growl. And that, more than anything, convinces me something is wrong.

I spin back, but Colton is already walking away.

Shit.

With a frustrated growl of my own, I turn and head toward my truck, trying my very best to put Colton out of my mind. The man doesn't give a damn about me. So I don't know why I even care if he's not his usual scowling, chipper self.

I plunk down behind the wheel of my truck and groan, setting my sandwich on the seat beside me. I care because this isn't business. It's one thing for the man to hate me for doing my job and doing it well. It's entirely another if he's struggling because of whatever the fuck sparked off between us.

Not that there's an *us*.

I curse every deity I can think of as I pull out my phone.

"Fuck," I mutter aloud. "Fuck, fuck, fuck."

I send a text.

Me: It's okay to admit you liked it.

If I know anything about Colton—which I'm frustrated to say I do—he won't respond well to consideration. He's already shown me as much.

Better to get his ire up a bit. Then he might let something slip.

His response doesn't surprise me in the least.

Colt: I did like it. Just not you.

Well, don't I feel the love.

Me: Keep talking like that, little Colt, and I'll put you on your back the next time I see you.

He takes longer to respond this time. I check the clock, but if I eat while I drive, I'll make my next appointment just fine.

Three pings come through rapid-fire.

Colt: There won't be a next time.

Colt: And you can't say shit like that.

Colt: Jesus.

A smile curls my lips.

Me: Would you rather I put you on your front instead?

I can practically hear Colton's outrage, and I chuckle to myself. Am I an asshole for provoking him? Probably. But he still hasn't told me to stop.

Colt: You're such a dick.

Me: If you want my dick, Colt, baby, all you have to do is ask.

I freeze, staring at the text I just fired off. *The fuck?* Baby? Really? I wish I could snatch the word back before Colton has a chance to see it, but it's too late now.

At least it doesn't mean anything. He has to know that.

My heart pounds as I start my truck, tossing my phone beside my sandwich on the passenger seat and cursing yet again.

Colton isn't wrong about one thing. There shouldn't *be* a next time.

The only problem with that is I'm not nearly done with the man. I want the pleasure of seeing Colton down on his knees. Want those scowling lips wrapped around my cock. I want to know if he'd let me fuck him. Want to witness him helpless and pinned, begging me for things he's too scared to admit he wants in the light of day.

I want to ruin Colton goddamn Darling.

Thoroughly.

Irreversibly.

And then, maybe, I'll be able to let go of this anger I've held on to for far too many years. It's well past time I put Colton Darling behind me. For good.

I unwrap my sandwich once I hit the road out of town, the mountains stretching in my rearview. Their peaks are still white with snow that probably won't melt until June, even though the ground down here is fully thawed, spring well underway and color sprouting from the dirt.

The memory of flower crowns flits through my head, the accompanying pang expected.

Walter said he wonders what his life would have been like had he not chosen such a solitary existence. Have I been doing the same? Not truly putting myself out there for fear of losing what I might gain, the same way I lost my parents?

They weren't perfect, but who is? The important part is they always tried. They showed their love—to me, to each other—in little ways and big. And I took that for granted as a child, as, honestly, any child ought to be able to.

Admitting I want that for myself, to share love and life with another person, isn't easy. But I'd be lying if I said there isn't a part of me desperate for what my parents had.

So why the fuck am I messing around with Colton Darling?

Why is it so hard to stop?

My phone finally pings as I'm turning onto the dirt drive for my next client. It's an exercise in restraint not to check my messages right away. But I keep my hands on the wheel, navigating past the open metal gate and over potholes and muddy tire tracks. I get a couple waves from the farmhands as I park near the barn. Looks like they're rounding up sheep for shearing.

As I'm reaching for my phone, it starts to ring. My pulse picks up, and I answer immediately, assuming it's Colton.

"Hello?"

"Hi. Is this Noah King?"

Disappointment hits at hearing the stranger's voice, but I do a quick mental recalibration. Of course Colton isn't calling. Why would he?

"That's me," I answer. "How can I help you?"

"I just got a horse from auction," the guy says, sounding young, "and he's got a bad shod. The other farrier...Darling? He can't come until next week. Can you fix it sooner? I really don't wanna let this horse loose until he's got new shoes, but he's getting real antsy in his stall."

For the first time in—*Christ*—ever? I feel a twinge of guilt about the idea of grabbing a client out from under Colton. But this *is* business, and I'm available to help when Colton isn't. So I put my personal feelings aside, confident Colton himself would have no problem whatsoever doing the same in my shoes, and answer.

"I can be there tomorrow afternoon if that works."

"Oh, *thank* you," he says around an exhale. "I'm Gabriel, by the way. Nice to meet you."

"You, too," I say with a chuckle. "All right, lemme just take down your address..."

Once I have Gabriel all set and on my calendar, I swipe over to my text thread with Colton. The last message I sent, goading Colton to ask for my dick, is still onscreen, that *baby* glaring at me. His response is simple and concise.

Colt: Never gonna happen, King.

I let out a slow breath. Now why the fuck does that feel like a challenge?

Work is waiting for me, and there are a million things I should be more focused on than feeding this *preoccupation* with Colton. But I can't quite resist sending off one final text.

Me: We'll see, little Colt.

Chapter 19

COLTON

"I can't believe I'm doing this," I mutter to myself, glancing around before sneaking into the horse barn. The door creaks, and I freeze before realizing how ridiculous I'm being.

Squaring my shoulders, I walk inside, my boots thudding lightly against the floor. It's pitch-black out, but I make my way by memory to the mini-fridge where we keep some fresh produce for treats, among other things. Light gently illuminates the area around me when I open the fridge door.

My heart gives a great big *thump* when I spot the carrots, and I nearly slam the door shut again.

"Ah, fuck it," I hiss, grabbing a moderately sized carrot. Before I can step back, I notice something on the shelf nearby. I snag the saddle butter, tuck both it and the root vegetable inside my shirt, and get the fuck out of there.

The ground is soft as I walk briskly back toward the ranch house, rain having hit yesterday. My boots are going to be muddied all to hell, but I'll deal with it later.

The house is dark as I approach, which is expected considering the late hour. Even still, I'm careful to open the back door into the dining room slowly, not wanting to make any noise. I take off my boots while on the porch, carrying them to the mudroom to deal with later. And then I practically sprint past the carrot-free kitchen—I checked—and race up the stairs.

I'm out of breath when I shut and lock my bedroom door, the soft click like a gunshot. The items I grabbed from the barn rest against my stomach, held in place by my hand over my shirt. I carefully remove them, staring down at the carrot with a mixture of dread and intense curiosity.

If I ordered a...*fuck*. A *dildo*. And any of my family found the package before me? I'd never, *ever* live it down. It would haunt me to the ends of this earth and beyond.

I can't risk it.

"Jesus," I grumble, tearing off my pants before I can chicken out.

It's no big deal. I just want to know what it feels like. I want to know, and then that will be that. It'll probably be horrible, and then I can drop this whole curiosity thing once and for all.

I kick my pants and underwear toward my hamper, leaving on my shirt and socks so I don't get cold. With another glance down at the carrot in my hand, I make the decision to grab a condom. I'm not going back downstairs to peel the dang thing, and would that even be safe? To stick a freshly agitated root vegetable up my ass?

No freaking idea.

With my heart racing a mile a minute, I drop onto my bed, comforter tossed aside. My hands shake as I unwrap the condom, and a near-manic laugh bubbles up from my throat.

Good Lord, if anyone could see me now.

I scowl thinking about Noah. Bet he'd enjoy catching me like this. Getting ready to fuck myself with a carrot of all things.

"If you want my dick, Colt, baby, all you have to do is ask."

I suck in a breath, those words all too easy to hear in the man's voice.

"Not a fucking chance," I mutter aloud.

I'm glad for the saddle butter as I roll the condom over the carrot. I don't have lube, but this will do just fine. Heck, the stuff is basically oil, all natural and safe, made from beeswax and tallow. I've never put it up my ass before, but I suppose there's a first time for everything.

My cock perks as I rub the saddle butter over the condom-covered carrot, and I take a minute to stroke myself, my eyes closing as I harden in my fist. That electric current is back, the same one I've had anytime I've contemplated this over the past couple days.

I just want to know. There's no shame in that.

Slowly, I guide the carrot where it needs to go. It's not overly large, certainly smaller than Noah's dick, which is a damn good thing. Plus, it's tapered enough it should be easy going, right? The tip is the same size as my finger. It's a little awkward keeping the condom in place, but I manage, stilling as the end of the carrot presses to my ass.

I breathe out, pushing gently. It glides in, and I freeze.

My heartbeat feels like a herd of horses galloping away inside my chest. There's something in my ass. A very small something, granted, but still. I plant my feet a little wider, the angle somewhat awkward to maintain. Slowly, I push the carrot a little further.

A gasp falls out of my mouth, the invasion feeling odd. The carrot itself is stiff and cold, not at all like a real dick would be. Probably not that much different than a toy, though, right?

I shake my head, giving my cock a few strokes to stay in the game. It's fine. It doesn't hurt.

I press the vegetable a little further, my ass strangling it on instinct. Wincing a little, I try to relax, but *fuck*. This is weird. It feels so...impersonal.

There's a goddam carrot up your ass—what did you expect?

I growl at my conscience, forcing myself to relax. Stroking my cock, I maneuver the carrot around a bit, trying to find an angle that feels good. I manage to fit another half inch or so inside of myself, the pressure strange and not all that pleasant yet.

With a huff, I let go of my cock and grab my phone. Porn? Would that help?

I mean to go to my web browser, but somehow I find myself clicking into my text thread with Noah. I scowl, reading over our last interaction. The man thinks he's fucking God's gift to mankind. Like I'll beg him for his dick. Goddamn ridiculous. I have more self-control than that. And even if I *do* end up wanting to try real dick, it's not going to be Noah's.

Just picturing his face turning smug at the request is enough to have me nearly chucking my phone across the room. Incidentally, that causes both of my hands to tense, and the carrot lodges further up my ass. I go still, waiting for pain. There is none.

Breathing out in relief, I try fucking myself with the couple inches of makeshift dildo in my ass. It's not...*bad*. But it's not doing anything for me, either.

With a frustrated growl, I toss my phone aside. It hits the mattress, and I hear barely there ringing.

Oh, no. No, no, no.

I grab my phone, breath catching when I see the call in progress to Noah. I try to stop it, try to hit the big red button onscreen, but he answers before I have the chance.

"Colton?" the man says, sounding sleep-hoarse.

I panic, hanging up immediately. My pulse rings in my ears as I wait. He's going to call back. I know he is.

The second the call comes through, I swipe to accept it, not wanting to wake anyone in the house. "I didn't mean to call," I tell him, my voice a harsh whisper.

He makes a soft grumbling sound, and I try my hardest not to picture him in his sheets. "You sure?"

"Yes, I'm sure," I hiss. "I'd know if I meant to call you."

"Why are you awake?" he asks, rustling around.

"None of your business."

I go to sit up, and that's when I remember I have a carrot in my ass. I make a startled sound, the shifting having caused it to lodge deeper. *Oh fuck.*

"Colt?" Noah says, the word firm.

"It's nothing."

"Didn't sound like nothing. Are you hurt?"

I nearly laugh, biting my lip as I resist the urge to move the carrot any which way. "No. Not that you should care."

His grunt is frustrated. "Right. Why would I? Not like I have a heart or anything."

I frown. "Not when it comes to me, you don't."

"Jesus Christ, Colt. You make me wanna strangle you sometimes."

This time, I do laugh. It's not a happy sound. "Case in point. A person doesn't want to wrap their hands around the neck of someone they care about."

I regret the words the moment they leave my mouth, the memory of Noah's hand circling my throat leaving me flashing hot.

He chuckles darkly. "I'm not so sure about that."

My swallow is rough. "Well, whatever kinky shit you get up to, leave me out of it."

"I'm not all that kinky," he says. "Unless... Do you want me to tie you up with rope, little Colt?"

"What?" I sputter, my grip on the carrot making it shift in a way that has me fighting a groan. Okay, *damn*, that doesn't feel horrible. "I never said that. Stop putting words in my mouth."

"I can put something else in your mouth if you'd like."

"Holy *fuck*. What is your problem?"

"Well, see," he says slowly, "somebody woke me up. So I'm feeling a little testy."

"I already told you I didn't mean to call," I snipe back.

"So you say."

"You didn't have to pick up," I point out, squirming a little as I shift the carrot around. It's moving inside of me easier now, but I wish the condom wasn't there, as bunched as it is. Doesn't feel the best. In fact, this experience leaves a lot to be desired. Unless...have I just not gone far enough?

"What are you doing?" Noah asks, his voice low and curious.

I still. "Nothing."

"Are you...jerking off right now?"

"No," I deny vehemently, my cock bucking. I bite my lip hard, refusing to make a sound.

"Colt..."

"I'm *not*. Fuck off. Why would I call you while I'm—"

My words trail off into a moan as the carrot nudges against a place that feels *good*. Fucking *finally*. I was starting to worry my ass was broken.

Of course, my relief takes a hefty back seat to Noah's voice in my ear reminding me of his presence. "We already established you didn't mean to call," he says slowly. Carefully. "Which begs the question... If you're not jerking off, what are you doing?"

"Nothing," I huff, wanting desperately to nudge the carrot against that spot again that felt like fireworks.

"Colt," he says dangerously. "You think I don't remember what you sound like when you're being pleasured?"

My skin flushes hot. Every inch of me, up in flames in an instant. It's not embarrassment I feel, not exactly. But I'm not able to escape the reminder that Noah King, somehow, some way, was the one doing said *pleasuring*.

Which is so fucking ridiculous I want to scream. Or cry.

"Tell me," he demands, not letting it go. "Tell me what you're doing."

I shake my head, gnawing on the inside of my cheek, not wanting to give him the satisfaction. Not wanting to admit I was so desperate to know what it feels like to be fucked that I grabbed a carrot and took matters into my own hands.

But this isn't the same as being fucked. I know it isn't.

And the tears in my eyes are frustration over that fact. That's it. That's all.

"Colt," Noah says, his voice softer. "Would it help if I told you I'm stroking my own dick now? That the thought of you getting yourself off has me so hard I'm ready to blow?"

"What?" I breathe out. "Why?"

He huffs what might be a laugh, and I chance moving the carrot again. "Because, apparently, men turn me on. Even ones as annoying as you."

"Fuck off."

"There he is," Noah says, sounding almost...tender. Which can't be right. "Do you know what I'd be doing if I were there right now?"

My lungs catch, the tip of the carrot sending a wave of pleasure crashing through me as I fuck myself with it. "What? No. I don't...fucking care."

He hums. "I think you do. I'd stroke your cock for you, little Colt. Do you know why?"

I don't answer right away, biting the inside of my lip so hard I draw blood. My cock is leaking now, pressure building in my balls as I continue massaging what must be my prostate, right? That has to be what feels so damn good. "I'm not little," I finally manage.

He chuckles. "I asked you a question."

I growl, my hips hitching off the bed. *Fuck*, I wish the carrot was bigger. Warmer. *Something*. "And, as I told you, I don't care."

Noah tsks. "Manners, little Colt. I'd take your cock in my hand because the sight of you at my mercy?" He whistles lowly. "It's stunning."

I lose my breath. For a second, I simply can't breathe. "Hate you."

"I know you do. Are you about to come?"

"No," I grit out, my breath sawing out of me, my balls pulled so tight against my body and my spine so rigid I feel as if I could snap. "I don't... I'm not..."

"Come, little Colt," he coos. "Put your hand around your throat for me, and come."

I don't even have time to do as he asks before I'm falling over the edge. My cock jerks, cum pulsing onto my shirt as my muscles strangle the carrot in my ass. I feel out of my body, warmth blanketing me from the inside out, my nerve endings pinging and a wave of euphoria covering me so fully I want to sink into it and never escape.

It takes me a long moment to come back to myself. To realize I'm panting like I just ran a marathon. To notice my phone now lying beside me on the mattress. To remember the carrot in my hand, the tip of which is still lodged inside my ass.

Holy shit. Holy *shit*, holy shit.

I didn't even touch my dick.

I ease the carrot free and drop it on my sheets, not caring that I'll have to wash away the saddle butter in the morning. My hand shakes as I wipe away the lingering oil, my phone waiting like a bomb I don't want to trigger.

Could I just...hang up? Just hang up and pretend like this never happened?

The seconds tick by painfully. Finally, I ease the device around, praying the call is disconnected. It's not.

I bring the phone to my ear, listening.

"Was it good?" Noah asks.

I curse internally, trying to quiet my breaths. "Fuck off."

"Oh, I did. Quite nicely, in fact. Sounds like you did, too. A thank-you would be nice, little Colt."

My teeth grind together, my instinct to tell him where to shove it getting tamped down by the fact that there was only one of us who had something shoved up his ass just now. And it wasn't him.

Noah lets out a sigh. "Fine. Sleep well."

"Noah," I say before he can hang up. "I really didn't mean to call."

The second I say the words, guilt and regret trickle in. What the fuck? It's true, and it's not like I care about his feelings. It's not like he even wanted me to call in the first place. But still...

Fuck.

I open my mouth to—I don't know—apologize, maybe? But Noah's voice is back in my ear before I can.

"Got it," he says briskly. And then he hangs up.

I let my phone fall to the bed and groan. There's cum on my shirt and a condom-covered carrot lying near my leg. But all I can think about is Noah fucking King and the hurt I think I heard in those two words.

Fucking hell. What is wrong with me?

Chapter 20

NOAH

"All right?" my uncle asks.

Realizing I'd been stuck in my head, I nod and turn off the burner. The eggs are done. I plate up my own breakfast, as well as my uncle's, and take a seat.

"What's this?" he says, holding up a strip of bacon.

"What's it look like?"

"I dunno. That's why I'm asking."

I huff. "It's turkey bacon."

My uncle frowns in a way that manages to convey his deep disappointment. "Now why would you go and buy fake bacon when the real thing exists?"

"Walt," I say, unable to hide my chuckle. "Don't start. It's better for you."

He looks at me over the lens of his glasses. "And who said I need better? I've been doing perfectly fine."

Oh, your doctors, maybe? I keep the thought to myself. It's not a battle worth waging.

"Just eat your bacon. I'll get the real stuff next time," I tell him, knowing balance is better than attempting a complete overhaul of his system. The man is too stubborn for that.

"You sign up for that treasure hunt in a couple weeks?" my uncle asks, ignoring his bacon in favor of his eggs.

"Not yet, but I figure I might. It's for a good cause."

"Looks like fun, too. And Lord knows—"

"I could use a little more fun in my life," I fill in, deadpan. "Yes, I'm well aware of your feelings on the matter."

My uncle mumbles something that sounds like *stubborn boy*, and I shake my head.

Guess we've got that in common.

I leave Walter with a freshly cleaned kitchen and the morning paper as I head out for work. I'm scheduled to shoe Marie's temporary horses again today, which means there's a good chance I'll run into a certain farrier who's been radio silent for the past week. Not that I expected another call after that...unexpected conversation we had. But the man has been mysteriously absent, as if in hiding.

I wouldn't put it past him.

Marie isn't inside the spacious arena when I arrive, nor the adjoining stables, but I prepare an area and set to work, knowing the ropes by now. I'm on my second horse when the door at the end of the hall opens.

I don't even have to look up to know who it is. I can feel the shift in the air. The quiet tension as Colton walks forward, his footsteps heavy.

"Morning," I say just as he's passing.

He falters for only a second, but then he keeps on, grunting out what I assume to be his form of a greeting. His bag thunks lightly to the ground, some rustling following.

"Sleep all right?" I ask.

Absolute silence.

I look over my shoulder in time to see Colton's gaze darting away. He finishes taking off his jacket, draping it over a hook on the wall. "Fine."

The color on his cheeks has me smirking to myself. "No more midnight...distractions?"

His gaze whips my way. "What? No. None of your business."

I hum, going back to clipping my horse's hoof. After a moment, I add, "'Cause if you needed a hand—"

"I do *not* need your hand," Colton says hotly, slapping his chaps into place. He starts loading tools into the pockets, huffing as I chuckle. "Why are you like this? Why are you fucking with me?"

"Do I really needa spell it out?" I ask, grabbing my rasp.

Finally, Colton says, "Yes. I think you do. Because I can not, for the life of me, figure out what's going on here, Noah."

The sincerity in his voice has me setting down my horse's hoof and standing upright. Colton has his hands on his hips, his jaw set and lips in a straight line, but the fire in his eyes is dimmer than usual. Only a flicker.

I've known all these years that Colton was hiding a side of himself from me. I could see it in the way he talked to others. In the smile he never aimed my way. I *knew* there was kindness in him somewhere. That kindness just didn't extend to me.

What I didn't realize until recently is that Colton is also vulnerable. He's so quick to snap and snarl, but the man who melted at my fingertips inside my barn and trembled against me outside the club... The one who fell apart on a phone call he could have ended at any time if he wanted... He's fragile in a way I never expected of town golden boy Colton Darling.

I wonder if *anybody* sees this side of him. Anybody but me.

I can pretend I want to fuck with the man all I want. Hell, even the prospect of it has me smirking to myself. But the truth is there's something else that keeps me coming back, and it's not Colton's vitriol.

"Maybe I like seeing that flush on your cheeks when you're angry," I tell him. "Not to mention when you're turned on. Maybe I like making you fall apart."

His chest rises and falls in a big, swooping breath. "Why?"

"Because you let me."

His eyes rove over my face, as if searching for answers. "I don't..."

"You do," I say firmly, taking a step closer. "You know exactly what I'm talking about. I'm not ever going to force you, Colt. You've gotta know that. But sometimes I just wanna shake some goddamn sense into you."

He moves his head back and forth slowly, as if at a loss.

I step closer. "Why do you try so hard to hate me?"

"I don't have to try," he says quietly. "I've always hated you."

"Why? Because I was new to town? Because I was a threat to your business? To your standing here?"

He shakes his head again.

"I'm thirty-eight years old, Colt," I say with a huff. "I'm tired of bickering like kids."

"It's...it's always been personal with you," he says, brow furrowed. "Don't lie and tell me you haven't hated me just as much. All the times you've tried to screw me over. All the ads in the paper and...and the horses you've stolen from my care."

"Colton," I nearly growl, shooting my arms wide. "We're the only two goddamn farriers in town. It was never personal for me. It was *business*. *Is* business. You really expect me not to advertise? Not to try my best? I never had the advantage of folks knowing my name. Not like you."

"They know your name now," he shoots back, him stepping closer now. "Goddamn *King*. Well, you're not mine, you hear? I don't need you laughing at me from your throne—"

"When have I *ever*?"

"And I don't need *you*, period. Got it?"

"Then why the fuck is your hand wrapped up in my shirt, Colt? Why are you—"

His mouth slams against mine, bruising and filled with bite. "Shut up," he growls. "Shut up, shut—"

He kisses me again, snarling as he presses me against a stall. Metal digs into my back, Colton's hands tugging at my hair as he tries his damndest to convince me this is nothing but an attack.

"I don't need you," he says, biting at my lip, his leg driving between my own. "I don't."

I hear the words he's not saying. The ones he maybe can't.

I want you.

I wrap my hand in his hair, tugging his head back. His lips part, blue eyes staring at me. "You're going to drive to my house tonight when it gets dark."

"No."

"And you're gonna wait for me in the barn."

"Fuck you," he says, rubbing his crotch against me, his breath hot on my lips.

I grab his ass, stilling his movement, my hand in his hair tugging again. "You'll come to me, little Colt. Don't make me find you."

"You wouldn't," he pants.

"I will," I promise. "Do you believe me?"

He doesn't say anything for the longest time, staring at me with a mixture of anger and longing. It's the latter that allows me to let go. Colton stumbles back a step, and I straighten my shirt.

"Get to work, Colt. We both have a job to do."

He stands in place for a minute longer, his breaths evening out, his stare on my back as I resume filing my horse's hooves. Finally, Colton brings his first horse of the day out, not speaking a word to me. In fact, he doesn't say another word for the rest of the morning or afternoon.

But more than once, I find him watching me like I'm a puzzle he's trying to solve.

I take a shower when I get home. Cook dinner and eat with Walt. We even play a game of chess before he retires to his room to read.

I stay in the living room, occasionally looking out the window at the front of the house. My motorcycle is parked inside the garage, my truck in the driveway. The road is dark, no headlights passing.

He better come. If he doesn't...

Well, my threat to collect him was not an idle one.

It's half past ten when headlights pass through the sheer curtain. I hop up, watching as the lights go dark. Colton doesn't move from his truck for a long time. Several minutes, in fact. Finally, he opens his door and heads toward the backyard.

My pulse is heavy as I wait another minute. Two. Just to make sure Colton doesn't run back to his truck and hightail it out of here. Once I'm fairly certain he's waiting for me like I asked, I go out the back door.

The barn is open. The lights on. There's a good chance Colton is looking through my collection right now. Examining the secrets I've kept hidden.

It was a calculated risk. An invasion of my privacy I'm allowing in exchange for his trust.

Is it wise of me? Maybe not.

But none of this is wise.

I stop in the doorway, pulse hitching as I see Colton's fingers drifting carefully over the unfinished metal crown on my workbench. He freezes when he spots me, his hand dropping to his side.

"Don't make it weird," he says as I approach. "This doesn't... It doesn't mean anything."

"I know," I tell him, taking his face in my hands.

His mouth pops open, his hands bracing against the table behind him. "It's not... I don't..."

"I know," I repeat.

When my mouth covers his, Colton groans. It sounds like relief, and I encourage it, lifting him onto the table and sliding in close. I keep one hand in his hair and undo his fly with the other.

"Shit," Colton murmurs, his grip tightening against me, his lips going temporarily slack.

I free his cock. Wrap my fingers around it. He stutters out a breath when I give him a stroke.

"Lemme hear you, little Colt."

He manages a single breathy, "Ahh," but that's it. I kiss him again, hard, before pulling back. When I spit down onto his cock, he lets out a string of curses.

"Should I stop?" I ask, gliding my fist over him smoothly, loving the way it makes me feel like a literal king to have this man's pleasure in the palm of my hand.

"No," he rasps, locking his heels behind my legs.

"Then tell me what you want," I say, tugging his head to the side so I can bite his neck.

He jolts, groaning against me, the sound near to a cry. "Want you to make me come, goddamn it."

"Like this?" I ask, twisting my fist on the upstroke.

"No," he says wryly, the one word endlessly sarcastic. "I'd rather have your lips wrapped around my cock."

I can tell he meant it as a taunt. He doesn't expect me to do it.

I give him a smirk before bending low and taking the head of his cock into my mouth.

Colton shouts, his hips jerking, his cock throbbing against my tongue. I've never had a dick in my mouth, but I don't hate it. I suck on the end as I stroke his base.

"Jesus fucking Christ," Colton yells, his hand grabbing my hair. I pluck it off my head, pulling both of his hands behind his back and holding his wrists tight. Without an extra fist to stroke him, I let my mouth do the work, bobbing once, twice.

Apparently, that's all it takes.

Colton shoots into my mouth with a hoarse grunt, his hands and thighs shaking, his heels digging against me.

"Fuck, fuck," he mutters. "Shit. What the fuck was that?"

I pop off his cock, spitting his cum out onto the ground before letting his hands go to wipe my chin. "Told you all you have to do is ask," I tell him, unbuttoning my pants. I take myself in hand, grabbing the side of Colton's neck and rubbing over the small bruise I left there.

His eyes rake over me, wide, before he flicks my hand off his neck and tugs me closer with his heels.

"Fuck," he mutters again, and then he's grabbing my cock. He stares right into my eyes as he strokes me, defiant almost, like he's waiting for me to do or say something to piss him off.

I have no intention of pissing the man off. Not when he's playing so nice.

"Fucking good, little Colt. Your hand feels perfect wrapped around my dick."

He looks surprised by my words. But he doesn't stop stroking me. And he doesn't protest this time when I trace the bruise blooming on his neck.

"Like seeing you hurt for me," I say, pulse hopping as his grip tightens. "I could make you hurt so good."

"Fuck you," he breathes, the sentiment falling flat considering he's still willingly stroking my dick.

"Mm. I think maybe you first."

Colton's shocked—*aroused*—face is all it takes to have me hurtling over the edge fast. I don't even have time to warn the man, only grab hold of his hair to anchor myself as I spill over his fist. The sound he makes is full of wonder and need, as if it's him painting his shirt instead of me. The man is too fucking innocent for his own good, and it makes me want to dirty him all the more. To see how far his curiosity extends. To find the limit of what he'll allow me to do.

When I heave out a breath and lean back, Colton's eyes flick up to mine before darting away. I can see the shutters pulling down, see the way he's already trying to protect himself.

I don't stop it, but I do hand Colton a rag to wipe his shirt.

"You couldn't have aimed elsewhere?" he grumbles, shoving his soft cock into his pants and attempting to clean the cum off his clothes.

"Who had a hold of my dick, hm?"

He shoots me a glare, tossing the rag aside before running his hands through his hair. "You mind?" he says, motioning to me.

I wait with a raised eyebrow, his legs still clasped around my hips. He flushes, unwrapping them and pushing me away so he can drop to the ground.

For a second, he looks like a lost lamb. And I don't know if my instincts are one of the shepherd...or the wolf.

He's halfway to the door when I say, "See you tomorrow, little Colt."

He pauses. "What?"

"Marie's. We both have more work to do."

"Right," he says on an exhale. "Yeah, uh. Yeah."

I chuckle to myself as Colton heads out of my barn, and I know, from the fleeting glance he throws my way before he's out of sight, this bad idea we're both indulging in is far from over.

Chapter 21

COLTON

"So you live here in town?"

"I do," Noah answers, his voice even.

I peek out through the bars of the stall I'm in, watching his interaction with one of Marie's new students. A handful of them arrived today for the start of their dressage course. All women. All young. College-aged, if I had to guess.

I scowl, going back to my work.

"Whereabouts?" the girl asks.

"Would you know if I told you?" Noah replies.

She titters like that's the funniest thing. "No, guess not. Been doing this job a long time? You look like you know your way around."

"Over fifteen years," he answers.

Would it be rude to tell this girl to kindly fuck off? Probably. But Christ. I don't know how Noah hasn't gotten fed up with her questioning by now.

I peek out of the stall again, appraising them both. The girl is dressed in typical riding apparel. Tight pants. High boots.

A collared shirt because Marie likes her students to always look ready to show. She's not wearing her sleek helmet, but it's tucked at her side.

Noah, like usual, is in jeans, a t-shirt that's seen better days, and chaps. His boots are dusty and worn in, and although he's not wearing his white hat, it's resting nearby. He hasn't stopped working as he's withstood the girl's chattering, so he's currently bent over a hoof. But even so, he's far bigger than her. More rugged by leaps and bounds.

Clearly, she likes what she sees. Is it his size? The damn tattoos that make him look almost dangerous? The stupid hair that's shaved at the sides?

Is Noah...handsome? Like, conventionally handsome?

I've never thought much about it. He's not terrible to look at, I guess, even though his attitude could definitely use some work. He does have unique eyes, the way they almost shine like woodfire, the coppery color far lighter than his hair. And he's proportional, I suppose. Folks like that, right?

He's definitely fit. Arms for days. Muscles visible beneath his thin t-shirt. I mean, the man was able to hoist me right over his shoulder, for fuck's sake. He's clearly strong.

And his ass, now that I'm thinking about it, is—

Oh fuck.

Nope. No, no.

I dive back within the safety of my stall, focusing on Peanut. He allows me to lift his hoof without issue, and I check it over carefully. I can't see any evidence of his prior injury, which is good. It means he can be trimmed without issue.

I lead him out of the stall, trying not to pay attention to the conversation happening nearby.

"How often are you here?" the girl asks.

Oh, fuck off already.

Noah hums. "Every four weeks or so. Unless something pops up."

She makes a sad sound. "So I won't see you for another month? We'll have to fix that. I'm only here six weeks, after all."

"Hey, Noah?" I say loudly.

He looks over at me, a brow raised. The girl looks my way, too.

"You got an extra pair of nippers?" I ask. "Can't find mine."

His lips twitch. "In my bag."

"Thanks," I mutter, making sure Peanut's lead is secured before I head that way. I drop down, rummaging through the bag, not in any rush. "How's, uh…" *Shit, I need a name.* "Daphne? Your girlfriend?"

Noah is outright smiling now, looking amused. What-fucking-ever. If he's too polite to tell this girl to get lost, I can handle it. And yes, Daphne may be his motorcycle, but it's the first name that popped into my head.

"Daphne," he replies leisurely, "is doing just fine. Thanks for asking."

"Mhm," I mumble, finding the spare pair of nippers I don't actually need and standing. I notice the girl's frown as I walk away.

Hah. Take that.

"So, uh, have you seen Mrs. Doherty?" she asks.

"Should be in the arena," Noah answers.

"Right," the girl says. "I'll just go check then."

Noah hums his agreement, and Marie's new student walks off. I can feel him watching me, but I don't look.

"Daphne?" he asks.

I shrug, starting to work on Peanut's hooves. I clip the ends of the horseshoe nails off with a little more force than necessary.

Noah makes a thoughtful sound, and I glance over at him, wondering what the fuck he has to be thoughtful about. He's focused on his own work, the arm that's covered with rope and flowers flexing. I peek at the other, not having gotten a good look before. The rope continues on that side, but it ends above his elbow. It's hard to make out the rest of his tattoo sleeve from here, but I think I see...antlers? We do have elk in Montana, so that could be it. A thorny crown, maybe. And...numbers. Dates?

I wonder again about the horseshoe that peeks out from the collar of his shirt. Does he have more tattoos covering his chest?

I force my gaze away, frustrated with myself for staring. I don't need to concern myself with Noah King's tattoos. Or his *anything*, really.

"Why do you figure Marie keeps such a large flock of chickens?" I ask, looking for something to keep my mind occupied. "Seems like the horse business keeps her plenty busy."

"The chickens were her husband's before he passed," Noah replies. "She never got rid of 'em."

"Oh," I say, my chest panging in sympathy. I knew Marie's husband passed some years back, but it happened before I took her on as a client. I didn't realize the farm was her husband's, not her own.

The realization that Noah *did* know because he, once upon a time, was Marie's primary farrier adds another layer to the ache in my chest. One I don't want.

I fucked up losing Noah this job. And this—the fifteen horses he's taking care of through the summer—isn't enough. It's not enough to make up for the fact that he should be the one here in my place.

Noah was right. It's one thing for a client to switch to another farrier of their own volition. It's entirely another to slander one's name so badly the client drops them.

God fucking *damn* it.

"What?" Noah asks, apparently having sensed my tension from down the hall.

"Nothing, it's just..." I heave out a sigh. "I'm sorry, all right? I'm sorry for losing you this job."

Noah is quiet for the longest time. "All right."

"All right?" I ask, whipping my head his way. "Just...*all right?*"

"Yeah," he says, rasping down his horse's hoof with efficient movements, the *sht, sht, sht* rhythmic and familiar. "I appreciate the apology."

What in the ever-loving fuck?

"That's it?" I ask.

"I mean, you would've looked better saying it down on your knees," he drawls. "But I'd be happy to accept a redo if you'd like."

Oh, the fucker.

Noah smirks, enjoying the hell out of himself. I shake my head, not knowing what to make of his easy acceptance. It doesn't fit what I know of the man.

But do I really know him all that well?

No, I don't.

I don't even know what the dates on his arm are. Only how his cock feels in my palm. And the taste of his lips on my tongue.

Ah, hell.

I put up a mental blockade to keep out all things *Noah King* as I refocus on my work. I get so lost in the repetitive process of shoeing, in fact, that I succeed in tuning out the man. It's not until sometime after noon that I look over at his station to find him gone.

Probably taking his lunch break.

After returning my finished horse to her stall, I wash up and head to my truck to grab the food I brought from home. Ash made mac and cheese yesterday, along with these delicious little cherry tarts. I pop one in my mouth on my way back to the stables. Noah isn't in his own vehicle, which means he must be inside.

Not that I'm looking for him or anything.

There's a break room near the arena that has a kitchenette, so I head that way to heat up my food. Unsurprisingly, I find Noah there, seated at the small table. I head to the microwave, putting my mac and cheese inside and setting the timer.

Noah doesn't say anything. I eye his lunch, but he looks to be mostly done, on to dessert now.

"What's that?" I ask.

He angles the container my way. "Strawberry cream pie. Want a bite?"

I shiver, taking an involuntary step back. "Oh, hell no. Can't stand the stuff."

Not after eating so much of it on my tenth birthday that I spent the entire following day in the bathroom.

"That so?" Noah says, a soft smirk on his face. He takes another bite.

What's he so happy about?

The microwave beeps, and I take my food out. I debate whether I should stand or sit before deciding I'm being ridiculous. Not sitting would be like letting him win.

Win what, I'm not sure.

I plunk down in a seat.

"Smells good," he says.

I eye him as I chew. "Why the fuck are you being so...nice?"

He's been like this all morning. Affable. Smiling and in what I can only describe as a *good mood*.

Noah is never in a good mood. He's a surly bastard.

He raises an eyebrow, leaning back in his seat. "I'm always nice."

I bark a laugh. "Fuck off. No, you're not."

He sighs, closing his eyes for a second before setting his container down. "Your experience is not universal, Colton. Usually, I *am* nice."

I frown. So he's just *not nice* to me. That shouldn't sting as much as it does.

Why am I even surprised, though? It's not news that Noah and I have a relationship built on rivalry and downright animosity. Of course Noah isn't nice to me.

Except—he has been today. What does that mean?

I flush, recalling last night in Noah's barn. Is he...buttering me up? Being nice so I'll come to heel when he calls?

Why the fuck doesn't that piss me off like it should?

"Well," I say, clearing my throat. "It doesn't mean I trust you."

Something flickers in his gaze before he crosses his arms. "Do you need to?"

Yes, I think to myself.

"No," I answer. "Why would I?"

He hums.

I don't think about the fact that I must trust him to some degree, right? Otherwise there's no way I'd let him do the things he has.

Unless I really am just that fucked up.

I'm not sure I want the answer either way.

Noah crosses his ankle over his knee. Leaned back as he is, arms folded over his chest, he looks utterly at ease. Like the cocky asshole I've always known him to be.

"You coming over tonight?" he asks, voice low.

I freeze. Absolutely turn to stone, not a single part of my body moving except for my lungs and heart.

Noah bounces his foot. "You're coming over," he says confidently.

"No. I'm not."

"Yes, you are."

"Where do you get off—" I start, only to lose my voice when I meet Noah's gaze and find him smiling at me. *Smiling.* Like he's genuinely happy to see me—what? Squirming at the end of his metaphorical leash?

Not that there *is* one. No leash. No reins. Nothing whatsoever tethering me to Noah fucking King.

"I'm not," I reiterate, putting as much bite into the words as I can manage and trying desperately to believe them. "I've got a life, you know. And the last thing I want or need is…"

"My mouth around your cock?"

Fuck. Just *fuck.*

"You can't say shit like that," I hiss, glancing toward the door. No one's there.

"So you say," he says nonchalantly. "I think I'll make you beg for it next time, little Colt. I do so love to hear you beg."

I'm up and out of my seat before I even realize I'm moving, my heart pounding and my traitorous dick responding to Noah's words. He chuckles as I rush out the door, the rest of my lunch in hand.

I'm not going to do it. I'm *not.*

I'll stay home tonight. In my own bed, where life is safe and normal and rote.

No begging.

No Noah.

And certainly no more hickeys I have to hide from my family.

I don't want a thing to do with Noah fucking King. Never have. Never will.

If only I trusted my own convictions.

Chapter 22

NOAH

The park near the town square is packed, folks having shown up in droves for Darling's first-ever treasure hunt. It's only eight in the morning, but vendors are already set up along the sidewalks, selling donuts, coffee, and other easy to-go breakfast foods. My uncle stayed home today, but there are plenty of people in the crowd I recognize.

Including the Darlings.

Colton is standing beside his parents, Hank and Marigold. Remington is nearby, although he's looking at his phone, seemingly preoccupied. I don't spot Lawson or his daughter. But Jackson and his blonde boyfriend Ashley are talking to one another, Jackson with a small smile on his face I'm not used to seeing on the man.

Colton doesn't notice me, not right away. I wish he'd look over here, if only so I could see that blush spread across his cheeks that's been a near constant these past couple weeks. For going on nearly forty, the man is surprisingly...pure. Not in a sexual sense. There's nothing innocent about the way he pleads with me to make him come with my hand, my cock on his, or even my mouth.

But as soon as the deed is done, he turns almost...bashful. Embarrassed, maybe? Is he still struggling with his sexuality?

Somehow, I don't think that's it. He's only gotten bolder in that regard. If anything, he seems downright eager to get his hands on me every time he visits my barn, even as he assures me with breathily spoken words that he hates my very guts.

Message received.

Yet, for all the ways Colton claims to despise me, he still blushes when I tell him how good he feels. Or when I threaten to put him on his knees.

When I call him little Colt.

And that, well... I'm not sure I've ever felt anything as satisfying as making Colton Darling show his begrudging arousal.

Part of me says it's because I've found a weakness of his to exploit. That's all.

But the truth is—seeing Colton look at me with something other than contempt for once? It feels like a battle I've been fighting for years.

And finally, I've won.

Colton still doesn't notice me, so I head over to a table with donuts, shedding my jacket as I go. It's plenty warm today, even this early in the morning, and it'll only get warmer as we move into summer. The maple trees in the park are fully leafed out now, their green foliage spanning out like stars.

I eat a custard donut as I wait for the contest to begin.

"Hi there, Noah."

Wiping my mouth, I turn to find Marigold Darling appraising me. Her brunette hair, mixed heavily with silver these days, is loose, reaching just below her shoulders. Her eyes are a shrewd yet warm brown. I see a lot of Colton in her. The squared jawline. The shape of their noses. Even the crinkles at the corners of their eyes.

"Ma'am," I reply, cleaning the sugar off my fingers with a napkin.

"Haven't seen you around since the Shoein'," she says.

I simply nod.

"It was quite the sight watching you and my son compete. I know he wishes the results would have swung in a different direction, but there's no denying you did a fine job with that horse."

"Thank you, ma'am."

She snorts lightly, a small smile twisting the corner of her lips. "You can call me Marigold. Not that it matters one way or another, but are you self-taught or did you go to a farrier school?"

"I took courses back in Wyoming," I tell her. "Horseshoeing, blacksmithing, animal husbandry, and the like. Got my business degree there, as well."

She nods thoughtfully. "No wonder my son found such a worthy adversary in you. I hope you two keep pushing each other."

I raise an eyebrow, but Mrs. Darling doesn't give me a chance to respond.

"Glad to see you're doing well, Noah. Good luck today."

"Thank you, ma'am."

Marigold walks back toward her family, and I lock eyes with Colton, who's looking at me with a furrowed brow. There's a question there, one I don't have an answer to. I'm not sure why his mother came over to talk to me.

I pull out my phone, looking away only to type.

Me: Ready to lose?

Colton looks surprised as he grabs his phone from his pocket. He reads my text, and I swear the corner of his mouth twitches before he flips me off, attempting a scowl.

I snort.

Oh, it's on.

After signing in for the event, I wait where the other couple hundred clue-finders are congregated, near the stone statue of a horse reared up, a rider on its back. There's an actual padlocked chest near the foot of the statue, presumably holding the winner's reward.

I'm guessing the final clue leads to a key.

Mr. Yadav from the board, the same man who called the Shoein', introduces the event. There are twenty clues spread throughout town, he explains, each leading to the next in line. The winner must collect *all* the clues before opening the chest, so there's no jumping ahead.

"Now," Mr. Yadav continues, "the clues are placed such that it's possible to finish the event in three hours. That being said, we suspect it may take longer. There will be plenty of refreshments offered for those who wish to stop back for lunch or a snack. If no one has come to collect the prize by six this evening, the event will come to a close and the individual who's amassed the most clues will win the prize. All clear?"

There's a bunch of nodding and excited murmuring from the crowd.

"All right, then," Mr. Yadav says. "Let the Darling Treasure Hunt begin!"

Raising a bullhorn in his hand, he lets out an ear-splitting blast.

"Jesus," I mutter, rushing to the basket where the first clues are waiting. My ears ring as I unfurl the small scroll, everyone around me doing the same.

The clue is printed in looping typeface, the entire thing no bigger than the palm of my hand. I hold the paper carefully as I read.

A head with no legs.
It hops but doesn't jump.
What is it?

Hops. A head…of foam? *Beer*. The distillery.

People all around me are scattering, running every which way. A few take off down the street toward the Darling distillery, but many go in other directions. I hesitate for all of a second before trusting my gut.

I'm not the first one to reach the distillery, but I can't tell if anyone has found the clues yet. A bunch of people are going through the front doors, so I head around back, hoping to get lucky. My pulse jumps when I see a barrel set beside the back door. A couple of folks run past me in the opposite direction. Did they already find the next clue?

I jog over to the barrel and lift the lid, a grin lighting my face when I spot the small scrolls. I snatch one up and take off before reading it, not wanting to lead anyone else to where they are.

The morning sun casts a hazy glow over my hands as I stop behind the bakery and unroll the paper.

It sees many but owns none.
Once broken now undone.
A mustang is just one.
What is it?

A slow smile curves my lips.

Cars. A mustang is a car. And who fixes broken cars but doesn't own them? This clue must be for the mechanic's shop.

Shit. Walter was right.

This *is* fun.

I make my way to my bike, tugging my jacket back on before strapping on my helmet. Daphne purrs to life, and with a twist of my wrist, we're off.

Ratchet, the mechanic, lives near the border of Darling. His shop is on the same plot of land as his house. I've been there a time or two for my own vehicles. When I pull up now, a few other clue-finders are scattered around. I try not to worry too hard about all the people I see, knowing there's plenty of time still to get ahead.

I pull Daphne to a stop and lean the bike's weight against the kickstand. I don't bother taking off my helmet, just look around for an object that might be holding clues. The folks here are all near their own vehicles or leaving, so it takes me a minute, but I finally find the little scrolls inside a massive wheel at the side of the building.

I head back to my bike and read.

Hard as a stone and soft as butter.
Bruise it, and it doesn't change color.
Yet dry, it becomes another.
What is it?

This one takes me longer. Several minutes, in fact. But finally, I think I have it.

Plums are a stone fruit with soft, purple flesh, like a bruise. Dehydrated, they become prunes. It's gotta be Plum's Grocers.

And just like that, I'm off.

I do find the next clue at Plum's, and after that, I head to the antiques market and then the community center. Everywhere I go, I see other teams working to solve their clues. And it's always teams. Adults or adults with kids. I seem to be the only person working solo. If there are others, I haven't run into them.

I don't let it get to me, determined to see this thing through to the end, whether or not I win. Which, let's face it, is a long shot with so many participants.

Around noon, I stop for a few minutes in town, eating a quick lunch before moving on. It's past the three-hour mark at this point, but the chest is still sitting below the statue, locked tight.

I keep at it for another hour and a half and am at clue number fourteen when I spot a familiar truck.

Colton's. He's here with Jackson and Ashley.

They look up at me as I pull my bike into the parking lot of the alpaca farm. My engine cuts out, and they go back to discussing what's on their clue, but Colton's gaze holds mine for a good long moment.

I head past them toward the shop where wool items are sold and folks can buy tickets to see the animals. I'm not buying any tickets today, but I hit jackpot near a display of scarves. A thick rope basket is filled with scrolls, and I breathe out a sigh of relief at seeing so many.

I grab a clue before glancing at the scarves again, remembering Walter could use a new one for winter. I pick one out in a blue I know he'll like and head to the register to pay.

"Enjoying the treasure hunt?" the owner, Ms. Bellevue, asks. She flips the handmade tag over, checking the price on the scarf before entering it into the register.

"I am," I tell her, wondering briefly if she remembers me from the one time I visited her farm when I was seventeen. I don't ask, knowing it was long ago and she has plenty of visitors come through. "Have many folks stopped in yet?"

Ms. Bellevue smiles, the outsides of her eyes wrinkling. "Well, now, I'm not sure if I'm supposed to tell you that. But since no one told me not to, no. There haven't been many. That'll be twenty-two dollars."

"Thank you," I say, passing over cash as she bags my purchase.

"Mhm. You have a good rest of your day now. And good luck."

I thank the woman again before exiting the shop. Colton's group is still near his truck, whispering amongst themselves. I stash the scarf in one of my saddlebags before unfurling the next clue.

Wings incapable of flight.
Hurry you must but gander you might.
Heed, five are waiting.
What is it?

Wings incapable of flight. A flightless bird?

Five are waiting. Does that mean the final five clues? But why would they warn us, unless...

Wings incapable of flight.

Which means walking. Where do you walk with the intention of looking around?

Holy fuck.

It's the trails. The last five clues are near the mountain trails.

"But which one?" I hear hissed from nearby. Someone makes a *shh* sound, but that's the question, isn't it? Which trail?

Hawk Hollow? Or Eagle Back?

"We'll split up," Colton says, voice quiet. "It makes the most sense. Your truck is on the way there anyhow."

"Yeah, all right," Jackson agrees. "You'll take west? We'll go east?"

"Yeah," Colton says. "Let's go."

I glance up as the men get into the truck, Colton's eyes snagging on me for just a moment. West. He's taking Hawk Hollow. The smart thing to do would be to go east to Eagle Back. Except, if I choose wrong, and Colton chooses right...

I get on my bike, taking to the road. I don't bother speeding ahead of Colton's group, knowing it's not necessary. They split off before long for Jackson's truck, and I get my head start.

I make it to Hawk Hollow trailhead fifteen minutes later, not a soul in sight, although there is a single vehicle parked in the lot. I pull off my helmet to search the area, guessing wherever the next clue is, it'll be close, not down any number of diverging paths into the mountains. I find the metal barrel hidden away behind a tree.

My adrenaline is high as I head back to the parking lot. The clue this time is a picture. A map of the trails that loosely form the shape of a hawk. There's a single blue dot at one wing tip, a spot just over two miles from here down accessible trails.

I look that way, the sun high overhead. The intention is to walk, I'm sure of it. But...

There's an access point a few miles down the road. It's closed to vehicles, but my motorcycle could manage. I'd get there quicker.

Making a snap decision, I hop back on my bike and head that way. I can feel the thrill of competition thrumming through my veins, the desire to win heavier now than it was in the beginning. It only takes a couple minutes to reach the access point, and I ease past the metal guard rail and onto the dirt path. Technically, there are no markers prohibiting motorcycles, so I pray like hell I'm not making a mistake.

I see the shape of a box a mile down the path. A smile forms on my lips.

And that's when my back end fishtails roughly.

The loose stones underneath me make it impossible to correct my momentum in time, and my bike goes down, me with it. I grit my teeth as the metal frame rolls over my leg, but then it's skidding past, the beautiful red body skating over dirt and stones as I watch on in dismay. I wasn't going that fast. I'm not terribly hurt.

But *fuck*.

My bike.

With a wince, I push myself to my feet, wiping dust and stones off the side of my pant leg. Another wince has me checking my palm, which is scraped up but not bleeding all that badly. The cuts are shallow.

"Fuck," I mutter aloud, stepping over to my motorcycle.

Daphne has a blown tire.

"Goddamn it," I groan. Her scratched exterior is the least of my worries if I can't even drive her out of here. The fuck am I going to do now? Walter can't come get me. I could call a tow truck, but that would put me out of this race.

Of course, there is one person I know is close by. One who could help load up my bike without much time wasted for either of us.

I don't expect him to answer, not right now, but Colton picks up on the second ring.

"Hello?" he asks slowly.

"Colt. Hey."

"Uh, King?"

I nearly roll my eyes. "Yeah, it's me. I need a favor."

Colton is quiet, so I go on.

"I crashed my bike. Can you come get me?"

"Holy fuck," he says, sounding far more alert. "Are you all right? What happened? Are you hurt?"

"I'm fine," I tell him, brushing my fingers against my sore palm. "No big deal. But I'm a bit stranded."

"Yeah, no, I..." A pause, and then, "Where are you?"

"Near the Hawk Hollow access point on Mason?"

"Yeah, I know it. I'll be right there."

"Thank you, Colt. I owe you."

"Um, yeah," he says quietly, and then he ends the call.

With a defeated sigh, I pick up my busted bike and walk it back toward the guard rail.

So much for my lead.

Chapter 23

COLTON

It takes about fifteen minutes to reach Noah's location. I was already headed in that direction toward the next clue, but once I got his call, I picked up the pace.

Noah looks up once he hears me, his head on a swivel when he realizes I'm approaching from behind him, not streetside.

"What...in the actual fuck?" he asks, pushing away from the guard rail.

I pull Clementine to a stop, dropping down out of the saddle. "Where are you hurt?"

He gapes at me. "You rode here. On a horse."

"Wonderful observational skills you've got," I deadpan, stalking his way. "Now where the fuck did you get hurt, Noah? Are you bleeding out? Did you hit your head?"

"What the fuck?" he mutters again.

I slap his forehead once I reach him, and he blinks in shock. "Focus, King. Do I needa get an ambulance out here?"

"Jesus. No," he says, swatting my hand away when I try to check his pulse. "Fuck, Colton. I thought you'd bring your truck."

"I was already on Clem when you called. The ranch is a straight shot east from here, and if the next five clues are on the trails like I think they are, I figured I'd get through them much faster on horseback. Now tell me where the fuck you're hurt before I do a damn strip search."

He shakes his head, copper eyes wide. "My palm," he finally answers, holding out his hand. "That's it. Maybe a bruise on my leg. But I'm fine."

His hand is streaked in a series of shallow cuts, dirt and blood dried over the surface. I wince, doubling back to grab the small first aid kit I keep in Clementine's go bag. Noah looks dumbfounded as I walk back his way.

"This is Clementine," I tell him, opening the small kit. "My horse. Clem, this is that asshole Noah King I was telling you about."

Noah looks unimpressed, but he doesn't pull his hand away when I take it between my own.

"Don't bite my head off," I tell him, using an alcohol wipe to clean the skin.

He doesn't even flinch. "What are we gonna do about my bike?"

"We can come back for it later," I tell him. "After I win this contest."

Noah scoffs.

I raise an eyebrow, meeting his gaze. "Something to say, Mr. Come Get Me? I certainly don't need to be dragging you along, you know."

"Wait... You expect me to ride with you on that horse?" he asks.

"Unless you feel like hanging here for the rest of the afternoon. Your choice."

I finish cleaning Noah's hand and apply some antiseptic. He hisses when I wrap a bandage around him tight enough to keep the wound clean.

"*Fuuuck*," he groans, long and low. "One horse, Colton. You have *one* horse."

"And?"

"You don't see the problem here?"

"Clem can handle it," I tell him assuredly, closing the first aid kit. I stick it back in the saddle bag, put my foot in the stirrup, and swing onto Clementine's back. "Coming or what?"

"Jesus Christ," Noah mumbles, heading my way. "I guess we're—what? Working together?"

"Guess so," I say, pulse hopping when Noah grabs hold of the saddle behind my hip, sticks his foot in the stirrup I vacated for him, and hauls himself up. He settles behind the saddle, since there's no way the two of us can both fit in it. I try not to flush as his heat lines my back, able to convince myself it's the Montana sun roasting me, not the man who, for whatever reason, called *me* when he needed help.

That's not something I'm going to examine.

"Gimme back my stirrup," I tell him.

He makes a huffing noise and pulls his foot free. I slot mine back in and pull the reins to the left, getting Clementine turned around.

"I saw a box about a mile up ahead," Noah says. "Pretty sure it's the next clue."

I nod, having noted the location on the clue I picked up on my way here.

We're quiet for a while, Clementine at a brisk walking pace. I don't dare put her into a trot with Noah riding what equates to bareback.

"What, uh, happened to your bike?" I ask.

"Spun out," he says. "A tire blew. Rolled over metal, maybe? I couldn't find anything."

I hum, acutely aware of Noah's legs brushing mine. Maybe he was right. This might not have been the best idea, after all.

Probably should have left the bastard behind.

"How'd you know her name is Daphne?" he asks. "You said it before. How'd you know?"

I squirm a little. "Must've heard you mention it."

"Hm."

"Where, uh, did the name come from?"

Noah is quiet for a second. "It was my mother's middle name."

Was.

"Sorry," I say quietly, my chest tight.

I can feel Noah shrug, his hands resting on my thighs now. When the fuck did they get there?

"It was a long time ago," he answers.

I nod, chewing my lip as we move along. I don't know what to say. This is awkward as fuck.

Noah lets out a small breath, perhaps feeling the same. "My ass is gonna pay for this later."

I snort, frankly having no sympathy for the man.

He leans closer, his chest lining my back and his voice beside my ear. "We *could* share the saddle."

"Fuck right off," I tell him, willing myself not to get a boner. Not right now, for Christ's sake. "There's no room."

He chuckles, his fingers slipping through the rips at the top of my jeans. What the fuck is he doing? "Bet there would be room with you on my lap," he whispers.

My inhale is sharp, the suggestion in his words impossible to miss. "I swear to God, Noah, I will leave you on the side of this mountain without a single ounce of regret."

He snorts, leaning back slightly. His fingers don't leave my thighs.

I glance down at my jeans. At Noah's fingertips disappearing under the denim, his touch hot against my equally scorched skin.

I'm grateful when we reach the clue box.

Noah lets go of me and slides down off Clementine, grabbing two scrolls from within the box. He closes the lid before getting back behind the saddle.

"It's another map," he says, handing me one of the scrolls.

Instead of a dot on the trail like last time, this one is a visual depiction of stairs leading to an overlook, an X placed on top. I recognize the spot, having spent a lot of my youth exploring this land. These are the closest public trails to the ranch, this mountain range visible from the house. The overlook indicated on the map is near Hawk Hollow's beak, a beautiful view beyond it.

"It's this way," I say to Noah, giving Clementine a gentle press of my heel to get moving.

He's suspiciously quiet behind me, his hands resting on my thighs again, fingertips edged under the fabric of my jeans as if in search of a home.

Clearing my throat, I say, "No one would believe this, you know. The two of us getting along."

He hums. "If anyone asks, I'll say you kidnapped me."

"*Rescued* you," I put in, punching his leg best I can from this position.

He merely snorts. "I do appreciate the pickup, Colton. Not that *this* is what I expected when I called."

"Beggars can't be choosers," I chide.

"Colt," he says quietly, his tone of voice putting me on high alert. "I think we both know, out of the two of us, I'm not the beggar."

I close my eyes and let out a slow breath, wanting so badly to be rankled by his words. Only I can't muster up the outrage. He makes me *want*. Even though it's *him*. Even as I'm mortified by my own terrible, wrong attraction and the fact that I *enjoy* begging. Because every time I ask anything of him, Noah gives it to me. He makes me feel *good*.

Why? Why is he doing this? Why *me*?

"Lost your tongue?" Noah asks, his tone softly teasing, his fingers trailing over my thighs again. He damn well knows the effect he has on me, and that pisses me off, too.

Or, at least, it should.

"No," I say, a surge of perverse courage making me add, "Just wondering when you're finally going to make use of it."

Noah goes still apart from the flexing of his fingers. "Is that so?"

Oh, fuck.

That voice.

Part of me wonders what the fuck I'm doing, but it doesn't stop my words from spilling free.

"You keep threatening to put me on my knees," I point out, my pulse thrumming wildly as I lead Clementine around a bend in the trail. "But so far, that's all it is. A threat."

Noah curses behind me, the sound almost too quiet to pick up. "Oh, little Colt. I don't make idle threats."

I shrug, trying to pretend my heart isn't attempting to beat right out of my chest. I shouldn't want Noah forcing me to my knees and feeding me his cock. But *fuck*, I can't stop thinking about it. I've jerked off to the thought more times than I can count.

That and what he might feel like in my ass.

If someone had told me a year ago that I'd be desperate to know what it's like to be dicked, let alone by the man I've hated with a fiery passion for a decade and a half, I'd have laughed. Hard.

I guess desperation makes fools of us all.

I try to drum up some of that fiery hate now. Something to remind me why it's a bad idea to provoke this man wrapped around my back. But all I feel is frustration that we're not in his barn right now.

Is this what it feels like when people fall for their captors? Have I been unwittingly ensnared by Noah King?

I let out a sigh as I come to terms with the fact that this isn't Noah's fault at all. I can't blame him, much as I want to. Even before I understood these urges, I couldn't let it go, could I? I kept pushing, pushing, *pushing*.

Noah just gave me the tiniest tug to drag me over the edge.

"All right?" the man asks, probably having heard the audible evidence of my internal crisis. Although is crisis the right word? More like awareness.

"Fine," I mutter.

Nothing like realizing I've been subconsciously craving my archnemesis's dick. Not any guy's. *His*. For whatever fucking reason, it's him and has been from the start.

At least my boner is gone, withered up and died right alongside whatever leftover denial I'd been carrying.

I'm attracted to Noah King.

Want him to do unspeakable things to me.

I get off on this man treating me with kindness under the guise of animosity or whatever it is still thriving between us.

And, maybe most shameful of all, I don't want it to stop.

Is it so bad? Letting this man I harbor such conflicting emotions for take what he wants from me when all I want is for him to take it, too?

Would anyone understand it? Do I?

"We're here," Noah says, cutting through my thoughts.

I nod, pulling Clementine to a stop. This time, we both get down, and I'm grateful for the reprieve from my own head, as well as Noah's proximity. We ascend the wooden steps, coming to a stop at the overlook built onto the side of the short, yet steep, mountain.

"Wow," Noah says, looking out over the field full of wild-flowers between the shadows of two peaks on either side. The ground is filled with color. A beautiful, undisturbed micro-cosm.

"The sun hits it just right for a couple hours every day," I tell him quietly, not wanting to disturb the still air. "It's why so many flowers are able to grow here."

"Yeah," he breathes, staring intently.

My eyes trail down the ink on his arms, and I recall the unfinished metal crown inside his barn. It'd be so easy to ask him about it. The flowers. Why they're clearly so important to him.

But I can't get the words to leave my mouth.

I head over to the wooden box nearby and lift the lid. It's filled with more clues. I pull out two but open one.

"Another location," I tell Noah.

He lets out a soft sigh before turning from the railing. "We should probably get moving then, huh?"

I nod, even as I want to tell him it's okay if he'd rather stay a while. But why would I? We're competing in a time-sensitive competition. Of course we shouldn't linger.

"Sure," I say, handing Noah his scroll. "We're heading north."

"Lead the way," he says, following me back down the stairs.

We get atop Clementine, heading in the direction of the next clue. And even though I know I should be grateful I'll only be stuck on this horse for a short while longer with Noah, I can't seem to find the expected relief anywhere.

Chapter 24

Noah

Being tucked up against Colton's ass is a distraction.

For assuming I was straight not that long ago, it's impossible now to miss the appeal in the man settled at my front.

The strong, sturdy lines of him. His scent, like leather and oranges with an undercurrent of *man*. The tan skin of his neck below the brim of his hat and the hair curling gently there, a hint of sweat visible that I want to wipe away with my tongue.

Colton isn't dainty, nor gentle. And I've been with my fair share of women that weren't either. But Colton is different than all of them. The way I *want* him is different. It's harsher, like freshly juiced lemonade versus prepackaged mix. He's tart, damn near irresistible.

How do I go back to anything else having tasted him?

"What're you doing?" Colton asks, his voice hitching.

I curse myself, realizing I'd moved my hand to his abdomen, poised to—I don't know. Slip down to his crotch, maybe. I move my hand back to his thigh, unable to resist slipping through the holes in the fabric there.

Colton makes a displeased sound, but he doesn't make a single move to stop me, which has my lust ratcheting up a notch. This prickly man. Doesn't he realize by now I'll give him whatever he wants?

I groan softly as I resituate, the sound not one of pain. Not exactly.

"Are you...hard right now?" Colton asks in shock. He tries to look back at me.

"Hard not to be with you rubbing up against me," I point out.

"I'm not...*rubbing* anything," he says, scandalized. "What are you...stop that."

"Stop what?" I ask, finding a second spot on his neck to nip.

"Stop nibbling me," he says, squirming. "Fuck, Noah. You can't give me a boner on top of a horse. I'm not that depraved."

I huff a laugh, grazing my teeth over a tendon that has him moaning. "What I hear is that you like me biting you."

"Oh, God," he groans. "Cut it out or I'll shove you off this horse, King. We haven't passed a single person, so I doubt anyone will find your body."

I huff a laugh, even as I pull back. "As you wish."

He cranes his neck to look at my face, his set in disgruntled confusion. I nearly laugh again, his scrunched nose almost...cute.

Christ. Cute? Colton Darling?

Clearly the heat is affecting my judgement.

After taking a few breaths and getting my hard-on under control, I reach for a distraction. "So, uh, Lawson is getting divorced?"

Colton nods, not seeming surprised that I caught the news around town. "Yeah. He actually signed the paperwork earlier this week. He'll officially be a divorced man before long."

I hum. "How's he doing with that?"

"Fine," he says almost shortly. And then, gentler, "Mostly. He'll be fine. Remi thinks he's lonely."

I wouldn't doubt it. "And what do you think?"

Colton lets out a breath. "I think all he knew of the world, of the life he saw himself building, got bulldozed right before his very eyes. And now he's having to rebuild, sweeping the rubble out of the way as he goes. Of course he's not fine. He's toppled and just trying his best to find even ground again."

The waver in Colton's voice makes me wonder if he's talking about his brother...or possibly himself.

"At least he has you all," I offer. "A family who supports him."

"I... Yeah," Colton replies, his voice quiet. "We're here."

Before I can climb down, Colton levers upwards, swinging his leg carefully over Clementine's head and sliding to the ground in a single fluid move. I watch, shocked, as he jogs the couple steps to the clue box.

"This one's a riddle," he says, tossing a scroll up to me. I catch it and roll it open.

A beat of its own.
Life within stone.
What is it?

"That's...concise," Colton mumbles.

"A heart. Right? There's a trail that leads to the hawk's heart within the mountains."

He nods. "And it's the last clue. We find this, and we're nearly done."

"Well, let's get moving then," I say, my excitement returning now that we're so near to the end.

Colton approaches the horse but stops at the last second.

My lips twitch as I understand his predicament. "What's your plan for getting back up?"

"I'm working on it," he says hotly. "Just...lean back."

"Oh, hell no. You're not swinging your leg over me."

"Come on," he practically whines.

"Nope," I say, dropping to the ground. "You first."

He huffs but sticks his foot in the stirrup. By the squeak he lets out, he's not expecting me to grab his hips and help boost him up. I grin, following him onto Clementine's back and settling behind the saddle.

Colton clears his throat. "Onward."

"Let's go."

The last clue box is nestled at the end of a trail that weaves through craggy, damp rock. The sun is blotted out here, the air wet and smelling of dirt and forest decay. The natural scents don't bother me. Colton lets me hop down this time, my boots crunching over pieces of shale as I grab our scrolls.

Once I return to the horse, Colton and I read the final clue in tandem.

The key is at the creation.
A name given now owned by all.
The dead may rest eternal.
But the child shall never fall.
What is it?

"Oh my God," Colton says after a minute. "It's talking about my great-great-great-whatever grandfather, Isaiah Darling. He founded the town. He gave it his name. And his child, this town, lives on." He huffs an incredulous laugh. "The key is at the statue. His resting place. It's right behind the chest."

"Holy shit," I realize.

"Yeah, holy shit. The treasure hunt literally ends at the beginning. Let's go."

Colton doesn't need to convince me. He turns Clementine around and, at a pace swifter than before, leads her down the trail. He veers off the marked path after a while, cutting through what I'm guessing is his family's land.

"Do you think anyone's gotten there yet?" he asks.

"No clue. Someone might've made it through before us."

He nods. "Or we're the first."

My pulse jumps, giddiness enveloping me. It's such a silly thing, this treasure hunt. But if we win?

"Fuck," Colton mutters. "Can you handle a gallop?"

"I'll need to hold on to you," I point out.

He huffs. "Don't pretend you won't like it."

I chuckle, not denying it in the least. Without another word, Colton urges Clementine into a trot. I wrap my arms around his stomach to keep steady, my thighs gripping the horse tight, and then, with a stutter step, we're off. There's no bracing against the movement without stirrups of my own. I let myself roll with it, the smooth, rhythmic *duh-dump* of hooves against dirt a metronome for our journey.

The sore ass will be worth it.

We pass through the woods for quite some time, and I'm astounded Colton made it to me so quickly earlier. He must have been moving fast coming through these woods before he got my call.

I try not to admire the man's ease in the saddle. This life is baked in his bones, the same as me. I may not have grown up with horses of my own, but they were always a part of my life, always near and dear.

It's why I thought, once upon a time, Colton and I might be friends. I thought we shared something. The same passion. That same lifeblood running through our veins.

But Colton and I were never friends. He made sure of that.

The bitterness rolls through me like Clementine's hoof-beats, there one second and then gone the next. I let it go, knowing I can't hold on to a grudge from another lifetime. It's not fair. Not to me.

Not to him.

Finally, we break out of the trees and onto an open field. The Darlings' ranch is bustling, even on the weekend. A few people stare as Colton and I rush past. Colton waves to a couple of the workers, but he doesn't stop.

We're both breathing a little heavily from the exertion of the ride as he slows in front of the horse barn. My eyes slip up to the hayloft door on instinct before I let myself focus forward again. Colton brings us to a stop, Clementine's tail swishing and a snorting breath leaving her as I swing to the ground. Colton follows quickly, and I give our ride a good couple rubs on her neck.

Clementine sure is a sweet horse. I'll give Colton that.

He quickly removes her gear, handing each item to me and directing me to toss them in the tack room for him to take care of later. After giving Clementine the quickest brushing in existence so she's comfortable enough, he leaves her with plenty of water, and we rush toward his truck.

"We'll get your bike later?" Colton asks as we jog.

I nod, certainly not wanting to take the time to do it now.

Colton unlocks the doors as we approach, and I hop into the passenger seat. "Shit," he says, starting the truck and reversing before pulling us forward onto a dirt drive. "My pulse is going wild."

"Yeah," I agree, pulling out my phone to see if anyone from town has mentioned a winner yet. "What do you think is in the chest?"

"No clue," Colton says, pulling roughly onto the road. He guns it, not caring about speed limits. "Probably not cash, right? It's a fundraiser for the new playground. So it's likely something donated."

"Or multiple somethings."

He nods. "I hope there's whiskey."

I snort a laugh, but I don't disagree. Colton tasted damn good with whiskey on his tongue.

He slows once we get close to town. Pedestrians are still out, many looking as if they camped out in the park, making a day of the event as they wait for the winner to appear. I crane my neck as Colton finds the first available parking spot.

"The chest is still closed," I say, my pulse racing.

"Holy fuck," Colton mutters, tugging up the parking brake.

We lock eyes before bursting from the vehicle.

A few people look over as we sprint toward the chest, no stopping us now. I don't know if Colton is feeling as wild and reckless as me, but I laugh at the wonder of it. How something as simple as a grown-up version of a childish game can make me feel so...weightless.

Or maybe it's simply this man at my side.

"Is that..." Colton says, his words cutting out.

I look over in time to see Jackson and Ashley sprinting toward the chest from our right. It seems impossible that they'd have the clues necessary to collect the prize, but there's no mistaking their goal.

Colton growls. "Go," he calls to me, veering off toward the duo. "Get the key."

I don't stop moving, even as Jackson shouts. The next second, Colton is tackling him to the ground, the two spinning over the grass as Ashley stops to bark out a laugh.

I accept the distraction for what it is and rush to the statue, my breathing loud, my pulse heavy. I start high up, figuring the key has to be hidden somewhere we couldn't see it before. There's some cheering from the crowd when they realize what's going on, and then Colton yells, "He's coming!"

I look over just in time to see Ashley running my way. Colton is still on the ground, his hands around Jackson's ankle. I hasten my search, stilling when my fingers roll over something far less smooth than stone. Plucking the key from the top of Isaiah Darling's cowboy hat, I drop to the ground.

Ashley curses, but he doesn't try to take it from me. Which is good because I honestly don't know how far I'd be willing to go to keep it. As is, my hands shake as I walk the couple steps to the chest. I fit the key into the lock, the two melding together seamlessly, and then I find Colton's gaze.

He nods, still holding his brother back, his eyes sparkling and so very blue.

With a twist, I open the chest.

Folks cheer in earnest now, and a foghorn blasts for a second time today, nearly deafening me. I shake off the echoing in my ears and look inside the chest to find...

"What the fuck?" I mumble.

Colton pants heavily as he catches up to me, dropping to his knees on the grass. "What...what is that?" he asks, sounding just as confused as I am. "Fake money?"

I reach into the chest, which is indeed filled with paper cut uniformly to look like fake bills.

"They're Darling coupons!" Mr. Yadav declares, coming up behind us. "You can cash them in for goods and services all over town."

I pick one up, examining the words on it. "Free oil change at Ratchet's," I read aloud.

"That's right," the board member says. "There's nearly two grand worth of prizes in there. Congratulations! I take it you two will be splitting the spoils?"

"We will," I answer, not for a second considering denying that Colton and I were working together. Colton doesn't even look relieved, like he hadn't considered I might betray him, either.

It warms me more than I want to admit.

"I'll just need to see your clues to verify," Mr. Yadav says.

I pull all the papers I collected out of my pockets as Colton does the same. As the board member goes through them, Colton pulls another coupon out of the chest.

"A free visit to the petting farm at... Oh, for fuck's sake," he mutters. "At the Darling Ranch. This one's yours."

I accept the coupon with a chuckle as Jackson reaches us, grass stains on his jeans.

"Look," Colton says to his older brother, tone victorious. "See all my prizes? Not yours, but mine. Aren't they pretty?"

"You're an ass," Jackson says mildly.

"How'd you guys even finish the treasure hunt?" I ask. "We didn't pass you on the trails."

"We were wondering the same thing," Ashley says. "Were there clues at Hawk Hollow? Because we followed the final five at Eagle Back."

"There were," Mr. Yadav says, returning. "The trail diverged with two possible conclusions. Clever, right? You gentlemen are all set. Your clues have been confirmed, which means the chest is all yours. Let us know if you need any help wheeling it out of here."

"It's...incredibly light," Colton says, testing the weight of it. "But thank you."

I snort.

"Well, I guess now I know why you never called to meet back up when your trail ran cold," Jackson says, raising an eyebrow. "Your trail *didn't* run cold."

"Hey, you didn't call either," Colton points out. "You were planning on finishing without me."

"Uh, guys?" Ashley cuts in. "Maybe let's not play the blame game when we're all guilty of the same thing?"

"Point," Colton says, sighing. "Anyone wanna grab some food? I'm fucking starved."

We all agree, and Colton and I field some congratulations from the townsfolk before closing up our chest and locking it in his truck.

The four of us head down the sidewalk to get dinner. And all the while I can't stop wondering why, when it mattered most, Colton helped me win the treasure hunt instead of his own brother.

Chapter 25

COLTON

Noah and I are quiet as I drive him back to his motorcycle at the Hawk Hollow access point. I keep looking over at him, but his gaze is trained out the side of the truck, his elbow propped against the doorframe and his chin in his palm.

He's been reserved ever since we finished the treasure hunt. Not that he's a particularly boisterous person to begin with, but I get the impression there's something on his mind.

I don't quite know what to make of it. Or the thoughts in my own head.

I pull off onto the gravel in front of the guard rail, careful not to hit Daphne. There's a tug in my chest when I remember he named the bike after his mother. I know nothing about his parents, and I feel guilty for that now. I couldn't take a minute to ask him a few questions about his life?

Noah pops the door open once I come to a stop, and I follow after him. As he brings the bike around to the back, I lower the tailgate. Since we grabbed a board from the ranch, it's not too difficult to push the bike up into the bed of the truck. Noah sets it down carefully. Reverently.

I nearly wince seeing the evidence of his spill on the side of the red frame.

"Thanks," Noah says, hopping down.

I nod, following him and sliding the board up before hoisting the tailgate back into place. The drive to Noah's is just as silent as before, and I start drumming my fingers against the wheel, nerves eating at me.

It's not quite dark when I pull into Noah's driveway. Not like the other times I've come here. With the help of the board, we get the motorcycle down, and Noah stores it inside his garage, shaking his head a little like he's disheartened to see it looking worse for wear. Once he lowers the garage door, his eyes meet mine.

"Come on," he says, heading for the front of the house.

I stand there, my keys in hand, confusion and indecision warring.

"Colt," Noah says. Just my name.

My feet carry me forward.

Noah stops inside the front door, kicking off his boots. I take mine off, too, feeling like I'm having an out-of-body experience. The small foyer inside leads to a living room to the right, and a large doorway to the left opens into the kitchen. There's a stairwell directly in front of us, curving up and to the right, and a narrow hallway that leads straight back.

"Walt?" Noah calls lightly.

"Back here," Noah's uncle says in return.

"Just getting home. You need anything?"

There's a brief pause before Walter says, "Not a thing."

"I'll be upstairs," Noah says. And that's it. He heads up the stairs, expecting me to follow him.

I do.

My pulse is heavy as I trail Noah through his home. Although small, it's well-loved with homey touches that speak to the life Noah has here with his uncle. I don't know why it surprises me, the evidence of Noah's life. As if I—what? Thought he existed inside a sterile box while plotting my demise?

I'm probably a blip on Noah's radar. He's likely never thought much about me. Not like I've thought of him.

He turns right into a bathroom, looking over his shoulder to make sure I'm still behind him. "Strip," he says as soon as the door closes.

I stare at him, fairly certain I'm having a mild cardiac event. We don't...*do* that. I've never even seen the man with his shirt off, let alone naked. He's never seen me, either.

Noah lets out a sigh. Not one of disappointment but understanding. Somehow, he understands. "Colt," he says softly, "I'd really like to get you in this shower. It's been a long damn day, half of which I spent nestled close to your ass. If you wanna go, you can. I won't stop you. But if you decide to stay, I'm hauling you into this shower, got it?"

I let out a breath, my stillness this time a choice.

Noah nods to himself before grabbing the hem of my shirt and wrestling it off my body. I consider fighting it, consider putting off the inevitable out of principle alone.

But, like Noah said, it's been a long day. And I think I'm done fighting.

Noah tosses my shirt on the ground and grabs my waistband, opening my fly. My jeans follow, hitting the floor, and then my briefs meet the same fate. Noah is squatting on the ground now, looking his fill as he lifts each of my feet up to remove my clothes, my socks the last to go. I feel utterly exposed. More than naked.

Noah stands with smooth fluidity, turning on the shower before staring me in the eye and unbuttoning his pants. My cock starts to plump the second I hear the zipper, and Noah smirks, a little more life entering his eyes. He makes a production of undressing, and I hate that I can't look away. Can't tear my eyes off the man for a single second as he removes his pants and underwear, his socks, the bandage around his hand, and lastly, his shirt.

My breath whooshes out of me when I see the ink flowing across his chest. The rope vines across, like I'd imagined, moving from one arm, across his pecs in beautiful motion, to his other arm and down again. Flowers are intertwined with the rope the entire way, creating a colorful tapestry over his skin, that horseshoe I kept getting a peek of hooked over one loop. It's as if it's part of the design. Part of him, the curve of the metal right over his heart.

Noah steps ahead of me into the shower, and my gaze dips down. I about buckle as I come face to face with the man's ass, his cheeks firm and dimpling at the sides as he moves.

Fuuuck.

My mouth feels dry as he steps under the showerhead, his hair darkening to near black, water dripping down his back in rivulets. I step in after him, and Noah turns to shut the curtain. What the fuck am I even doing here? What is this? Why do I want it so much?

Noah tugs me forward, no hesitation in the man. He maneuvers me under the spray, his fingers sinking into my hair as he tips my head back an inch, the water drenching me. He hums, seeming so pleased by something so simple.

I'm afraid to open my mouth. Afraid, if I do, I'll fuck this up. Afraid he'll stop. Afraid that I don't want him to stop.

Noah's hand wrapping around my cock is an immense relief. It's what I'm used to from him. What I expect. He gives me a couple slow, slippery strokes before stepping in closer. It takes me a second to realize he's grabbing his soap, not moving in to kiss me, and the disappointment that hits is unwelcome.

But then Noah is squeezing soap out onto his palm, and the man's hands are back on my skin.

"You look like a scared kitten," Noah remarks, his voice low but still startling following our silence.

I don't have a single comeback, and Noah raises a brow. How he expects me to speak with his palms running slow circles across my chest and shoulders is beyond me.

"Have I broken you?" he asks.

I clear my throat. "Never."

"Good," he rumbles, reaching around to rub soapy palms over my back, the move slotting us neatly together. "I much prefer you alive and kicking."

"That's a surprise," I manage, trying to keep the groan from my voice as his hip moves against my cock. "Didn't think you liked when I kick."

He huffs a laugh, his palms smoothing down toward my ass. "On the contrary. I like the fight in you, little Colt."

"Yeah?" I breathe, my brain going haywire as his fingers slip, testingly slow, down between my ass cheeks. "Why's that? You like the challenge?"

My hands are on his waist now, holding steady, my pulse a fast cadence in my ears beside the noise from the shower.

Noah hums, his palms so fucking big as he covers my ass, his fingers continuing to tease, dipping just inside my crack. "I like that moment you give in," he practically whispers. "When you stop fighting yourself."

His words make me freeze, but then all thoughts scatter as Noah's fingers rub purposefully over my hole. They stay there a moment before slipping down and cupping me, fingertips close to my balls. He holds me, pressed so close it feels like a hug.

"You want me to stop," he says, "you say so."

I shake my head the tiniest bit, not wanting him to stop. He can't. Not now. I'll fucking punch him if he does.

He must catch the movement of my head, because he makes a sound of smug approval and slides his hand back up again. This time, when his fingers rub over my hole, I nearly fall against him. I use his body as support, keeping my face hidden, practically shaking with the way I want those fingers inside of me. I threw out that damn carrot, not caring in the least for the impersonal and cold quality of it. But I haven't been able to bring myself to buy a toy. All I've had are my fingers, and somehow, I just *know* Noah's will be better.

Warmer. More fulfilling. Just...*more*.

And his cock?

Ah, fuck.

"Little Colt," Noah breathes, his hand in my hair holding tight as he circles my rim, seemingly content to torture me as always. "Do you know what it's like to feel you shaking in my arms?"

"Fuck off," I try to mumble. The fact that my lips are pressed to his shoulder makes the words come out muffled.

He huffs, his fingertip pressing against me the tiniest bit. *Oh fuck, oh fuck.*

"It makes me feel powerful," he says, retreating and then slipping the tip of his finger back in place, his aim clear. "The control you give me..." He cuts off, pressing inside of me, only just. I let out a keen, pushing back against that digit, beyond caring what I look or sound like right now. Noah groans before finishing with, "I never want to give it up."

I can barely follow along, all of my focus on the finger edged inside my ass. It's not enough. Not nearly enough.

Noah slips away, his hand sliding upwards. I rear back in outrage, but his fingers in my hair soothe, rubbing against my scalp like a gentle massage.

"Calm, little Colt," he says with that infuriating smirk. "Finish washing up, and I'll give you exactly what you need."

"I don't need you," I say weakly, the response automatic.

Noah's smile quirks as he hands me the soap, setting to work on his body now. "Want," he amends, the motion of his hands hypnotizing.

I can't even find it in me to argue.

It feels unbearably intimate washing alongside Noah, letting my eyes wander, taking him in in all his naked glory. I hate to admit the sight is one I appreciate, but what's the point in pretending otherwise anymore? I'm standing here of my own free will, aren't I? Sharing a *shower* with the man.

Noah finishes before me, stepping out and grabbing a towel. He dries his hair first, leaving his ass uncovered, the ink along his arms flexing with his movements. I take a quick moment while he's rebandaging his hand to slip a finger inside my ass, washing myself perfunctorily before shutting off the water.

Noah grabs a second towel for me, holding it out, his cock bobbing as he takes me in without shame. I pluck the towel from his hand, hiding the blush on my face.

He waits until the towel is around my waist to open the door. I scoop up my clothes and follow him across the hall into what must be his bedroom, feeling like a damn teenager sneaking around. Although it's not like the barn was much better.

He shuts and locks the door behind us, flicking on a floor lamp before walking back my way.

My pulse is thrumming, electricity licking over every inch of my skin.

Noah lets his towel drop and tugs me closer by my own. "On your knees," he says, not a request.

My cock fills so rapidly, it leaves me lightheaded. "Make me," I spit out, unable not to.

He wings up a brow before grabbing my shoulder and pressing down. Instinct has me shoving his arm away, but he anticipates the move, grabbing the back of my neck in a tight hold. I arch toward him, my towel falling, my cock rubbing briefly against his before Noah is shoving the heel of his foot behind my knee.

I go down in an instant, my knees hitting the plush towels, Noah's cock in my direct line of sight as he straightens out, a challenging look on his face like he's waiting for my next move.

"Now," he says evenly, "are you going to stay there, or do I needa hold you down?"

Ah, fuck.

My eyes slip shut, and Noah's fingers thread through my hair. "Fucking gorgeous," he says. "Open your mouth."

My eyes open, breath ragged as I stare down Noah's cock. I don't know what I'm doing. I've never done this. Don't even know where to start.

Noah grabs the base of his dick, one hand still in my hair as he guides me closer, his cockhead tapping my lips. I grab onto his wrist near my head, holding tight, not pushing away.

"Open, little Colt," he urges. "Lemme take what I want from your mouth."

Somehow, that makes it easier. The demand in his voice. Knowing I can let him lead. I don't know what it says about me that I want him to, but I open my mouth and wait.

Noah takes his time, running his cock agonizingly slowly over my bottom lip. His own lips are parted, brown eyes dark, that coppery blaze like flames licking into the night.

"Smack my thigh if it's too much," he warns.

I don't move an inch.

Noah slides his cock onto my tongue, and I have to hold back my groan. "I was right," he says, smug. "You look good down there."

He doesn't let me off his dick to fire off a retort, and even that has my cock bucking.

"Christ," he says, hips flexing, the smooth glide of his cock through my lips making me dizzy. "My cock looks right at home inside you. Just imagine what it'll look like in your ass."

I can't stop my moan this time. I just can't.

Noah grins, his thumb running over my cheek before his fist is back in my hair, tugging me down on his dick.

"Ask me for it, little Colt. If you want it, ask."

He pulls me back, his cock popping wetly from between my lips. "No," I breathe.

He hums, sliding himself back into my mouth, punching his hips a few times, his dick grazing the back of my throat and making me gag.

"Beg me," he says.

"Fuck you."

His grip tightens, the sting bringing tears to my eyes. My own cock leaks onto the towel below my knees, Noah's taste on my tongue overriding all other senses. He tastes and smells woodsy, like the soap in his shower.

"Beg me to fill your tight virgin ass with my cock, little Colt. Say the words, and it's yours."

Tears roll down my cheeks, whether from Noah's grip in my hair, the blowjob, or the fact that I know I'm going to ask for it like he wants. I knew weeks ago I'd do whatever Noah needed to get him to fuck me. To find out, once and for all, what it feels like to be full of the man, overwhelmed and overloaded, consumed in a way I never have been before.

All he needs is the words. He needs my consent. That's it.

"Please," I breathe when Noah pulls back.

"Please what?" he asks gently, rubbing a tear away with his thumb.

I kiss the head of his cock, my eyes slipping closed. "Please fuck me."

"Colt, baby," he says, his voice so quiet I'm not sure I'm meant to hear it. "Anything."

Chapter 26

NOAH

Colton looks like a rugged dream, his hair hanging damp around his face, tears littering his cheeks and his cock flushed and hard, straining toward me.

The man would knock me off my feet if I allowed it. As is, I'm barely keeping it together, everything in me desperate to toss Colton onto my bed and cover every inch of him with my tongue and teeth. I want to mark him, taste him, pull whimpers and pleas from between his lips.

I want *everything* he'll allow me.

"Up," I tell him, giving his hair a gentle tug.

He gets to his feet, letting himself be led as I drag him over to the mattress. He falls back against it, his cock bobbing, his chest rising and falling as he pushes up to his elbows.

"Have you played with your ass?" I ask, going to my nightstand for lube.

He lets out a breath, but he doesn't answer.

"Colt?" I prompt.

"Yeah," he finally says. "Little bit."

Fuck.

"So you know how to let me in?"

"Assuming you stretch me enough, I'm sure you can find your way in," he shoots back.

I huff a laugh, enjoying the bob of Colton's throat as I climb onto the mattress. I drop the lube and condoms beside his hip and tug the man flat onto his back. "I'm damn well gonna enjoy pinning you to this bed."

He swallows again, eyes wide. But he doesn't look scared. He looks wild. Like an animal willing to fight for its last meal.

"Turn over, little Colt."

"Not little," he mutters, spinning under the cage of my body.

"Admit it," I tease, knowing he'll do no such thing. "You like being my—"

My voice chokes out when Colton completes his turn. He freezes before groaning loudly.

"What the fuck," I breathe, my fingers tracing over the letters inked at the top of Colton's right ass cheek.

"God," he moans, the sound barely audible, pressed to the sheets as it is.

"When... When did you do this?" I demand.

"After the Shoein'," he says, face turned enough for me to hear him. "I wasn't about to back out of our bet, was I?" He sounds pained when he adds, "You won fair and square. So...I got that."

That being the word "King" tattooed in beautiful script on Colton's ass. I never thought... I didn't think he went through with it. He's had this for two months? Two months, and I had no clue.

"Fuck," I grit out, dropping my mouth to Colton's skin. I lick over the word—*my name*—before biting down.

Colton jolts, pressing up against me. "Jesus fuck, you can't just—"

I bite him again, an inch over, and he groans.

"I can't believe you did this," I rasp, covering his ass with my teeth and my lips, one bite and kiss at a time. "Fuck, Colt. *Fuck*."

"Noah," he groans, rutting against my sheets.

I work on the other ass cheek next, biting, licking, but I sit up before long, needing to see my name again. Needing to see the evidence of myself etched permanently on his skin. I roll my thumb over the letters, my heart thrashing about wildly.

"You're never getting rid of it," I growl.

"How the fuck would I?" he counters. "Aren't tattoo removals like—"

His words cut off when I squeeze his ass cheek hard. "Never, Colt."

"Jesus," he gasps, squirming, his cheeks bright red when he looks back at me. His inhale is sharp, whatever he sees on my face enough to have him staring at me another few seconds longer. "Yeah," he breathes out. "It's not going anywhere."

Satisfied, I lean down to run kisses up the length of Colton's spine. He's stiff for a second, but then he melts into the bed, smelling like my bodywash and a little bit like himself. It's a heady combination.

When my crotch reaches Colton's ass, I nestle my cock between his cheeks, snug against warm skin. "I need you to do something for me," I tell him, my voice hoarse. I grab the lube as I roll my hips.

"What?" he says, the word all breath.

"I need you to be quiet this time. Can you do that?"

I'm sure he understands why. My uncle is somewhere in the house, and I'd rather him not hear my sexual explorations with a man he knows I hate. Or did.

"How about when you start doing something worthy of moaning about," Colton says dryly, "I'll try my best to keep it down."

"Cheeky fuck," I mutter, moving down his body.

"Yeah, well. Maybe you could get between my cheeks and—*oh fuck.*"

"What was that?" I ask, swiping him with my tongue again.

He shifts against me, his back heaving. "I'll be quiet."

"Good," I breathe, licking over his hole before grabbing the lube. Colton spreads his legs, opening himself up for me, one leg hitched up at the knee. His hand goes to his cock, and I realize it's the first time I've seen him touching himself. There was that phone call, but it's different seeing it in person.

"Have you done this before?" he asks as I circle his rim with lube-wet fingers.

"What?"

"Fucked an asshole."

I huff a laugh, pressing a finger inside of him. He stills for only a second, and then he's stroking his cock again, his hips moving almost imperceptibly. The sight of my finger disappearing inside his body is mesmerizing.

"Fucking beautiful," I mutter before answering his question. "Not a man's."

He nods against the sheets, his hair covering his face from my view. "C'mon. Two. I can handle it."

I groan at the direct request, leaning down to fit my teeth over his tattoo again as I slide a second finger in alongside the first. His body is warm, tight but accommodating. It's clear he *has* done this before, at least this part. Because Colton is shifting back against me, seeking more from my fingers, knowing exactly what he wants and going after it.

"Goddamn sexy," I tell him, my knuckles brushing his ass cheeks as I stretch him out. "Watching you fuck yourself on my fingers might be the sexiest fucking thing I've ever seen, little Colt."

He groans, turning his face back against the sheets. "Less talking."

"You don't wanna hear what you look like swallowing my fingers?"

"No."

"How about how gorgeous you are laid out on your stomach, begging me for what you want without words?"

"Fuck. Off," he breathes.

I lean over him as I work my fingers in deeper, teeth nipping his ear. "I think you like it. I think you like hearing how stunning you are when you give yourself over to me. When you get exactly what you want."

He shakes his head. "Just fuck me already."

I ignore his attempt at avoidance, sliding a third finger inside his body. He groans at the invasion, the sound almost broken. "You can hide your face all you want, but it doesn't change anything, Colt. I understand you. And this thing you want? There's nothing wrong with it, and I won't ever mock it. Do you know why?"

His breathing is labored, the long line of his back arched, his ass lifted into the air and my fingers moving inside of him with ease now.

"Because I want it, too," I tell him fiercely. "I wanna fuck you so good you have trouble walking for weeks. I wanna give you every goddamn thing you need so you keep coming back to me for more. You *are* beautiful down on your knees. Because you like being there. And you're beautiful like this. Opened up for me. *Trusting* me."

He shakes his head again, but the movement is weak.

"Don't you get it?" I ask, my frustration leaking into my tone. I ease my fingers out and grab a condom, hands shaking as I tear open the package and roll it down my cock. I'm so hard it hurts, but it's the ache in my chest that has my voice coming out strained. "I can't stop thinking about you. You're in my fucking head. Invading my life. You're everywhere I goddamn look. Everything I see."

I line up my cock as Colton pants, his asshole glistening with lube. Almost subconsciously, my thumb rolls over the ink on his skin, and I grab on tight.

"And I'm not letting you run anymore," I husk out. "You're mine, Colton Darling. You. Are. *Mine*."

Colton sucks in a breath as I press my cock past his tight ring of muscle. His body clamps down on me for only a second, and then he's bearing down, the invitation evident, his stuttered moan a match for my grunt. I ease inside of him in increments, his body fitting my cock like a glove, the sight of me disappearing inch by inch between his spread cheeks more satisfying than it has any right to be.

When my hips press tight to his ass, my body rolls in a shiver.

"Noah," Colton gasps.

"Yeah?" I say, running my hand over the swell of his ass, my other anchoring at his hip, thumb pressing tightly into my claim on his skin.

"Please, *please* fuck me now," he begs. "I can't... I need you to..."

"Yeah, baby," I tell him, brushing his hair behind his ear. "Don't fucking hide."

He swallows roughly, nodding once.

With my hands on his hips, I ease out, the clasp of Colton's body lighting every one of my nerve endings on fire. When I roll forward, it's as if each of those flickers bursts into flames.

Colton lets out a breath, and another when I do it again. "Oh, fuck," he says, hand fisting the sheets, his other still around his cock. "Oh, God."

"King," I correct, his ass shaking every time my hips slam forward.

"What?"

"It's 'Oh, King.'"

Colton laughs, a raspy thing, as he strokes his cock. "You're an absolute dick."

"You like my dick."

"Fuck off."

"Admit it," I goad, pulling him back onto me, fucking him harder, his ass feeling like absolute heaven. "You fucking love this."

"Hate you," he mutters, even as a smile curves his lips.

"Oh, baby. Then you're really gonna hate this."

Colton scrambles when I tug his hips upright, forcing him to let go of his cock and get his knees under him. He looks affronted for all of a second, but then I'm clasping my hand around his dick and slamming deep, and his outrage dissolves into a reedy groan.

"Quiet," I remind him, my thumb rolling over the head of his cock as I punch repeatedly into his body. There's one way he's far different from a woman when it comes to this. Well, two, taking the cock in my hand into consideration. And if I can just find it...

Colton cries out, his cock jerking. "*Fuck.* Fuck, fuck," he mutters.

"Still hate it?"

"*Ahh*," he moans in response, his face pressed into my pillow to muffle the noise. I keep at the same angle, driving against his prostate, wondering what it is he's feeling right now and curious to find out for myself someday. Right now, there's nowhere else I'd rather be.

"If it's so bad," I tease between breaths, "I can stop."

"Don't you fucking dare," he growls. "I will make you"—a grunt—"rue the fucking day, King."

"If you don't want me to stop, then what *do* you want?" I ask, jerking his cock in earnest now.

He groans, his muscles shaking, a small tremor running through his body. "You're gonna fuck me until I come. Or I swear to God—"

He cuts off on a gasp, his neck tasting sweet when I sink my teeth against his skin. He jerks again, my thrusts shallower at this angle, but the man sturdy enough to take my weight over him. For a second, as he falls silent, I worry I went too far. Bit him too hard, maybe.

But then he's sucking in a great big mouthful of air, the tightening of his ass around me preceding the swell of his cock.

"*Oh fuck*," he says on a moan. And then he's coming.

Colton's ass wrings me as the man spills onto my sheets. I can't see it, but I can feel his orgasm pulsing from him, hear the anguished bliss in his tone as he groans into my pillow. I bite the inside of my cheek to keep from drawing blood on his shoulder or neck, fucking him through his release in short pumps of my hips, trying to hold myself back from the edge.

It's the husked-out, "Noah," that makes that impossible.

I tuck my face against the back of Colton's neck as I shatter apart. It's a blast so heavy, it flares outwards for only a moment before the weight of it crushes inward again, my body locking tight. It's torture, and it's bliss, and I empty inside the condom as I wish I was painting the inside of Colton's ass instead. I want him to take a part of me with him. To fucking *keep* me.

And with startling clarity, I realize he will. My name is forever imprinted on his skin, the black lines forming four letters the most remarkable thing I've seen in my life. So unexpected. So achingly perfect. And even if it didn't mean for Colton what I'm coming to fear it means for me, it doesn't matter. I'm still there. The memory of me immortalized on the one man who I swear only a few months ago would have done anything to be rid of me for good.

And now, he never will be.

I trace my fingers over the letters as I come back to myself, my skin still buzzing, my cock nestled inside Colton's ass. He's breathing harshly below me, but his face is turned, a single lock of hair resting over his cheek. He looks...soft. For once, he's allowing me to see him without guards. Or maybe he simply can't hold them up.

I press a kiss to his shoulder before easing back, holding the condom as I slide out of his body. The sight is almost as enticing as when I slid in, and I let out a groan, already anticipating the next time. And there *will* be a next time.

"So," I say, getting rid of the condom as Colton lies sprawled out on my bed. "Was it as horrible as you expected?"

"Worse," he mutters.

I hum, rolling him onto his back so I can see him better. He doesn't stop me, but his eyes look wary.

"No running," I remind him, brushing his hair back, letting my thumb stroke down his cheek to his jawline. I pluck up his chin, raising an eyebrow.

He swallows, but he doesn't look away, and, slowly, I bring my mouth to his. His lips tremble beneath mine, this man who's strong and brazen and a little wild sharing his vulnerabilities with me, whether or not he intends to. He's soft against my mouth, and I want to tell him he *can* be. That it's okay, and I won't hurt him. That we'll figure this out.

When I break from his lips, I tuck myself over Colton's body, tugging him close. It takes a moment for him to relax, but then his hands are smoothing over my back, and he holds me just as tight.

As the sky turns dark, I search inside of myself for the answers I think I already have, my fingers stroking rhythmically over the ink resting indelibly on Colton's skin.

Chapter 27

COLTON

The sun is shining through the window when I crack my eyes open. I'm hot, and it takes me a second to realize why.

Noah is plastered against my side, his big body wrapped around me like an overgrown koala. I turn my head the smallest fraction to look at him, and my throat catches.

He's naked, as am I. His leg is trapping my own, his arm holding me captive, and the curve of his ass is on display just above the white sheet that's tangled near his calf.

Ah, fuck.

I squeeze my eyes shut, willing myself not to react. But then they shoot wide again.

It's morning.

As in I slept the night.

As in I'm still at Noah fucking King's house after the man fucked me into his mattress. Oh, God.

I attempt to extract myself from his octopusing limbs, but he rolls with me, trapping me under his body as he rumbles his approval, his cock now slotted against my ass.

Fuuuck.

"Noah," I croak.

"Mm?"

"It's morning."

"And?"

"*And,*" I say, "it's light out. As in the sun is up, and I'm still here."

"It's the weekend," he says casually, his stubble bristling my shoulder.

"So? Have you met my family? This isn't going to go unnoticed."

"You're a grown man," Noah rumbles, his hand slipping down between us until it's covering my ass. He makes a sound of approval, and I realize he's petting my tattoo again.

Fucking hell.

I will not get a boner. I will not. I will not.

"You're freaking out," he says calmly.

"Why aren't *you?*"

He shrugs, kissing just below my ear. "I've accepted it."

I go still. "Accepted what?"

"I think you know."

Like hell I do.

"I have to go," I say, weaseling out from under him. My pulse is pounding as I look around the floor for my clothes, finding them in a heap near the foot of the bed. Noah is quiet as I dress, but he sits upright, his legs over the side of the bed, the man rubbing his eyes as his cock lies heavy against his thigh.

I quickly avert my gaze.

"When did you get all those fucking tattoos?" I wonder aloud, shoving my legs into my pants and trying my best to ignore the ache in my ass. It doesn't hurt. Not exactly.

"College," he says, cracking a yawn.

"Why flowers?" I ask, my pulse sprinting.

He hums softly, blinking his eyes open and watching me. "My mom liked them."

I swallow roughly, pulling my shirt over my head. Noah doesn't say a word as I tug on my socks and zip up my fly, but he speaks before I can walk out the door.

"Colton," he says, the one word causing my eyes to slip shut. "We said no running."

"You said," I fire back, my hands curled into fists at my sides.

"I meant it."

"I don't know what this is," I rasp.

"You'll figure it out."

"Oh, fuck off," I say, turning in his direction, his calm tone pissing me off. "Don't say it like that, like I'm some sort of...*foal* who's just learning how to walk. I'm not that green, King."

"No," he says, smiling now. "You're certainly no foal. You're my colt."

I scowl at the man, and his smile broadens.

"What are you so afraid of?" he asks, tone gentle despite his words.

I throw my hands in the air. "Goddamn everything? I'm afraid you're fucking with me. That you're... That we..."

"Shh," Noah says, standing and walking over, still entirely nude. He wraps his arms around me, his lips near my ear as my pulse pounds so heavily I can feel it coursing through my veins. "Settle, little Colt."

I let out a grunt, and he sifts his hands up into my hair. I can't tell if this is a hug or if Noah is reminding me he holds my reins.

Not that he does.

"There's no rush," he says. "Call me. Text me. I'm not going anywhere. And I'm not letting *you* go anywhere."

I don't know what he means by that, but he places a swift kiss near my ear and steps back, walking to his closet to get dressed. I stand in front of his door until he's done, and then we wash up in his bathroom and head down the stairs.

My plan is to walk right out the front door, but we only make it as far as the entrance to the kitchen when Walter's voice rings out from inside the room.

"Well, good morning."

I sigh, turning my head to find Noah's uncle sitting at the kitchen table, a mug of what I presume to be coffee in front of him and a wide grin on his face.

"Morning, Walt," Noah says mildly. "You know Colton Darling."

"Sure do," he says, inclining his head my way. "Been a while."

"Nice to see you again, sir," I mumble, wishing the floor would swallow me whole.

"You having breakfast with us?" Walter asks, his question clearly for me.

"Uh, no. Can't stay. Sorry."

He makes a small sound of acknowledgement. "Maybe next time."

"Walt," Noah says, tone warning.

The older man chuckles before taking a sip of his drink. "G'day, Colton."

"Sir."

Noah walks me to the front door, waiting until we're out of sight to ask, "All right?"

"Nope. Not in the least," I whisper harshly.

He huffs what might be a laugh, his eyes damn *soft* as he looks at me. Since when does Noah fucking King look at me *softly*?

"See you soon," he says, as if it's a foregone conclusion. "Save some of those coupons for me."

Right. The chest is still in my truck.

I nod, and Noah stands there for another second before nodding back and rounding the corner into the kitchen. I tug on my boots, Walter's voice carrying quietly, although I'm more than positive I'm not meant to hear it.

"Was wondering if you were ever gonna tell me about him," he says to Noah.

Oh, God. Noah's uncle knew? Of course he did. How many times have I parked in his damn driveway?

I shake my head, tugging on my second boot.

"I would have told you when there was something to tell," Noah says back, which *ouch.* Why the fuck does that sting so much?

I don't wait around to hear more. I tug open the door and head outside, squinting against the sunlight as I walk briskly toward my truck. The treasure hunt feels like a lifetime ago, not less than twenty-four hours in the past. How was it just yesterday afternoon that Noah and I were riding horseback together, working to solve the final clues? So much has happened since then. A world's worth of change in mere hours.

I let Noah fuck me. Wanted it. *Asked* for it.

And it was everything—*everything*—I was afraid it would be.

How do I go back now? Can I?

When I get home, I park in my usual spot in the lot outside the ranch house. Seeing as it's the weekend, there are less vehicles here today, a skeleton crew on duty as opposed to the full twenty or so we have on a typical weekday. I check myself in the mirror before grabbing my hat and heading toward the house, leaving the chest for later.

I hear voices once I step inside and cringe. Maybe I can sneak past? I toe off my boots as quietly as I can, shut the door, and make my way down the hall.

My family goes quiet the moment I pass in front of the dining room. My mom, my dad, Jackson, and Remi are all inside, silent now and staring at me, frozen in place. My mom's hands are midair, halted in conversation. Remi's eyes ping quickly between me and the rest of our family, checking for words he may be missing. Jackson raises an eyebrow, surely noticing I'm wearing the same clothes I was before.

"Morning," I say and sign before hurrying past.

Fuck, fuck, fuck.

It's fine. It could've been any one-night stand. Any one-night stand with a girl from town or someone passing through. Or a *guy*, even. Anyone. Not a single person in my family is going to assume it was Noah King.

Even though it was.

I lock myself in the bathroom, stripping out of my clothes so I can shower off any potential evidence of my night with Noah. My chest pings as I scrub away the woodsy scent from his bodywash, replacing it with my own.

When I get in my room, I change into fresh clothes and sit my ass on my bed, my head in my hands as I try to parse through my racing thoughts. I'm not the least bit surprised when there's a knock at the door.

I know it's Remi. I just do.

I stand up and walk over, letting him in. He's not wearing his processor, which isn't uncommon at home.

A quick, *'Spill,'* tumbles from his hands as he leans against the door. His eyes shift to my neck, and I groan, walking to the mirror in front of my dresser.

Fucking Noah. He left another goddamn hickey.

I plop back onto my bed, looking at Remi, at a loss. *'I don't know what to say.'*

'Try.'

I let out a breath, hands moving more swiftly than the words inside my head can form. *'I've been hooking up with Noah King.'*

I spell out Noah's name, secretly hoping Remi will assign him a name sign one of these days that denotes his *asshole king* status.

Remi's mouth drops open. *'Since when?'* he asks, hands cutting swiftly through the air.

I try to count backwards. *'Since that time he jerked me off in his barn?'*

'Months,' Remi supplies.

'Months,' I agree.

"The hell?" Remi says aloud, switching back to ASL to ask, *'Why didn't you tell me?'*

And *fuck*. He looks hurt.

'I was embarrassed,' I admit. *'I didn't know what you'd think of me for hooking up with a guy I don't even like.'*

I frown at the present tense, not sure if that's even true anymore. *God*, I'm so confused.

Remi pushes off from the door, coming over to sit beside me on the bed. *'You're an idiot.'* He flicks my forehead when I lift my hands in protest. *'I'm your brother.'* He repeats the word, looking me straight in the eyes as his hands come together. *'I'll always support you. And I won't ever think less of you because of who you choose to sleep with.'*

'But he's...' I pause mid-movement.

He's an asshole? *Is he?*

He's my competition and business rival? *That's true enough.*

He's my...enemy? *Is he still?*

Swallowing heavily, I leave my sentence unfinished and ask something else, my hands shaking slightly. *And if it's more than sleeping with him?*

Remi's eyes bounce wide. *You like him.* It's not a question.

I don't know. I shouldn't.

Says who? Remi combats.

I've always seen him one way, I try to explain to my brother. *How do I change that?*

He lets out a breath, hands on his lap before he casually lifts them again and knocks me on my ass. *Don't you think the man deserves to be seen as he is now, not as he was fifteen years ago?*

Fuck.

And who is Noah King now?

A man who gets under my skin. One who has no problem pushing me around a little when I ask for it. One who held me last night after fucking me and calling me gorgeous. Telling me I'm in his head. Claiming I'm *his*.

Who the fuck is that man? Where did he come from?

I scrub a hand over my face before telling my brother, *I feel lost.* The admission is painful.

Is it his gender?

I pinch my fingers together in a quick *no*. *It's him. He...*

How do I even explain it? He overwhelms me? But not necessarily in a bad way. It's just new. He's *so much*. His presence is big, and he's always been there in the background of my life, needling me without even trying. But now...

Now I can't escape the man. And I'm starting to worry I don't want to.

I need to tell the family, I sign to Remi. Quickly, I add, *About being bisexual. Not...Noah.*

"Now?" he asks aloud.

I nod. It's something I can do. Even if everything else feels so uncertain right now.

Remi gives my arm a squeeze, and we stand. My parents and Jackson are still downstairs in the dining room, talking business, and they look up when the two of us enter.

"Hey," I say, rushing on before I can chicken out. "There's something I need to tell you all."

"Is everything okay?" my mom asks, worry weighing her hands and her expression.

I nod, pulling out a chair and taking a seat at the long dining table. "Yeah, but... Can we call Lawson?"

My parents exchange a brief look. Jackson is the one who pulls out his phone, dialing our brother.

"Jackson?" Lawson says when he answers the call.

"Hey, Law. Colton has something he wants to tell us. You're on speaker."

"Okay?" he says tentatively. My dad interprets for Remi.

I let out a whooshing breath. *Fuck*. Just say it. "Turns out... Uh. I'm bi. Bisexual."

There's a beat of silence in which Remi squeezes my arm again, and then Jackson grunts, nodding as if he expected as much. *What now?*

"Colton dear," my mom says, her hand going to her chest. "You nearly gave me a heart attack. I thought you might be dying."

"No, uh, just bi," I answer, a little dumbfounded.

My dad nods several times. "Huh," is all he says.

"Welcome to the club," Jackson puts in.

"Congratulations, sweetheart," my mom adds. "Does this mean you'll be introducing us to the man who's been leaving bite marks all over your neck?"

"Oh my *God*," I groan, scrubbing my neck harshly, as if that could erase the evidence of Noah's bruises. "No. Nuh-uh. That's not a thing. We're not talking about that."

My mom only smiles, my dad snickering.

"Y'all are the worst," I mutter, even as my chest fills with something that feels suspiciously like warmth.

"Doing all right?" Lawson asks, the first time he's spoken up.

"Yeah," I tell him and the rest of the family. I meet Remi's eye, and he gives me an encouraging smile. "It's been a surprise, and I'm still tryna figure out a few things. But I'm good."

Jackson reaches across the table, giving my hand a squeeze in a show of supremely uncharacteristic affection.

"Shit," I realize. "I forgot about Ash."

"I can give him the news," Jackson offers, to which I nod.

"So," my dad says, slapping the tops of his thighs. "Who's making lunch?"

Conversation starts up again, the lot of us saying goodbye to Lawson even though we'll surely see him this evening, my dad putting in that *enchiladas sound good if anyone would be so inclined*, to which my mom suggests my dad get on it.

And all the while, there's a smile on my face. Maybe I do still have some things to figure out when it comes to a certain farrier here in Darling.

But I couldn't have asked for a better family by my side.

Chapter 28

NOAH

"Check."

I grunt, eyeing the board.

My uncle sits back in his chair, hands folded over his stomach. "Is it serious?"

"Walt," I warn.

"I'm allowed to ask about it," he says primly. "I'm your family. And he's been coming round for a while now."

I shake my head, reaching for my rook before finding a flaw in my plan and setting my hand back on the table. "I shouldn't be surprised you noticed."

He snorts. "No, you shouldn't. You two kept sneaking around like teens. Confident like teens, too, thinking you wouldn't be caught."

"I wasn't trying *not* to get caught," I respond. "I was just...trying to be discreet."

"For whose benefit? Mine?"

I sigh. "Partially," I admit. "But also...for his."

I can feel my uncle's eyes on me, but mine are on the chessboard.

"He's skittish," I explain. "And maybe, at first, it wasn't...anything." At least, I tried to convince myself of such. "But now... I need to go slow."

Walter hums. "So it is serious."

I raise a brow his way, but my uncle only smiles back. "He's Colton Darling," I tell him a little hotly, knowing he's perfectly aware of all that means to me. "Excuse me for taking a minute to come to terms with it myself."

"I'm curious how it happened," my uncle says, waiting patiently on my move. The way he doesn't ask outright tells me he's not going to pry.

But I don't mind telling him the truth. "Pure accident," I say, finally plucking my queen off the board and moving her three spaces over. "I kissed him on accident."

My uncle barks a laugh. "Must've been one hell of an accidental kiss."

I let out a laugh. That it was.

"Checkmate," my uncle says.

I groan, and he chuckles lightly.

After Walter demolishes me in chess, *twice*, I head out to the barn to work on the metal crown. It's nearly finished, and I'm anxious to put the final touches on the piece. The smaller details that will bring it all together.

I flick on the lights and start up the forge before pulling out my phone. Colton's name stares back at me for a long moment as I wonder how the fuck we went from...what we *were* to what we are. Steeling myself, I send him a message while I wait on the forge to heat.

Me: Doing all right?

It doesn't take as long as I'm expecting to hear back. I'm just pulling my tools off the rack when my phone pings.

Colt: Fine.

I hold back my sigh at the perfunctory response, wondering if we've already taken a step back. But then another text comes through.

Colt: I told my family I'm bi.

My brows pop up, something akin to hope settling in my chest right alongside my surprise.

Me: Were they good to you?

Colt: Jesus, I don't get you sometimes.

Colt: Yeah, they took it well.

I release a breath.

Me: That's good.

Colt: You left fucking marks all over me, you dick. My ass looks like a Rorschach.

I bark a laugh, fingers moving swiftly.

Me: Send me a picture.

Colt: Fuck off.

It's only a couple seconds before he adds...

Colt: Hold on.

My pulse beats heavily as I wait. Is he really going to send me a photo of his ass?

I get the rest of my metalworking supplies out, setting everything up on my workspace. The forge is at temperature now, but I wait to start working on the crown, not wanting to miss Colton's message.

Finally, my phone pings.

It *is* a picture. I click to expand it, my breath catching in my throat. Colton's pants and briefs are tugged down on one side, exposing his right ass cheek. Mottled bruises pepper his skin.

Nothing too outrageous. Just small blooms of color I sucked to the surface of his skin.

But just above the marks, visible below the tugged-up hem of Colton's shirt, is my name. *King.* I trail my finger over the letters on the screen, heart pumping viciously.

Me: Gorgeous.

I'm not the least bit surprised by Colton's response, but I laugh all the same.

Colt: Oh, fuck you, you possessive prick.

I am possessive of the man, aren't I? Possessive of his pleasure. Of his pain. Possessive of those marks I left all over his body and the way he looks when his scowl drops and I see the man beneath all that anger, feigned or otherwise.

But I'm not the only one guarding this thing we've stumbled into. And I'm not going to apologize for it. I wouldn't ask him to, either.

Me: Maybe next time some girl who's far too young for me starts flirting, you can show her your ass.

It's a mental image that has me chuckling.

Colton doesn't respond for the longest time, so I give him a prod, wanting him to know I'm teasing. Mostly.

Me: Don't worry. Jealousy looks good on you, little Colt.

He calls, much to my surprise.

"Hello?"

"I wasn't jealous," he spits in greeting. "And she *was* far too young for you."

"That's what I said," I point out, amused. "And *you* invented a girlfriend to get her off my back. What d'you call that?"

"Helping you out," he replies, making me huff a laugh. "Why didn't you tell her to stop?"

Oh, did I hit a nerve?

Not jealous, indeed.

"It was harmless," I answer. "Nothing was going to come of it."

"She didn't know that."

"Did you?" I ask carefully.

He's quiet, not answering.

"Colt... I won't be flirting with anyone else."

"None of my business," he mumbles.

Oh, hell no. "Nuh-uh," I tell him. "You listen and listen good, Colton Darling. What I said the other night? That wasn't a lie. You're mine until you tell me otherwise. So this prickly, indifferent thing you're trying to pull off? Just know I see through it. I see *you*. And I'm telling you I won't be flirting with anyone else. Got it?"

He's breathing hard enough for me to hear. "You're not letting this go, are you?"

"No."

"We're wrong for each other, Noah. We don't fit."

"I disagree."

"And you just know everything, don't you?" he asks, the frustration in his voice directed at himself, I suspect, and not me.

"Hardly," I allow, leaning against my workbench. "There's a lot I don't know. But I'm trusting my gut on this."

"And your gut?" he says, a question.

"Has latched on to you."

He scoffs. "Like a lamprey. I sure have the evidence all over my ass. *And* on my neck. Thanks for that."

"You're welcome."

"Dick," he mutters before sighing. "This is so fucked. I don't even like you."

"Is that so?"

He groans, and my mouth quirks into a smile. "I *am* sorry about the job at Marie's," he says, seemingly out of nowhere, but it's clear he's still harboring guilt over it.

"I know," I tell him softly. "But it won't happen again, will it? We'll be careful moving forward. And we'll talk things over if we have concerns."

"Yeah," he agrees. Hesitantly, he asks, "Will you still advertise?"

I let out a breath I'm positive he can't hear. "If you need me to stop, I will."

My business is stable. I have enough clients, and like Colton said, folks in this town—and even towns over—know me well by now. Sure, I might miss out on the occasional new resident or someone with a brand-new horse looking for a farrier.

But is getting their business worth losing Colton?

The answer to that earlier this year would have been a resounding yes. Because the man wasn't even mine to lose.

Now?

Colton makes a noise in the back of his throat. "No," he says quickly. "You can't just... Don't stop putting out ads because of me."

"It won't bother you?" I ask, surprised.

"Of course it will," he says without venom. "They're terrible. *King this* and *King that. For the royal treatment, go King.* I wanna punch you in the face every time I see one, but..."

"But?" I ask, a smile curving my lips.

"I wanna win fair and square," he says. "If you stop trying, it'll feel like taking candy from a baby. And don't you *dare* bring up the Shoein'. That was *not* an accurate representation of who's the best farrier in this town. You won on a technicality."

I'm grinning outright now. "Did I ever show you my trophy?"

"You did *not* get a trophy," he says, appalled. "The fuck?"

"A kid drew it for me," I tell him. "It's hanging on my fridge."

"Well that's just the fucking worst," Colton grouses. "I can't even be mad about that."

I laugh, and Colton grumbles something I can't quite make out. There's a pressure in my chest as I listen to him on the other end of the line. I rub over my sternum, picturing his hair curling at his neck and the blue fire in his eyes as he complains about the outcome of our *friendly* competition. I picture the bruises on his ass and those on his neck.

I picture my name tattooed across his skin for the rest of his—and my—life.

"What was that noise you just made?" Colton says, his previous ramblings cut off. "Why do you sound so pleased?"

"It's nothing," I lie. "Just a happy memory."

He makes a dubious sound. "What, uh, are you up to right now?"

Apparently, still talking to you.

I keep the thought to myself, not wanting to scare the man off.

"Just getting ready to play around a bit. With my forge," I explain.

There's a brief pause. "The sculptures?"

"Mm."

"What, uh... Why do you do those? Do you sell them?"

"No," I answer. "They're just...for me, I guess."

Another pause. "They're really good. What I've seen of them, at least."

There's that pressure in my chest again. "Thanks, Colt."

He makes a noise like he's allergic to the T-word. I snort a laugh.

"What are you doing today?" I ask in return.

Was it really just this morning that Colton was hightailing it out of here like there was a firecracker in his ass and I was holding the lighter?

"You're gonna laugh," he mutters.

Well, that piques my interest. "I won't," I promise.

He lets out a long, drawn-out sigh. "I'm doing makeup tutorials with my niece. At present, I have one cat-eye, one that's called natural, even though there's a pound of makeup on there, and she did something called contouring that took near an hour and made me look literally no different."

I choke back my laugh.

"You're laughing," he whines.

"I'm not," I say quickly, charmed beyond words. *Fuck*. "Is she waiting on you now?"

"I'm taking a break to wash it all off. And then she'll start again," he says, trying to sound put-out and failing.

"Would you send me a picture?" I ask, already knowing the answer.

"Not a fucking chance in hell, King. And breathe a word of this to anyone, and I'll... I don't know. Kick you in the balls, maybe."

"Wouldn't want that," I mutter around a smile.

He heaves a breath. "I should go."

"Yeah," I agree, the forge waiting behind me. "Hey... How's your ass?"

He pauses. "Pretty sure you already saw for yourself."

I smirk, even as I shake my head. "That's not what I meant."

"Oh," he says, and I can practically see the blush spreading across his face. "Good. Fine. Shut up."

I huff a laugh, and Colton groans.

"See you soon, Colt," I say gently.

"Yeah," he mumbles. "Fuck. This is weird. See ya, Noah."

When Colton clicks off the call, I set my phone down on my workbench and run through possibilities. Would it be so bad if Colton and I were to...date? Our rivalry is known around town, being that we're the only two farriers here, but I'm fairly certain no one save the two of us and our immediate families know of the animosity we've held for each other. I imagine folks would be pleased to see us together.

Is Colton ready for that?

I don't want to keep this a secret forever. It doesn't feel right. Maybe, in the beginning, it was the only way for us to be. I certainly didn't know what we were doing. Didn't even know what I wanted.

But now that this thing between us has become starkly real in a way I never anticipated, staying hidden and sneaking around until the end of time isn't an option. At least, it's not one for me. But Colton is still wary.

Like any colt, he needs an outstretched hand. Encouragement to move forward.

The man would certainly knock me on my ass—or try to—if he heard me making that comparison, but it's an apt one. He's been scared from the start. Like his father told me before I truly understood what he was trying to say, Colton is afraid of asking for the things he wants. The things that *matter*.

Because what if the answer is no?

I won't tell Colton no. Not ever. What he wants from me, he can have.

But until he's ready to ask for it, I need to be the one propelling us forward.

Donning my gloves, I pick up my unfinished crown. A few thorns for balance. Evening primroses that only open at night. A sprinkling of forget-me-nots for the man who refuses to leave my head.

I work on the additions long into the evening. And when I set the finished crown down, a weaving of past and present in one, I'm certain I've made my choice.

Colton goddamn Darling is going to find out what it means to be mine.

Chapter 29

COLTON

"What in the fuck is this?" I mutter, slowing on my way to the sandwich shop.

Noah's truck is idling beside the curb.

I approach slowly, and the passenger side door opens. "Get in," comes Noah's voice.

I peek inside the cab, finding the man waiting for me with an arched eyebrow. "Are you...abducting me?"

"There's a roast beef panini on the seat," Noah says in lieu of explanation. He lets off the brake long enough for the truck to squeak an inch forward. "And technically, you kidnapped me first. In or out, Colt."

He rolls another inch down the street, and I hop into the vehicle, shutting the door after me. "This is coercion," I point out.

"I'm not above a little bribery if it gets me what I want," Noah says, pulling immediately into the lot behind the businesses on this stretch.

I look over at him as he parks. "Quite the ride."

"Eat your sandwich, Colt," Noah says, looking—and sounding—smug. He grabs his own lunch off his lap, peeling back his sandwich wrapper before taking a large bite.

With a grumble, I open up my roast beef panini, groaning at the first mouthful of warm gooey deliciousness. "Fuck, that's good. Don't tell Ash, but Louise makes the best paninis. It's the commercial press."

Noah hums.

"Ash is a damn fine cook, though. We lucked out getting him at the ranch."

I take another blissful bite. *Damn*. That's delicious.

"And look," I say, keeping my mouth mostly closed as I talk, "I'm not gonna thank you for kidnapping me, but this sandwich *is* my favorite, so—"

My words cut off when Noah takes my chin in hand, forcibly directing my face his way. He presses his mouth against mine, licking over my closed lips, and I about bite my tongue.

Leaning back, he looks me in the eyes, his more than a little wild. "Fuck, Colt. You moan the same way eating that sandwich as you do when I fuck you."

"Beg your fucking pardon?" I rasp.

"Is it really that good?"

Noah makes a grab for it, and I pull the sandwich out of reach.

"Maybe you're just that average," I shoot back.

He smirks at me. *Smirks*. "That's not it. Gimme a bite."

"Fuck you," I bark, curling my body to block the last half of the lunch Noah is trying to steal. Never mind the fact that he got it for me in the first place. One does not steal another man's panini.

"Colt," he says in warning.

"No-ah," I warn right back.

His hand lands on my thigh. I freeze as he rather pointedly runs his palm toward my cock. The next second, Noah is snatching the sandwich out of my grip and ripping off a bite with his teeth. I stare at him in shock.

"That was fucking dirty!"

"Mm," he hums with a grin. "Very good."

I swipe my sandwich back. "You absolute dick. Hate you."

He chuckles, a sound that does *not* go to my cock. "I'll buy you another one."

I wait for him to exit the vehicle and follow through on that promise, but he doesn't move. He goes back to eating his own lunch as I glare at him.

"And when, precisely, would that be?" I ask, finishing off my much smaller sandwich.

He shrugs. "Maybe tomorrow. If you're lucky."

I gape at him. "If I'm *lucky?*"

His smile is disarming. One minute, the man is teasing me, albeit good-naturedly. And the next, he's looking at me like...like *he'd* be the lucky one to buy me lunch again tomorrow.

I clear my throat. "Does that mean you're gonna kidnap me again?"

"You could always come easily."

"Usually do around you," I mutter.

Noah barks a laugh, apparently having heard me. "Colt, if you think you've been *easy*, you need to readjust your system of measures. You are the most infuriatingly stubborn man—"

"Am *not*."

He raises an eyebrow. "Stubborn man I've ever met. And pulling you in has been the exact opposite of *easy*."

I squirm as he holds my eye, confused by the wash of disappointment I feel at those words. What? Like I care if Noah thinks I'm too...difficult?

"Colt," the man says, tone far gentler than I would've thought him capable of in the past. He seems to read what's on my mind, because his hand clasps my neck, and he squeezes tight. "I never asked for easy. I don't need it. But if you ever get tired of fighting, it won't change anything. All right?"

He waits as if there's a simple response to that. As if Noah telling me I can be any version of myself around him is a simple fucking thing.

"Come here," he says, not waiting for me to move, simply tugging me in by the back of my neck.

His lips meet mine again, less forceful this time but no less terrifying. There's a stutter in my chest I'm starting to worry is permanent around this man, and Noah only makes it worse when he rumbles low in his throat like I'm the best thing he's ever had the honor of sampling.

When he pulls back, I feel exposed. The same way I did the first time I stripped down in front of him.

"You're having dinner with me and Walter tonight," he says, crumpling our trash into a cohabitating ball.

My indignation wars with...I don't even know what. "Oh, I am, am I?"

He doesn't seem to mind my snarky tone. His lips twitch up, and he answers with a concise, "Mhm."

"And what if I don't want to?" I ask, my throat clicking when I swallow.

"I could always drag you there myself," he says, eyes glimmering with a hopeful edge.

"Do you like reminding me you're bigger than me?" I ask, even though I've come to realize that's not it at all.

"No," he says simply. "What I like is when you let me prove just how much I want you. And how far I'll go to have you."

Fuck.

It takes me a second to get my mouth in working order. "Why? Why *do* you?"

I can't bring myself to say the words *want me*, but Noah clearly understands. He shifts toward me in a way that causes his horseshoe tattoo to flash before his shirt settles. The reminder of all that's stood between us feels like only a whisper of what it once was.

"Do you want an honest answer to that?" he asks.

Jesus, do I?

I look out the windshield for a moment, my heart beating swiftly. Soon enough, I'll leave this truck and get back to work, shaping hooves and shoes to be an equal match. Doing the things I do every day. What follows is the difference.

Before, going back home to the ranch was a given. Spending my evening around my family, heading to bed alone, barring the occasional instance of me finding a woman to keep me company for the night.

I was drifting along my comfortable path, not questioning all I was and all I wanted, even as I knew something was missing from my life. Or, maybe not *missing*, exactly. But I did want companionship that lasted longer than an evening, didn't I? I wanted to find what my brother found with Ash.

Someone to care about me: smooth, jagged parts, and all. Someone to *love* me.

And now, I have...Noah. I have a man who's telling me he wants me around. Who, for some inexplicable reason, went from frowning at me every time I was near to *smiling* like he can't get enough of me. *Me.*

I'm terrified of what that means. Because how can this man be the one I was looking for? How is that possible when he's been under my nose this entire time?

And I simply didn't see him.

So do I want to know why it is that Noah wants *me* when I don't feel remotely worthy of that interest? What have I possibly done other than be cruel and undeserving?

"I don't know," I finally admit. Because if he only likes the thrill… If I'm simply a conquest to him…

I'm not sure I could stand it.

Noah doesn't let me travel down that depressing train of thought for long. "When you're ready," he says, voice calm, "you lemme know."

I nod, the motion feeling jerky. "Am I free now?" I ask, trying to make the words sound light.

"Your kidnapping is over," he confirms. "Just…one thing before you go?"

"What's that?" I ask cautiously.

"Show me again."

A bolt of lust shoots straight down my gut, even as I shake my head. "No fucking way! Look where we are."

Noah makes a point of glancing around. The parking lot has plenty of vehicles, but no one is walking past at the moment. "Looks fine to me."

"Anyone could catch us."

"Would that bother you?" he asks, seeming curious about my answer.

"Yes," I say too quickly, too harshly. "I don't need people seeing my *ass*, Noah."

"And is that the only part that would bother you?" he persists, scooting closer.

My pulse hops.

"I won't let anyone see," he promises, his scent—overlaid with the work we both do—crossing my mental barriers and clouding my brain. Making me think of the last time that scent was surrounding me.

It's the only explanation I have for why I shift around enough for Noah to have access to my right hip. He rumbles his approval, tugging down my jeans, his other hand pulling my shirt out of the way.

I feel like a rabbit—fragile, heart pounding—as Noah's fingers trail over my skin. Mapping out his name.

I was pissed all to hell when I got that tattoo. Pissed at Noah for winning. Pissed about my obsession with the man. Pissed, even, at all the emotions I couldn't name when it came to this *King* I thought I hated. I *did* hate him. For a long while.

But I still got his name tattooed on my ass. It was a point of pride. Of not wanting Noah to see me as weak for backing out.

I don't feel weak now. Even rabbits have a powerful purpose, don't they?

They nourish the wolf.

Noah's fingers dance over me reverently, his soft sound of satisfaction and wonder making me feel like the most powerful being alive.

"Are you done stroking me?" I ask when my cock starts getting interested in the proceedings.

Noah huffs a small laugh, his fingertips skating over me once more before he tugs my pants back into place and lets go of my shirt. "I'd be happy to stroke you again later."

"Not sure your uncle would appreciate that," I note.

He snorts. "Consider it a private dessert. For just you and me."

I swallow roughly. "I needa go."

"Mhm. See you tonight at six-thirty."

I get out of Noah's truck and head to my own on the other side of the lot, not even bothering to tell him *we'll see about that.*

"Oh, God," I groan to myself, walking the short path up to Noah's front door. His *door.* "What am I doing? What is this? Why am I even here?"

"Hopefully to have dinner," Noah says, nearly startling me out of my skin.

"*Fuck.* Don't sneak up on people, King!"

"I was standing here the entire time," he says calmly, holding the door open wide. "Wasn't sure if you were going to get out of your truck."

"Yeah, well... Can you blame me for being...*confused* about all this?"

He closes the door once I pass, a thoughtful expression on his face. "No, I suppose not."

I thrust the bottle of wine I brought at him before tugging off my boots. "I think I figured it out."

"What's that?" he asks, motioning me toward the kitchen. I can smell savory herbs and what I desperately hope is pot roast simmering away inside the room.

"This," I repeat, motioning between us and then encompassing the entirety of his house and my existence. "I fell off Clementine. I fell and hit my head, and all of this is just a dream."

"A good one, I hope," Noah says, setting down the wine before sidling up close and placing his hands on the outsides of my hips. Like that's *normal*. Him and me.

"Fuck," I mutter, keeping my voice down, even though I don't see Walter anywhere. "Don't you think this is weird, Noah? You're being all...polite and shit. And I'm..."

"Spiraling?" he supplies, tucking his face against my neck and unerringly finding the spot that makes my knees want to give out. He sucks on it, and I do wobble, just a bit.

"I'm not *spiraling*," I hiss. "*Christ*. Say something mean. *Please*. Please assure me I'm awake right now 'cause I honestly don't think I can—"

Noah's grip slips up into my hair, and he tugs my head back hard enough to shock me into silence. "Later," he says, voice low and full of promise, "I'm going to find out how much of my cock can fit inside your throat, little Colt. I'm gonna fuck your mouth, wait for the tears to slide down your cheeks, and only then will I give you mercy. You'd like that, wouldn't you? To worship at my feet?"

"*Jesus*," I groan. "That wasn't mean. That was..."

My "ungh" has Noah's hand flexing in my hair. He leans closer, lips at my ear. "Beautiful Colt. How could you possibly think you're not mine?"

With that, Noah's fingers skim through my hair before he lets me go. He steps over to a pot on the stove as I waver for a moment, feeling as if my world has gone hazy.

"Do you like carrots?" he asks.

"What?" I nearly squeak. He can't possibly know about the...*carrot* incident, right?

Noah looks at me over his shoulder, eyebrow raised. "Carrots?" he repeats, holding up a ladle, which has a stout, chopped carrot sitting next to a large piece of potato.

"Oh," I breathe, shaking myself loose. "Yeah, I like 'em. Is that pot roast?"

"Sure is," he says, that satisfied smirk back on his face, as if he *knows* how much I love it. As if he could.

"The best pot roast," Noah's uncle says, walking into the room. His gait is slow, but he seems to manage just fine with his walker. "Recipe was his dad's."

"He'd hunt," Noah fills in for me, pulling plates from the cupboard. "When he could, he'd make the dish with venison. Sometimes elk meat. This one's beef."

"Is that why you have antlers on your arm?" I ask.

"It is," Noah says, pouring glasses of wine. "Have a seat. Dinner's ready."

I sit down in the chair Walter pushes out for me. "Good to see you again, Colton," the man says.

"You, too, sir," I answer, even as it feels surreal to be sitting in this kitchen. In this house. With these men. "Thank you for having me."

"Oh, you're certainly welcome anytime you'd like," Walter says, humming happily when Noah sets a steaming plate of pot roast in front of him. "Isn't that right, Noah?"

Noah's gaze meets mine, the man setting a plate in front of me, too. "That's right," he says, no artifice in his tone, no hint of tease or anything at all but complete and utter honesty. "Anytime."

I let out a breath as Noah takes his seat beside me. For the first time in a very long time, I eat dinner with someone—two someones—who aren't family. One of whom I could have sworn was evil incarnate.

He's not, it turns out. Not even close.

Either that or the devil managed to get me under his thrall, after all. Because I can not, for the life of me, find anything at all to hate about this moment.

Chapter 30

NOAH

"Has Remi always been Deaf?" I ask Colton, the two of us out behind my house, sun beating down our backs as we work on the garden. I hand him another clump of bellflowers, which he takes before wiping his wrist across his forehead. The smudge of dirt he leaves behind has me smiling to myself.

"Yeah," he answers, setting the hearty perennials into the hole he prepared at my instruction. It feels like a small victory, Colton being here with me during the day. We're making progress, slowly but surely. "He got his cochlear implant when he was two. Am I doing this right?"

"Mhm. Now pat the dirt back into place."

"Can't believe I'm planting flowers," Colton mumbles, following my directions and covering the roots of the plant. The simple act has my heart clenching in the best way, memories of my mom doing the same surfacing.

"You're doing very well."

"Oh, fuck off," he says. "Don't humor me."

"So prickly," I murmur, positive he can hear the fondness in my tone. His look of befuddlement confirms it.

He shakes his head, continuing with his task. "He grew up speaking and signing equally. Signing was mostly done around the house, since, you know, our town is pretty tiny. Deaf community of one."

I nod, pulling another clump of bellflowers from its container.

"But it was pretty obvious, even early on, that Remi wasn't the biggest fan of his implant. It's why we all learned ASL. As our mom said, the least we could do was learn Remi's language, the same as he was learning ours. That always stuck with me."

I hum, my respect for Marigold Darling growing.

"The dates," Colton says, sitting back on his haunches. "On your arm. What are they?"

Ah.

I hold out my forearm so he can better see the tattoos. "This is my mom's birthday. And this is my dad's."

"To remember them?" he asks.

"Yes." Although their birthdays aren't the only tattoos I have to remember them by. I trace the thorned crown that fits my forearm like a band. "This was my very first ink."

I got it while I was still grieving, just over half a year after my parents died. It felt fitting at the time. A king devoid of life. It was how I felt inside. Hollow. Stripped down to nothing but thorns and bone.

The flowers came after that. New life. Growth. Repair. The rope a lifeline to pull me back to the person I knew myself to be.

It took a while, but I got there.

"How'd they pass?" Colton asks, his question so very soft.

"Accident," I tell him. "Car crash."

He makes a small sound. "Seems so unfair."

I can't disagree.

"Did you ever go hunting with your dad?" he asks, wiping more dirt across his cheek. At this rate, I'll have to drag him into my shower before he heads home.

Shame.

"Sometimes, yeah," I tell him. "It wasn't just about sport to him. He respected the animals, always. Nothing went to waste."

"Noah," Colton says lightly, gentle laughter bleeding into his tone. "I'm not judging. You do remember my family raises beef for slaughter, right? I know perfectly well you can respect the creatures that are part of our circle of life."

I nod at that, not sure why I thought, even fleetingly, Colton would judge in the first place. I guess I'm used to the reaction from past relationships I've had. And I refuse to believe Colton and I aren't in a relationship.

I just have to get him to admit to it.

"Here," I say, handing over another clump of flowers, the garden's yearly revitalization nearly finished. "Back to work, Darling. Chop chop."

He snorts. "Remind me why I'm here again, letting you boss me around?"

"Because you couldn't resist the allure of my company," I tell him, tossing the empty transplant pots into the wheelbarrow nearby.

When I turn back Colton's way, the look on his face has me holding in a laugh.

"Are you just now realizing you like me?" I ask.

"No," he says quickly. "That can't be it."

"Certainly not."

"Oh, God," he mutters, dirty palms on his knees. The clump of bellflowers waits beside him.

"Take your time," I say, moving to Colton's other side to place the flowers into the hole.

"Oh, God."

My lips twist. "All right?"

"No. This is horrible."

"Is it?" I ask, patting the dirt into place.

"I can't."

Like me, I presume.

"I think you already do."

"So fucking cocky," Colton grumbles. "See? This is why I can't. Because you say shit like that, and you look at me like *that*, and I just wanna..."

I give in to temptation and wipe the dirt off Colton's cheek, my thumb lingering on his skin. "Shut me up?" I guess.

He deflates with his breath. "Well, yeah."

"There are better ways of shutting me up, Colt."

He sits with that as I bring the wheelbarrow back to the barn. I store it in the corner, having just enough time to turn around before Colton storms through the open doorway.

"You're just so..." he starts.

"So what?" I ask calmly as Colton strides my way.

He pushes my chest, dirtying my shirt, and energy zips down my spine.

"So full of it," he spits out. "So...*sure* all the goddamn time."

"And that pisses you off?" I ask, preparing for Colton to come at me again.

He does. Shoving my chest once. Twice. "*Yes*, it pisses me off. Why do you get to have it all figured out, huh?"

"I don't," I assure him. "I'm just not fighting it."

"Not fighting *me*," he amends.

"Is that what you want?" I ask, grabbing his wrists when he makes to shove me again.

He twists out of my hold, blue eyes wild. "I just want…"

The vulnerability in his voice and the way his chest hitches has me closing the distance between us in an instant. I take Colton's throat in my hand, and the man grabs on to my arm, his eyes feathering closed as his mouth pops open.

"This better?" I ask him roughly. "Need me to tell you to stop struggling?"

The sound he lets out is almost wounded. "I don't know what I need, Noah."

"Yes, you do."

His eyes plead with me, his hand grabbing my shirt, the fabric bunching in his grip as his knuckles graze my skin. "I can't."

"You can. Tell me."

He lets out a breath, the hand on my arm flexing. "I need you to kiss me."

The words fall between us, heavy, like stones. They're not what I'm expecting. They're so, *so* much more.

I crash my mouth into Colton's, and the two of us go stumbling, trying to maintain our balance. We don't manage it. One or both of us trips, and then we're on the ground, my elbow hitting hard enough I know it'll bruise but not caring one bit. Colton scrambles over top of me, pinning my wrists to the dirt as he bites my lip.

I'm about to pull my hands free, regain the upper hand, when Colton grinds down on my lap. His breath puffs against me, the groan that follows causing me to still. He does it again, grinding, his mouth urgent against my own in a way I've never felt from him before. Not like this. Not with him taking what he wants from me.

I tug my hands free, and Colton makes a tortured sound, but it turns into pure, aching relief as I hastily shove his pants down his hips. The doors are wide open, but I don't think either of us cares. The only one around is Walt, and I pray he stays inside the house for the next however many minutes.

Colton's kisses are bruising as I work my own pants low enough to take our cocks into my hand. His breath stutters and restarts, his hips moving against me as the both of us grunt.

"Admit it," I rasp out, one hand in his hair to keep him close. "Admit you like me."

"You," he pants.

It takes me a second to understand, but then I give the words freely. "I like you a whole fucking lot, Colt. Tell me you're mine."

"God fucking damn it," he mutters, his head dropped forward, hair concealing his face. I tug it back out of the way, but his eyes won't meet mine. "I want to hate you."

"I know."

"I don't want to hate you at all."

My heart kicks. My cock, too. "I know, baby."

"*Fuck*," he hisses, leaning down to catch my lips again. He rolls against me, the pressure and dry rub of our cocks bordering on uncomfortable. It doesn't matter. I'm so close to the edge, the hint of discomfort only spurs me on.

I stroke us together, Colton raining kisses veering on attack down on me. I accept them all, the air around us scented with fresh earth and citrus, the man on top of me everything I had no idea I wanted.

When he leans back enough to hastily push my shirt up to my chin but not take it off, I falter for all of a second. But then Colton is crying out, his hand planting on my shoulder as his cock kicks against mine, his release coating my stomach and chest.

I follow him like it's my sole purpose in life.

My orgasm is brutal and sharp, and I adjust my grip, my hand squeezing my dick as if I could somehow call back the wreckage. It's no use. I feel like I'm splintering apart, pieces of me coming undone without my permission.

But then there are warm hands bracketing my neck. A face pressed to the side of my own. A familiar scent.

"I didn't want to like you," Colton whispers.

I heave a breath. Another. "I know."

"But I do."

I close my eyes, my hands on Colton's hips holding tight. "So what does that mean for us?"

"I don't know," he says around a sigh, sitting slowly upright. He looks around before popping up and grabbing a mostly clean rag from a table nearby, hiking up his pants as he goes. "I was kinda hoping you could tell me."

"Well," I say, accepting the rag he hands me and wiping my stomach and chest. Much to my surprise, Colton kneels back over me, tucking my cock into my pants. Having him touch me like that, so easily and without a hint of reservation, has my chest turning unbearably warm. "Here's what I think."

Colton sits on the tops of my thighs and motions me on.

I toss the rag to the side before easing up onto my elbows. "We're dating."

"We are?"

"Yes," I answer. "Exclusively."

He bites his lip before nodding.

"And whether or not that means going out in public, I don't care. But I'm not going to lie about us if anyone asks. And

I don't wanna hide." I pause before asking, "Is that all right? 'Cause I can give you more time, but it can't be a forever thing."

He nods again, slower. "No, that's all right."

My surprise must show on my face because Colton puffs out a breath.

"Christ, Noah. It's not that I care what other people think. I just... It's fucking throwing me, okay? You and me. It doesn't make sense to me, so how is it gonna make sense to anyone else?" He scrubs his face before adding, "But it doesn't need to, does it? *Fuck*. How did this even happen? How'd we end up here?"

"Well," I say slowly, rubbing Colton's thighs. "Pretty sure after spending half our lives hating and avoiding one another, kissing and fucking was simply bound to happen."

He stills before snorting a laugh. "Is that right?"

"Mhm. Laws of nature, you know."

"That's fucked up. You're welcome for not coming on your shirt, by the way. *Some* of us have some decency."

Colton is already standing by the time he finishes talking, but I tug on the backs of his knees, and he comes toppling back down, his face landing inches above mine.

"*Jesus.*"

"What are we doing tomorrow?" I ask him, slipping my hands up into his hair so he can't get away.

He attempts a scowl. "I already spent my Saturday doing manual labor for you, and now you want my Sunday, too?"

"Yes."

He scoffs, but he doesn't fight it when I turn his head to the side, mouthing his neck.

"Horses?" he says. "We can...go trail riding?"

I still before nipping his skin, enjoying his responding squirm. "Two horses this time?"

"Yes, two fucking horses," he says, sounding indignant. "You can have five horses if you want. We have plenty."

I hum. "I accept."

"You accept?"

"Your trail riding idea. It's a date."

"Oh my fucking God," he groans, sounding so absolutely disgusted by the word that I laugh.

"What time should I be at the Darling Ranch?"

He huffs another breath. "Eleven? And don't fucking call it the D-word in front of my family. We're not sixteen."

"I should hope not," I say, smoothing my hand down over his ass. "Otherwise, your parents would be horrified by the things I wanna do to you, little Colt."

He whips his head up in alarm. "You're not gonna *tell* them."

I snort, and his face relaxes.

"Not funny, King," he says, grabbing my arms and standing, pulling me with him. "None of my family needs to hear *any* of those details. And call me 'little Colt' while we're there, and you'll find out how it feels to have your nuts retreat up into your body. I'm not even kidding. The jewels will *not* be safe from me."

There's a grin on my face as Colton tugs me out of the barn, rambling all the while about how if his family starts razzing him, I'm not allowed to pitch in. *But* if the jokes are aimed toward any of his brothers, it's fair game. We finish cleaning up the area around the flower beds well before the sun has started retreating in the sky. And when Colton heads home for the night, he does so after allowing me to kiss him so thoroughly we're both starved for air by the time we part.

I'm floating on a cloud all evening and into the morning. So much so that by the time I arrive at the Darling Ranch at precisely eleven and make my way toward the horse barn, there's not even a pinch of worry as I catch sight of the hayloft door shut tight at the top of the structure. I trudge right through the open doorway, intent on finding Colton and leaving the past in the past.

Only Colton isn't here.

He's not in the hallway. Not inside Clementine's stall, although the horse greets me when I offer a pet through the bars. I wait a long damn time for the man to show, and, when he doesn't, I call his phone. There's no answer. And none of the ranch hands passing through have seen him all day.

The more time drags on, the more certain I become that this isn't some prank. It's not a cruel joke. Colton isn't coming.

So I do the only thing I can.

I turn around and trudge right back out of the barn.

Chapter 31

COLTON

"Shit," I mutter, placing a new ice pack over Remi's forehead as my brother curls in on himself.

"Bad one?" Ash asks from the doorway. I nod, and he says, "I'll make some tea."

I appreciate it, but I don't think Remi is resurfacing anytime soon. Not even for Ash's ginger tea.

I card my fingers through my brother's hair as Ash heads down the hall. I wish I could take away Remi's migraines. I wish this wasn't the norm for him.

I hum softly, some song I don't know the name to. Remi doesn't say anything, but his hand squeezes my foot in ac-knowledgement, his head resting in my lap.

When there's a bang from downstairs, like the slam of a door, I pause and listen.

I hear Ash first. "What are you doing here? Is everything okay?"

"Where is he?" comes another voice.

Is that...

I groan, reaching for my phone to check the time, only to realize I don't have my phone on me. Ash says something to Noah I can't make out, and then there's the stomping of footsteps up the stairs.

Noah King comes to a halt in front of the doorway, his eyes sweeping inside and landing directly on me. He steps forward, his hand shoving the door open so hard it knocks into the wall. I wince, knowing the sound won't bother my brother, but he's sure to notice the vibration of it.

"What in the ever-loving fuck, Colt?" Noah demands, more angry than I've seen him in quite some time. "Do you know what time it is? I—"

He cuts off abruptly, his eyes finally having trailed down to Remi. Confusion flashes across his face, followed by some sort of understanding and then immediate remorse.

"Remi has a migraine," I explain calmly. "I didn't realize how much time had passed. I'm sorry."

Noah heaves like a popped balloon. "I..."

"I know I should have called," I go on, keeping my voice low. "But like I said, I didn't realize. If you're staying, could you please wait in my room? It's the one next door."

"Colt, I—"

"I'll be there in a minute," I tell him firmly, not wanting to disturb Remi any more than we already have.

Noah rubs a hand through his hair, the dark strands flying every which way. With a jerk of his head, he walks down the hall, and Ash gives me a worried look from the doorway.

"What was that?" he asks.

"I'll explain later," I say, feeling utterly wrung out. "Would you mind sitting with Remi?"

"Of course," Ash says. "Let me just move the teapot off the stove."

I nod, and when Ash returns a couple minutes later, we swap places. Remi lets out a confused sound when I set his head on a pillow, but then Ash is holding the ice pack over his forehead and rubbing his back, and he goes quiet.

I take a deep breath in the hallway, shaking out my hands. When I push open my partially closed door, I find Noah waiting in front of the window, his fingers intertwined behind his head. He spins to face me, dropping his arms, looking both torn up and frustrated, like his residual anger is still rolling over.

Seeing the man standing inside my bedroom is beyond strange, but I don't focus on that right now. I shut the door and motion to my bed. "Wanna sit?"

Noah plops down, his big frame making the mattress squeak. "I'm sorry," he says immediately. "I shouldn't have rushed in here like that. I just..."

He blows out a breath, and I sit down next to him, feeling incredibly turned around right now. Usually, I'm the one freaking out, and Noah is the one gently talking me down. The reversal is throwing me.

"Guess that answers the question of whether or not your threats to come collect me were real," I point out.

Noah huffs what might be a laugh. "Very real."

He drops his elbows to his knees, looking far smaller than usual.

"Is that normal?" he asks. "The...migraines?"

I nod. "They're bad. I know he doesn't need me to stay by his side through them anymore. He's a grown adult, but..."

"But he's your brother," Noah fills in. "And it helps if you stay, which is why you do it."

The simple fact that he gets it has me blinking fast. *Fuck.*

"You were really upset," I note.

He doesn't say anything to that, only looks down at his hands, which are clasped now between his knees. His leg is bouncing, and it strikes me that he's *seriously* upset. A lot more than I first realized.

"Jesus, Noah. Are you okay?"

He opens his mouth, but nothing comes out.

I'll admit I'm the last to understand whatever the fuck is going on between us. I don't know the *right* way to help him. To soothe him. I'm still learning. Learning who Noah is and who we are together.

But I go on instinct, tugging his shoulder around, not letting him hide because I have a feeling that's what he'd do for me. "Come here."

He doesn't need telling twice. The second I touch him, Noah all but falls over me, taking me down to the mattress and pressing his body over mine. There's nothing remotely sexual about it. It's...possession. Like covering your favorite toy so no one can take it away from you.

His face presses to my neck, his arms on the mattress above my head like he's blocking out the world.

"Okay?" I ask him, my heart beating double-time, my voice muffled in the cocoon I've found myself in.

"Better," he mumbles.

"What happened? You thought I blew you off?"

"Well, yeah," he answers. "But more than that, it was the goddamn barn, Colton. It messed with my head."

I frown. "The barn?"

"I know I overreacted," he goes on. "But I just..."

He lets out a big, huffing breath, and I rub his back. "I'll try my best to call or text next time. I promise. I'm sorry, Noah. I didn't realize..."

I didn't realize he was this serious about me. About *us*. To be nearly shaking as he all but pins me to my bed like he's terrified I'm going to, what—vanish right before his eyes?

"I'm sorry," I say again, a scared Noah scaring *me*.

I don't know when this fucking man switched the narrative, but the last thing I want is to pain Noah King.

Jesus. The Colton of a year ago would have been aghast.

"Not your fault," Noah rumbles against me. "I'm sorry, too. Just...please try not to leave me hanging like that, Colt. I thought, for a minute..."

"You thought what?"

A small tremor wracks through him. "I thought you were going to hurt me again."

I still. "What?"

"When you didn't show up at the barn," he continues, his nose pressed to my neck. "It was the same place, and... You just can't hurt me like that again, Colt. I know we were kids, but—"

"Hold up," I say quickly, trying to see his face. "What are you talking about?"

He rolls his head toward me, blinking. "When I moved here. We were seventeen, and—"

"Whoa, whoa, whoa. Um, what? You moved to town when you were twenty-two."

"No," he says slowly. "I was seventeen, nearly eighteen. Our senior year of high school."

I try to sit up, and Noah lets me, looking as confused as I feel. "What...the actual fuck?"

"Are you serious right now?" Noah asks at an even clip, his voice turning hard. "You know exactly what happened, Colt."

"Um, I most certainly do not. So I'm gonna need you to explain. Like, right now."

He scoffs, scooting away from me. "Senior year," he repeats. "I was the new kid at school. We hit it off talking about horses, and you invited me over. I came."

"And?" I prompt, even as my head reels.

"And you dumped a bucket of horse shit on me through the hayloft door."

I jump off the bed, my pulse racing. "What. The actual fuck, Noah. I did *not*."

"You did."

I let out a laugh that's entirely devoid of humor, and Noah seems to realize I'm serious.

"Are you kidding me?" he says, voice incredibly low. "You don't...*remember* me?"

My breath puffs out, and I bend at the waist. "Start over."

"*Jesus Christ.* I moved to Darling after my parents died. Stayed with Walter and finished out my senior year in school with *you*. I thought I'd met a friend, but instead, you made your thoughts on the matter very clear."

"I don't..." I shake my head. I would've remembered him, wouldn't I?

"I went by Junior back then," Noah says woodenly. "It's what my parents called me because my dad... His name was Noah, too."

Oh, fuck.

Junior.

"You looked different," I wheeze.

"Yeah, well... No tattoos back then. Hair was longer. Hadn't quite grown into my body yet."

I look at Noah now, his expression like stone. It's such a far cry from the kid who showed up for a few months at the end of my senior year, his cheeks rounded and a shy, if not troubled, smile on his face. I get that now. He'd just lost his parents, hadn't he?

He looks nothing like that boy.

"I don't understand," I tell him, my chest aching. "You ignored me."

He scoffs. "After you dumped a pile of horse shit on my head, yeah, I did."

I let out a pained sound. "I didn't. I didn't do that."

"You invited me over," he says.

"Yeah, I remember that part now."

"And when I got here..."

"No," I say again, trying to remember but *knowing* I didn't do what he said. I never would have. He was *nice*. And even if he wasn't, I wouldn't have.

It comes to me in fits and starts.

"Eddie," I realize aloud. "He said you couldn't make it or something? We played video games instead."

Noah's expression doesn't change.

"Jesus, you really think I'd do that?" I ask him, frantic now.

"Like I said, we were just kids."

As if that would excuse it. "Why didn't you *say* anything?"

"When would I have?" he all but shouts, standing up. "When I moved back to town? What for? What good would it have done, Colt? Should I have said something when I *kissed* you? When I jerked you off for the first time?"

"Oh my *God*," I groan, sucking in a breath. "That's why you hated me? Because you thought I..."

I can't even say the words. Bullied him? *Assaulted* him? Noah shakes his head harshly, heading for the door.

"Where are you going?" I ask in alarm, following after him.

He stops so abruptly, I have to pull up short so I don't ram into his chest. "All this time, and you had no fucking clue who I was. Unbelievable."

"That's not fair."

"Isn't it?" he asks, the hurt in his eyes palpable. "I needa go."

"Wait."

Noah opens the door, stomping down the hall as I trail after him.

"Noah, *wait*."

"I need to fucking think, Colt."

"But I didn't *do* anything."

He stops at the foot of the stairs, looking up at me, his jaw set in a tense line as he swallows heavily. "No," he says, voice deceptively soft. "All this time, you didn't do anything, did you? You simply hated me...for me."

I pull in a breath as Noah walks down the hall. Jackson's head peeks out from within the dining room, a frown marring his face, but I barely see it. I follow Noah to the front of the house, watching through the open door as he storms out of sight.

"Fuck," I mutter, pulling in another breath and then another. "Oh fuck, oh fuck."

"Colt," my brother says, his hand landing on my shoulder.

I shake it off, turning and heading for the stairs. I keep my steps light as I make my way back past Remi's room, only pausing for a moment to make sure he's all right. Ash is still with him. I find my phone lying on my nightstand and pluck it up, searching for Eddie's number.

I have no clue if he still has the same one. I haven't talked to the guy in over a decade, not since he moved out of Montana. Luckily, he picks up after the third ring, sounding curious but not unhappy to hear from me.

"Colton Darling? Is that you?"

"Eddie," I say on a gasp. "I need to ask you something."

"Yeah, all right," he says slowly. "What's up?"

I ease out a breath, feeling as if I might just jitter out of my skin. "Back in high school. Senior year. Do you remember a kid named Junior?"

There's a long pause. "Sure, I remember."

I look up at the ceiling as my vision swims. "You told me he didn't show up."

Another pause. Longer this time. "Yeah. I did."

"Did you..." *Ah, God.* "Did you really do that to him?"

I don't even need to spell it out. Eddie sighs, long and low.

"Why?" I ask, my voice catching.

"Christ, Colton. Isn't this ancient history by now?"

"No, Eddie. It's not. I'm dating the man."

He sucks in a harsh breath. *Fuck*, I hope I'm still dating the man.

"Are you serious?" he finally asks.

"Yeah, I am. So explain to me why you did that because..."

Because I'm terrified I might have just lost Noah? Because all of this *shit* that's been between us for the last fifteen years—the tension, the animosity, the goddamn rivalry—was from a conflict that never even happened in the first place?

Because he thinks I hated him. And I did. But I didn't. I never hated *him*. I hated the way he saw me. The way he *refused* to see me at all.

"Eddie," I prompt, the both of us having fallen silent.

"Colton, fuck. I had a thing for you, okay? I liked you back then, and I didn't want new competition hanging around."

What? "I...I never realized."

"No, I know," he says a little harshly. "You were pretty oblivious, man."

I shake my head. Still oblivious, it would seem. "What you did to him... Eddie, that was *so* shitty."

He lets out a sigh. "I know. I do, okay? Believe me. I've regretted it plenty."

That sure doesn't help me now.

"Do you want me to call the guy?" he asks. "I can call and apologize."

"No," I say weakly, knowing it wouldn't do any good. "It doesn't matter."

"For what it's worth, I *am* sorry. And...congratulations, I guess?"

I huff a pained laugh. "Bye, Eddie."

"See ya, Colton."

I hang up, letting my phone fall to my bed. Following it down, I press my face into my sheets and scream.

Chapter 32

NOAH

"Fuck," I say for the hundredth time, my voice getting lost to the wind as I take a turn on my bike. Daphne guides me along the outskirts of town as my mind runs winding paths of its own.

All this time... All this fucking time, and Colton had no clue who I am. Who I *was.*

The kid who moved in with his uncle, grieving and trying to acclimate to a new school months from graduation. One who'd hit it off talking about horses, of all things, with another boy from his class.

One who—hopeful he'd found some *good* in this fucked-up world—found himself learning another reality entirely.

It took me *so long* to forgive Colton for that. For kicking me when I was down. For being heartless and cruel when all I'd been looking for was a friend.

I did forgive him. Eventually. I had to let it go for my own sanity.

Even as I never forgot.

And now, what? It wasn't even him to begin with? He never knew. He never fucking *knew*. His coldness, his aloofness, all those scowls he sent my way for years... It had nothing to do with that prank pulled on me when we were only seventeen years old.

He didn't even remember me.

Fuck.

I take a corner faster than I should and immediately slow down, not wanting to wreck poor Daphne's body once more. I still haven't buffed out the prior damage, even as I fixed the tire.

My heart thumps viciously as I pull off onto the side of the road, needing a goddamn minute to process. My boots hit gravel and dirt, and I pace a few steps away, stopping in front of a railing that overlooks a small ravine. The sun is setting, painting the sky in red and orange and brilliant purple.

"Fuck!" I scream at it all, my voice echoing.

Pulling my helmet off, I do it again.

"God *fucking* damn it! Why him? Of all the goddamn people, why did it have to be *him*?"

The painted clouds offer no answer, the mountains stretching so high I can't see their peaks.

"I trusted him," I say, my voice cracking. "I forgave him, and I chose to trust him again. And you're telling me it was literally for nothing? That I was *so goddamn angry* at him for no *fucking* reason?"

I heave out a breath, my sides aching, my lungs feeling raw.

"It could've been anyone. I could have fallen for *anyone*. Why did you make me need *him*?"

My hands catch the rail, the metal supporting me. It takes me a moment through my blurry vision to see the rack of antlers appear below. Down past the guard rail, between a copse of trees.

The elk seems entirely unconcerned with me, weaving through branches, careful to turn his head just so to make his way through the world. I let out a disbelieving laugh. He's easily the biggest bull I've ever come across in the wild.

"What are you trying to tell me?" I ask, expecting no answer.

The elk looks up at me for a long moment, assessing, before he moves on.

Colton didn't remember me.

What's worse? Finding out the seventeen-year-old Darling boy I thought I knew never existed in the first place?

Or learning the only reason he ever hated me…is because of *me*.

My actions. My anger. Me.

A bugle cuts through the still air, the sound eerie and haunting. The elk cries again, and with it comes the memory of my dad.

"The elk never stops running," he told me once. *"Do you know why?"*

I didn't, not at the time.

"Every creature will find its end, my son. It's inevitable. But we never stop fighting while we're here. Like that elk, we fight because every moment we're on this earth, no matter how big or small, is worth fighting for."

I wipe under my eye as I turn from the railing, my gaze skipping down my arm. Tugging up my sleeve, I look at the antlers inked into my skin. The memory of my dad. Of the lessons he taught me about love and perseverance and *living*. He lived such a big life while he was here. He loved deeply. Me. My mother. He taught me compassion for the world around me. How to see through a lens that's not my own.

And instead of using that compassion, I held a grudge against the one person least deserving of it. I turned the man against me, made him my enemy, and then I fell in love with him despite it all.

What kind of sick, cosmic joke is that?

I pull my helmet back into place, swing my leg over my bike, and get on the road.

The lights are on when I pull into my driveway, the sky around me dark. A quick check of my phone shows several missed calls from Colton. Looking at his name makes the pain in my chest flare anew.

What do I say to him?

So many years of hurt. So much pain that could have been avoided.

Goddamn it.

I walk inside the house, closing the door behind me. "Walt?"

My uncle is in the back room when I find him. He sets down his phone and looks at me over his glasses. "Wondered when you'd be back. It's late."

"Sorry about that," I say, taking a seat across from him. "Did you get dinner figured out all right?"

He scoffs. "I'm perfectly capable of fending for myself, kid. Was more worried about you. Something happen?"

"You could say that," I mumble, scrubbing my face.

"Well?" my uncle asks.

I huff. "Just found out everything I thought I knew was complete bullshit."

"Colton?"

I raise an eyebrow. "How'd you guess?"

"Doesn't take a genius. So what'd you learn?"

My sigh is heavy. Weighted. "That I'm the villain in this story. Not him."

Not that he ever was a villain, not truly. An asshole, sure. But he had a right to be. Because I was an asshole to him.

My uncle makes a disagreeable sound. "You're not a villain, Noah. The world doesn't work like that. There's good, and there's bad, but there's no absolute."

"He's a good guy," I tell my surrogate father. This man who stepped up for me when I had no one else. I appreciate him more than I could possibly say. "He's always been a good guy, Walt, but he wasn't to me. And I thought... I don't know. I thought there was a reason, and I hated him for it. Because I didn't deserve that."

"No, you didn't," my uncle says softly.

"But neither did he."

The sound of crunching gravel has my head swinging toward the front of the house.

"Well," my uncle says, opening his book and nudging up his glasses. "Now's your time to make it right."

"What did you do?" I ask slowly, my heart thumping. "You called him?"

"He was blowing up my phone first," my uncle says, full of sass. "Now get."

Jesus.

I push out of my seat in time to hear the unmistakable sound of Colton's voice ringing loud and clear.

"Noah fucking King! Get your ass out here!"

When I pull open the front door, there he is. Colton Darling, standing only a couple dozen feet in front of me on the lawn. The light from inside the house barely illuminates him, but I can see the pain around the corners of his eyes. And...is that a shoebox under his arm?

"Colt," I start, heading down the porch stairs, an apology poised on my tongue.

The man storms forward before I have a chance to utter a word of it, stopping in front of me and dropping to his knees in the grass.

My breath whooshes from my lungs.

"Now you're gonna listen," Colton says, voice stern. "Because there are some things I needa say."

I nod numbly as he opens the top of the shoebox, tossing it aside. Inside are...pieces of paper?

"What is all this?" I ask, bending down and picking up one of the papers. The words on the clipping are familiar. "Are these...my ads from the newspaper?"

"Shush," Colton says, not answering my question. "You said I didn't remember you, but I *do*. I remember you. And I know exactly who you are. You're the dick who made me strive to be better just so I could say I'm the best farrier in town."

Colton tosses some of the clippings my way, the thin papers fluttering to the grass.

"You're the one who's been under my skin since the very first time I met you. I liked you then, Noah. I did. And I like you now."

He throws another handful of papers angrily.

"You're the guy who's been haunting me for years. *Years*. Don't you get it?"

Colton upends the box, the rest of the clippings falling at my feet, his blue eyes flashing in the limited light.

"Against all goddamn sense and reason, you made me fall brim over boot, Noah King. And now I don't know which way is up unless it's with you."

"Colt..." I say, my voice nearly lost, the vise around my chest so tight it physically hurts.

He shakes his head, dropping the box beside him and pressing his hands together in front of his face. "I'm down on my knees, willingly, because I just got you. I *just* got you, and I can't lose you. I'm *sorry* I didn't recognize your face from back then. I am. But *you*, Noah...the boy who asked to ride horses at my ranch." The sound he makes is wounded. Involuntary. "I know you deep in my bones. And I was so fucking scared of that when you showed back up in town. Because I *saw* that man. I saw you, and you wouldn't see me back."

I drop down in front of Colton before I have the conscious thought to move. I clasp his face in my hands, and he latches on to my wrists, holding tight. "Fuck, Colt. I see you. I do."

"I know that now," he says, his eyes wet. "You see me better than anyone. I don't know why the fuck all of this happened. Maybe in another life we could've been friends from the start. But...we're here now. We made it here. So *please* don't hold it against me, Noah. You look so fucking different than you did then."

My laugh is pained. He's not wrong. I was heavier as a teen. Add on to that the muscle I put on in college and the ink on my skin, and I'm a different person entirely.

"And I swear I didn't do it," he goes on. "I never wanted to turn you away. I never tried to hurt you back then."

I rub my thumbs over Colton's jaw, the prickling against my skin the best sort of pain. "I know," I tell him. Colton was horrified when I recounted what happened. As caught off-guard as me. I know he's telling the truth. "I'm not mad at you, Colt. I'm mad at...everything else. At myself. At Eddie, apparently. At all these fucking years I blamed you when there was no blame to be had. *I'm* sorry. You didn't deserve that."

The noise he lets out is full of confusion. "You're...*not* mad at me?"

"Do you want me to be?" I ask, my hands stroking over his skin. I can't seem to stop myself now that I've started. How did

I ever think this man cold when he's fire and heat beneath my fingertips?

"Well, no," he says. "But *fuck*, King. I'm not used to you not being mad at me."

I let out a breath, skating my palms down to Colton's neck, my thumb rolling gently over the column of his throat. "None of this is your fault. And I'm sorry I left like that. I just... I needed a minute to think so I wouldn't blurt out something I didn't mean. I made assumptions from the start, Colt, and that's on me. All of this is on me. You simply reacted in kind. Forgive me for that?"

"Jesus Christ, you asshole," he says, humor—of all things—in his voice. "If it's not my fault, it's not yours. How could you have known? For all intents and purposes, I was the dick who tossed horse shit on your head. I wouldn't have been friendly either in your place." He lets out a breath, one hand planting on the top of my thigh. His other moves to cover the back of my hand, shifting my grip to the front of his throat. "You hold my reins, King. So please. Tell me where we go from here."

My own throat feels tight as I swallow, the curve of Colton's neck a perfect fit against my palm. "We start over."

His eyes flare wide, alarm there. "What?"

"Shh, little Colt," I soothe, giving his neck a gentle squeeze before letting my fingers drift away. I hold out my hand. "Hi. I'm Noah King from Wyoming, and I'm a farrier. How about you?"

Colton lets out a wet laugh, his hand clasping mine tight. "Colton Darling," he says in kind. "Born and raised here in Montana. I'm a farrier, too. Small fucking world, huh?"

"It really is," I agree, my eyes stinging. "Wanna come inside, Colton Darling? We could talk some. Get to know one another better."

His blue eyes shut for only a second, shoulders heaving in a sigh before he nods. "Yeah. I'd really like that."

Our hands stay clasped for a long moment before we finally let go. Colton grabs the shoebox, and I help him gather the fallen clippings.

"So, uh," I say slowly. "My newspaper ads?"

Colton groans. "Shut it. They were hate mementoes, okay? Doesn't mean a goddamn thing."

"Mhm. Which is why you brought them with you as evidence of your infatuation with me."

Colton's mouth drops open. "I am *not* infatuated, you dick. If anyone's obsessed, it's you. I've got your *name* on my ass, and it isn't enough, is it? Pretty sure if I let you, you'd have an honest-to-God bit in my mouth and a bridle wrapped around my neck."

I still, and Colton looks up slowly, eyes meeting mine.

"No," he says shortly.

"You sure?"

"Fucking positive. Hard pass."

I snort, and Colton shakes his head, shoving the lid on top of the shoebox. "We never speak of this again. *Ever*. It's bad enough I have to be seen with you. No one needs to fucking know about...*this*."

"Sure," I agree easily.

Colton sighs, looking pained. "*Christ*. It doesn't actually bother me being seen with you, okay? Don't go all puppy eyes on me. It's just... We're gonna have to ease my family into it. No one is gonna see this coming."

"Puppy eyes?" I ask, helping Colton to his feet.

"You know you have pretty eyes. Shut up."

Colton groans as I laugh.

"Come on, King," he says, all business as he heads for my front door. "Fill me in on what I missed while I was too busy hating you."

There's a smile on my face as I glance up at the sky. The sunset is long gone, the stars having taken their rightful place, front and center. I wonder about the elk in the woods. If he found what he was running toward.

My dad was right about many things. But especially this.

We fight for what's important in life. Every big moment. Every small.

And love, well. I think that might just be the most important battle worth waging.

Chapter 33

COLTON

"I knew it!" Ash cries, looking around at my assembled family in glee.

My arms fall lax at my sides. "What? No, you didn't."

"I did," he says, slapping Jackson's shoulder. "Tell him I called it."

Jackson shrugs apologetically.

"Fucking hell," I complain. "This isn't news?"

I glance around the room, all of my family—sans Lawson and Wendy—staring back at me and Noah, not a single one of them remotely surprised. Remi's lips twist into a smirk.

"For fuck's sake," I grumble.

Noah rubs the back of my shoulder. "Thank you for taking this in stride," he says like a goddamn gentleman. Since when is Noah fucking King a gentleman?

I give him a glare, but he only smiles at me.

"Well, we're very happy for you both," my mom pipes up. I wait for the catch I know is coming. "Does this mean you two are done sneaking around?"

I groan again, and my mom taps her neck surreptitiously, thinking she's being subtle. Jackson laughs before covering it with a cough.

"Anyways," I say loudly. "Now that you've met my…Noah, we'll be on our way. Say bye."

"Hold on now," my dad says, resituating on the couch and clasping his hands in front of himself. "Noah, you ever seen a castration?"

"We're going," I say loudly, forcibly steering Noah out of the living room to a chorus of cackles.

I hear Ash mutter, "Do not recommend," amidst the noise.

"They seem nice," Noah says, clearly trying not to laugh.

"They're the worst," I assure him. "I love them terribly, but I'd trade any one of them in given the chance. *Eh*. Not Remi."

"Is he doing okay?" Noah asks, the two of us stepping outside onto the porch, the sun high overhead and the breeze blowing gently across the grass behind the house.

I nod, giving him a tug toward the horse barn. "He's better. Sometimes it takes him a day or two to fully recover, but you'd never know it. He's strong."

"I don't doubt that," Noah says.

When we reach the barn, I head toward Clementine's stall. Noah keeps pace with me, looking around curiously, even though I know it's not the first time he's been in here. My horse lifts her head immediately in greeting, waiting for me to open the door before headbutting my chest. I rub along her neck and scratch behind her ears.

"Clem," I say softly as Noah steps up beside me, "you know Noah King. Asshole extraordinaire. Good kisser. Kinda a decent guy."

"Quite the progression there," Noah deadpans.

I snort. "You're only allowed to bite him if he really deserves it, all right?"

Clementine kicks her head up in acknowledgement.

"And, uh," I say, giving Noah a little shove back into the hall. I lead him one stall over, to a bay roan whose tail is swooshing gently. "Noah, this is Hazel. She's been a workhorse for the last ten years, but after several spooks recently, we learned she's losing sight in her left eye. She's retired now and could use someone to care for her."

Noah stills.

"She can still be ridden just fine," I go on, "but a calmer life would be better for her. And I thought, well, if you wanna..."

I trail off, unsure of how to take Noah's silence.

He clears his throat once. Twice. "Are you asking if I want her?"

"Well, yes?" I say, opening the door to Hazel's stall. She's always been a real good girl, gentle and sweet, and I give her a pet along her nose that she accepts readily. "No pressure. But you mentioned how you've never had one of your own 'cause you and Walter don't have the land for it. We have plenty of space here, so—"

My sentence ends abruptly as I'm tugged into a sturdy pair of arms. Noah hugs me so tightly I can feel my bones creak, his hand in my hair not giving me an inch in which to move. His kisses my neck, stubble bristling, and my eyes flutter closed, my hands sliding to his back and hanging on.

Noah fucking King.

"Jesus, Colt," he says, sounding wrecked. "It's too much."

"It's not. We would've handled her care. But if you want her, she's yours. There's no one better for her."

He exhales shakily. "You got me a horse."

"I mean...only kinda."

"You got me a horse, Colt."

"Okay, yeah. I guess I did? Are you accepting her?"

"Fuck," he mutters, tugging my head back and claiming my lips.

I used to want to take my nippers to this man's balls.

What a fool I was.

Noah smacks away from me, looking flustered as he greets Hazel. He holds out his hand, letting her snuffle his palm as his other roams over her head, her neck, her shoulders. The smile on his face breaks my heart, even as it heals something I didn't even realize was fractured.

"Hey there, Hazel," Noah says, his voice quiet. "I'm Noah. You're a sweet thing, aren't you?"

In answer, Hazel kisses Noah's palm, her lips moving in a wiggle.

He lets out a soft laugh, the sound of it making me ache in the best way. "I think we're gonna be good friends. Would you mind me visiting lots?"

Hazel leans her head over Noah's shoulder, her approval clear as day. He holds her for long minutes, rubbing up and down her neck, speaking in a soft, soothing tone.

I step outside the stall, giving them a moment together. Noah finds me sometime later in the tack room, his arms crossing as he leans against the doorjamb. I finish straightening the row of bridles I was putting to rights.

"You realize this means I'll be here quite often," he says.

"Oh, really?" I mutter. "I hadn't, uh, really considered that."

"Uh-huh."

"We could probably go riding together sometimes," I point out. "Lotsa trails here."

"Mhm."

"And if you want, you're welcome to stay for meals. Although I understand if you'd rather share those with Walter."

Noah lets out a breath, walking closer. His hands settle to each side of my body as he braces himself against the table at my back.

"I will want to spend time with Walter," he confirms, and I nod, having figured as much. Noah's uncle is important to him, and I understand that fully. "And I hope you'll join us sometimes?"

I nod again.

"But yes, Colt," he adds. "I'll stay for meals here, too. You know how possessive I am of you. You really thought I wouldn't be all over you the minute you allowed it?"

As if needing to prove his words, he presses me into the table, his thigh wedging between my legs. My mind short-circuits as his hand slips under my waistband, unerringly finding the tattoo on my ass. *Oh, God.*

Noah's lips settle close to my ear. "You're mine, little Colt. Remember? You don't get to run away from me ever again."

"Like I'd want to," I breathe.

"Finally done fighting?"

I huff. "Not by a long shot."

Noah leans back to catch my eye. "Good."

His mouth comes down on mine, and I go boneless. A small corner of my mind wonders... If the past had played out differently, would Noah and I have found our way here sooner? In the end, it doesn't matter. We're here now. And this man I thought I hated is teaching me the ferocity of what it means to *yearn*. To want someone so deeply you'd embed them under your very skin given the chance.

I never wanted, never *needed*, another person the way I need Noah. It's no wonder I was so terrified to let him in. There's no going back from something like this.

When Noah spins me around, I don't even resist. The broad expanse of his body lines my back, and his hand finds its way to the front of my jeans. I groan as he palms my cock, trying to drum up enough brain cells to remember why this is a bad idea but failing spectacularly.

The saddle butter is right here on the table. We could easily...

"Oh, gross!" comes a cry. *Remi.*

Noah and I split apart in an instant, him brushing his hair into place and looking as put together as always while I frantically try to make sure my dick is inside my pants and no other suspect body parts are showing. *Shit.*

"Remi," I manage, turning around to find my brother standing there with both hands in front of his face.

"Gross," he mutters again.

"All clear."

He lets his hands drop, expression that of a disapproving parent. "Have either of y'all seen Lawson?"

"Um, no?" I say. "Been a little busy."

He huffs. "He didn't come home last night, and you *know* that's not like him. I tried texting Laura this morning, but... Oh, hold on. That's Wendy." Remi looks down at his phone, eyes widening. "He...left."

"Wait, what?" I ask. "What does that mean? Left where?"

"He's in Kansas."

Remi's gaze meets mine, and I understand instantly. *Oakley.* Lawson's best friend moved down to Kansas a few years back. Our brother took it hard, and I know he's been having a tough time with the divorce and everything changing, but would he really run off without telling any of us?

"What the fuck," I mutter aloud, trying to look past my own hurt to understand my brother's. "Has it really gotten that bad?"

Remi's pained expression is answer enough.

"Did he take anything?" I ask. "His stuff? He wouldn't just *leave*, right? His daughter is here. His job."

Remi shakes his head, even as he's texting. "His room looked the same, so he couldn't have brought much with him."

"He probably just needs a day or two to recharge," Noah offers, his hand squeezing the back of my neck. "I bet he'll be back before you know it."

"He better be," Remi mutters darkly, shutting off his phone and shoving it in his pocket. "You hear anything, you tell me."

"I will," I promise.

Remi is halfway to the door when he stops. "Oh, and Noah? Welcome to the family. Colton won't ever admit it, but he's incredibly sentimental when it comes to his birthday, so don't forget it. And he can't watch movies where dogs get hurt, so please don't make him try. He's got a very soft center."

"You shit," I gripe, making a grab for my brother.

He backs up out of reach, heading swiftly for the exit. "Leave a sock on the doorknob if you're fucking," he calls, tapping his processor. "That way, I can shut the two of you off."

"The next time Ash makes biscuits," I shout, "I'm eating every single one and leaving you none."

He signs a rather creative retort I'm sort of glad Noah can't understand.

"Rude," I mutter.

"Well that was...interesting," Noah rumbles, stepping up beside me.

I let out a sigh. "You haven't seen anything yet. Trust me."

At that precise moment, Jackson passes in front of the doorway to the barn, a donkey at his heels that he's grumbling to. I nearly bark a laugh, realizing we have *two* ornery asses at the ranch now.

"Was that...the Darling Donkey?" Noah asks of the senile donkey who's terrorized the town for years. The same one who, yes, spends much of his time now on our land, thanks to the dates Jackson feeds him in return for helping save Ash.

I let out a longer sigh this time, shoving Noah back toward the horses. "Come on. Let's saddle up, and I'll tell you the story. You see, once upon a time, there was this stubborn mountain of a man and the most sunshiny newcomer you've ever met."

"More sunshiny than you?" he deadpans.

"Har har," I say, shoving him again.

Noah laughs, and, frankly, it's a sound I could get used to.

With a start, I realize I'll have the chance to do exactly that.

When Noah and I get back to the house after a long day of riding, it's already past dinnertime. With Clementine and Hazel safe in their stalls for the night, Noah calls Walter to check in, and I raid the fridge for provisions. I find what I want quickly and load everything onto a plate.

"He all right?" I ask once Noah is off the phone.

He nods, the two of us heading upstairs. "Yeah. I probably worry about him more than I need to. But I can't really help it."

I get that. I'm the same with my own family. I set the plate of food on my comforter as Noah shuts the bedroom door. "You won't move away from him, will you?"

He looks surprised by my not-quite-question, but it quickly morphs to a sort of cautious concern. "I'm...not sure," he finally says.

"It's fine," I tell him truthfully, taking a seat and motioning for Noah to do the same. I stuff a piece of salami in my mouth, following it with a cracker as he sits beside me. "I'm not asking you to move in, Noah. It's just...it's the sort of thing people think about in situations like ours, isn't it?"

His lips slowly curve into a smile. "In situations like ours."

"Yeah," I say gruffly. "You know...*boyfriends* or whatever."

He looks downright amused at my sour expression. "Does it pain you to say that?"

"You know damn well it does. Number one, I'm thirty-fuck-ing-seven, thank you. The word feels ridiculous. Number two...it's *you*."

"Mhm," Noah hums, sliding our plate out of the way.

"My salami," I mumble.

Noah presses me back onto the mattress, blanketing my body, and I forget all about the food.

"Did you know," he says softly, "that your nose does this thing when you scowl at me. Right here. It crinkles."

"Does not," I mutter, Noah's finger tracing the edge of my nose.

"And your eyes," he goes on, his own blazing softly. Copper amidst earth. "They burn bright blue. But not the same way they once did."

I swallow thickly.

"I used to hate that scowl," he says, not sounding it one bit. "But now, I can just do this."

He drops his face to my neck, brushing his lips over my skin before opening his mouth. The sucking bite is expected, but even so, my head falls lax against my pillow.

"Just like that," he says in a satisfied whisper, eyes taking in my face. "Now you're all pliant and mine."

I want to deny it, but there's no use.

"Would you stay the night?" I ask.

Noah lets out a soft breath like the question pleases him on multiple levels. "Yeah, Colt. You ask, and it's yours."

I've never had someone make that promise before. Let alone follow through on it the way Noah has. And I believe him. I think if I *did* ask him to move in here with me, he'd do it, even as it'd pain him to leave Walter.

I'd never ask for that, though. Never ask Noah to do anything that would hurt him.

I think, when the time comes, I'll find a way to get him to ask me to move in with him. And I'll say yes. Because for as much as I love being close to my family, Walter is the only family Noah has left. And it's not like I'd be far. Not to mention our horses will stay here, so we'd come back all the time. I wouldn't ever truly be gone.

I never wanted to leave this ranch before. Never had a reason to.

But Noah... *Fuck*. I think he's going to be my reason for a lot of things.

"Come on," I say, giving Noah a gentle shove to move back. "Let's finish eating so we can wash up. And then I wanna test out that whole little spoon thing. I was too fuck-drunk last time to truly appreciate it."

"Fuck-drunk?" Noah asks, a chuckle in his tone as he sits upright.

"You know exactly what you do to me, King. Don't pretend otherwise."

"Does that mean you'll be begging for my cock again soon?" he asks, the evil, wonderful man.

"Dunno," I lie. "You might needa make me."

Noah's responding grin is far softer than I expect. "I think," he says, eyes tracing over my face in a way I wouldn't have allowed myself to see before, "that can definitely be arranged."

Maybe things could have been different. But this right here?

No. I wouldn't give this up.

Chapter 34

NOAH

"Thank you so much, Noah," Henrietta says, handing over my usual basket of goat milk products as I stand on the Brookes' front porch. "Quite the heat this summer, don'tcha think?"

I hum my agreement. July has reached some of the hottest temps in recent history. "Can't argue that," I tell her. "See you and Brownie again in six weeks?"

"You bet. Take care now."

I set the basket of goods on the passenger seat of my truck before removing my hat and turning the engine. The scent of bergamot wafts over from the handmade soap Henrietta made, reminding me instantly of Colton. Although his citrusy scent is laced with leather and something far more masculine.

The man himself texted me earlier to let me know he's bringing steak by tonight. Walter, of course, will love him for it. I'll just make sure there's some broccoli on the plate to even things out.

When I arrive home, I put away the basket of goods before hopping in the shower. I scrub the dirt and grit out from under my nails, letting another hard day's work wash down the drain. Despite the roughness of it, there's not a thing I'd change about this life of mine. Aches and pains included.

Especially now that a certain rival farrier isn't a rival at all. No, that man is entirely mine.

A smile graces my lips as I dry off and get dressed. Walter is on the phone when I come down the stairs, likely—by the tone of his voice—talking to Hank Darling. He and the man have developed a rather surprising friendship in the past month, even though my uncle is a good decade older than Colton's dad. I'm glad for it, truth be told. It's gotten Walter out of the house more often lately.

I never expected my relationship with Colton to help my uncle's loneliness. Just another thing I have to thank the man for, I suppose.

I leave my uncle to his phone call and head out the back door. I'm not surprised to find Colton here already, but seeing him crouched down in front of the garden we planted at the end of spring has all sorts of flutters setting off in my stomach and chest.

Colton goddamn Darling.

Wonders never cease.

"Hey," he says, popping up once he sees me. "Steak is in the fridge. Was that goat butter from the Brookes I saw?"

"It was," I confirm, stepping in close.

"Fuck yeah," Colton mutters. He's a big fan of that butter. "By the way, I found another coupon for free entrees in the treasure chest. Figured we could have dinner just the two of us this week. What d'you think?"

"It's a date," I tell him, slipping my fingers into the front pockets of his jeans. A little smile lights Colton's face as I tug him in close. "Caught you."

The glimmer in Colton's eye broadcasts his intent before he moves, but I still find myself grinning as he steps quickly back, forcing me to lose my grip. "Yeah?" he taunts. "You so sure about that?"

"Mm. How about this," I say slowly, taking a step closer as Colton takes an answering step back. "I catch you, I get to have my way with you."

"And if I get away?"

I press my lips tightly together, trying not to smile. "You won't."

Colton's gaze flicks to the side before he turns on his heel and runs. I'm after him in an instant, not the least bit surprised when Colton races toward the barn. He tries to shut the door, but he doesn't get it latched before I'm there, shoving it open again and chasing after him. Colton rounds my work tables, careful not to disturb any of the metal sculptures on top. His eyes are wide, wild. Prey, waiting for the inevitable.

Maybe I am the wolf. But I know for an absolute fact Colton Darling is more than willing to be my meal.

I catch Colton's arm as he tries to skirt away, but he doesn't go down easy. He slips my grip, making for the exit.

He doesn't get there in time.

I grab Colton around his middle, heaving him into the air as he laughs. My own smile is wide as I carry him over to the old blanket we keep in here to save both our asses from the hard ground.

The barn sees a decent amount of action.

I wrestle Colton down onto the blanket, tugging his shirt up as I drop my face to his stomach, bristling his skin. He groans, even as he tries to squirm away. I climb up his body and lock my legs over his hips, tearing his shirt off before he can object.

His chest heaves, all muscle and a smattering of dark hair, the man more rugged than my partners before him.

He's perfect for me in every way.

Colton tries to get the upper hand as I work off his jeans and underwear, and I let him tug my own shirt over my head, not minding the clothing being out of the way. But the second I have Colton's cock at my disposal, I drop low and take him into my mouth, and his fight is gone.

Colton's hips hitch off the blanket, his breath leaving him raggedly as I suck him down.

"Goddamn, Noah."

I hum, sliding upwards and then back down again, working him swiftly with my mouth. Colton lets out a sound of protest when I pop free. But then I'm flipping him onto his knees, and he groans instead.

He smells like soap and man as I drag my tongue down between his ass cheeks.

"Fuck, fuck," Colton mutters.

I swipe over him once. "Beg me for it."

"Aw, fuck you. C'mon."

I chuckle, licking him broadly before easing back. "Beg me, little Colt. Let me hear you."

He huffs out a breath, his ass waiting in front of me, a dusting of hair covering his balls as I roll them in my palm. *King* stares back at me from atop his right ass cheek, permanent and stunning.

"I want your tongue in my ass," he finally says, half huff, half moan. "Please. *Please*, King. Tongue me, and fuck me, and make me come so hard I forget my own fucking name."

I ease out a breath, kissing one ass cheek and then the other. Biting the tattoo. "After you fuck me."

Colton's sharp "*What?*" is lost when I bring my tongue back to his ass. He groans, long and low, the sound petering out into a whispered plea for more and *god fucking damn it, Noah, give me more.*

I tongue him roughly, grabbing the lube we stashed under the blanket and working down my pants. All the while, I make a blubbering mess out of the Darling native under me, the sound of his pleasure the most beautiful music I've ever heard.

Colton hisses out a "Yes" when I slip a finger inside his body. I loosen him with one and then two before flipping him onto his back. He blinks up at me blearily, hitching his knees up, ready and waiting. When I reach behind myself, working the plug out of my ass, those eyes pop wide.

"Noah," he gasps, breath catching when I press the tip of the toy to his own asshole. "What... *Oh, fuck.*"

"Okay?" I check, sliding the plug in slowly.

"Oh, fuck, fuck," he pants. "Yeah. Good."

I nod, watching each flicker of expression that crosses his face. The lust. The confusion. The interest.

When the plug pops in, settling, I grab the lube again. Colton's abs clench as I stroke my hand over his cock, spreading the moisture. I can tell when he gets it. His cock jerks, the man himself sucking in a breath so harsh I worry for his lungs.

I climb over his body, my knees at the sides of his hips. "If you come first," I say, holding the base of his dick as I feel out my position, "I get to fuck you, too."

"Oh, God," he groans, eyes shutting tight for a moment, his hands grabbing onto my thighs. "Jesus Christ, Noah. You realize that's not incentive for me to hold off, right?"

I huff a laugh, bearing down on his cock. Colton's expression shifts to mild concern, and he rubs soothingly over my thigh, even as the rest of his body is held stiffly.

"All right?" he checks.

I nod. It doesn't hurt, not after getting myself ready in the shower. It's just...different.

"Go slow," he says, the words gritted out as I sink an inch lower. "Fuck. Ah, God."

I do take it slow, letting myself acclimate to a cock in my ass for the very first time. But I've done the reverse enough to know what to expect. And using my fingers on myself has helped me get a feel for it.

The moment I bottom out on his cock, Colton lets out a breath.

"Fuck," he says in summation.

I hum, shifting slightly before bringing my hand to the front of his neck. Colton swallows harshly against my palm.

"Caught you," I say again, my voice a whisper.

The look in his eye is one I've seen many times before. It's this man, telling me he's exactly where he wants to be.

His voice is hoarse when he says, "And what are you gonna do with me?"

Ah, now isn't that a question.

"Love you," I say, rolling my hips.

Colton's eyelids flutter.

"Keep you," I add, doing it again, getting accustomed to the motion. Colton's cock is like steel in my ass, and it doesn't take long for me to find a rhythm that has my own cock perking from its half-hard state, the mild discomfort from the initial invasion shifting to something else entirely.

"Noah," he breathes.

"Not let you go," I tack on, keeping my hand around his throat as I ride him. "Never let you go."

"Please," he says, holding my wrist, his other hand digging into my thigh. "*Please.*"

"Little Colt," I murmur affectionately, tightening my grip. His eyes never leave mine. "Come on and paint my ass so I can fill yours."

Colton groans, the vibration of it traveling up through my palm, the man himself locking in pleasure as his cock throbs and releases inside of me. I grind down against him until he's done, the sensation so foreign and yet not the least bit unwelcome, and then I ease off his cock.

"Ah, fuck," Colton says, looking down at the cum coating his dick. His gaze, near reverent, snaps back to mine the moment I give the plug in his ass a gentle pull. "*Aw, fuck.*"

I tug the toy free, wasting no time before hoisting Colton's leg up, positioning myself, and sliding home.

"Holy fucking shit," he groans, neck arching back. "*Noah.*"

"Yeah, baby. Look at you. So fucking perfect on my cock."

"*Jesus Christ.*"

"You like being at my mercy?" I ask, pegging him hard, my arm wrapping around his leg so I can grab ahold of his cock. "You like getting caught and fucked and showing me how goddamn gorgeous you are when you let yourself have all the things you want? All the things you deserve?"

He groans, moving to cover his face, but I don't let him. I grab his hand, planting it against the blanket beside his head.

"You're beautiful, Colton. And you are mine. Let me admire you."

His cock is plumping again, and I stroke him with a firm grip. His eyes hold mine, his body and mine intertwined as I slow my thrusts, making each pass last, letting myself cool down as I work him closer to the edge.

"Say it," I demand.

He sucks in a breath. "Fuck you, you dick. You know I'm yours. I'm skewered on your cock right now, aren't I?"

I bark a laugh, leaning down to bite his lower lip. Colton groans against me. "Not that."

His eyes flutter closed for a moment before opening, bright and blazing blue. "I love you, too, Noah fucking King."

I smile against his lips. "That's better. Are you gonna come for me, too?"

"Fuck. Apparently so."

"Mm. C'mon, then."

Easing back, I shift Colton into the position I know drives him absolutely wild, and then I let loose. He takes over stroking his cock as I grab his hips and slam our bodies together, but his tempo falters quickly. His inhalations become shorter, murmured *fuck, fuck, fucks* leaving his mouth. When he bites his bottom lip hard enough to blanch the skin, his ass clamping down on my dick, I squeeze Colton's hand over his cock and enjoy the fireworks.

Colton paints his chest on a low groan, his muscles spasming around me as he loses his second battle of the night. It's all too easy to follow him over the edge.

I come inside his body, the privilege one I won't ever tire of. For long minutes, we stay exactly that way. Tied together. Catching our breaths. His fingers sifting through my hair as mine stroke where I know my name resides on his ass.

When Colton finally shifts, I ease back.

"Walter's gonna know what we were up to," he says on a sigh.

I huff a laugh, watching my cock leave his body, Colton's expression when I catch his gaze telling me he knows exactly how much I'm enjoying the visual. "Not if we sneak past," I point out.

"Christ. *Fine*. But you're cooking the steaks."

"Deal," I tell him, dropping down on the blanket, not in any hurry to move.

"The butt plug?" he asks.

I snort. "Bought it online. You like it?"

"Mm."

"Got a leash, too," I say. "And you can't be mad because it's not a bridle."

His head rolls my way slowly. "You did *not*."

No, I didn't.

I break into a grin, and Colton shoves my shoulder.

"You fuck," he mutters. "Don't know why I possibly love you."

"I have some idea," I say, my gaze catching on the finished metal crown sitting on a shelf at the edge of the barn. Standing, I walk over to it, my fingers tracing along the top edges, across forget-me-nots and thorns and dainty leaves reminding me of so many summers past.

I pluck the crown up, walking with it back to where Colton is still lying. Going down on my knees, I nestle the crown on top of his head, the size just right, the metal a bright contrast to the brown locks curling around his ears and against the nape of his neck.

A smile touches his lips, his head shifting lazily to see me better. "Do I look like a king?"

I pull in a breath. Outside, the evening sun shines, lighting the barn we're in, and steaks wait for us inside the kitchen. The whole world waits, days stretching out before us. Years, even. But right now, there's only him. My Colt. The man I'll gladly spend the rest of my life fighting for.

Does he look like a king?

I give him a smile, leaning down to press my lips to his.

You look like you could be one.

Epilogue

COLTON

THREE YEARS LATER

"You're going down, King."

"That so?" my rival asks, lips twitching as he stands across from me. "Last I recall, *you* were the one who lost. So I don't think I have anything to worry about."

I scoff. "Won the year before that, though, didn't I?"

Noah only hums.

"All right, gentlemen," Mr. Yadav says with some amusement, cutting into our bickering. "Why don't we start this competition off with a friendly handshake?"

I hold out my hand, and Noah clasps my palm tight.

"I'm not going easy on you," I tell him.

He puckers his lips, blowing me a kiss. "Love you, too, Colt, baby."

I grunt, and Mr. Yadav starts us off. The crowd cheers as Noah and I race toward our respective horses for our fourth annual Darling Shoein'. Noah may talk a big game, but I came prepared this year, and I am *not* losing.

The minutes tick by, the gathered townsfolk murmuring amongst themselves as the sound of our tools fills the air around us. I don't dare look over at what Noah is doing, not wanting to get distracted. We've both forgone the speed approach. Yeah, it gives a good chunk of points. But, in the end, the finished product is what wins the race.

I'm almost surprised when I hear Noah announce he's done, but a quick check his way shows his horse shoed and polished to perfection. Not a problem. He's still not winning.

I finish polishing my horse's final hoof, and then I bring out the big guns. Noah barks a laugh as I pull the ribbons from my bag, his eyes twinkling when I look his way.

"My ace," I tell him, shooting him a wink.

He shakes his head. "You're gonna pay for that later."

Oh, I won't mind that one bit.

I take my time, braiding my horse's mane and tail, incorporating the ribbons like Wendy taught me to. When I stand back, my horse looks as radiant as a damn unicorn. All that's missing is the horn.

"Done," I declare.

There are chuckles and hoots from the crowd, but I catch more than one appreciative comment about my horse's appearance. Damn right. I've got this in the bag.

The members of the town board come out from behind their judges' table to check our work. Noah heads my way, shaking his head again.

"Really, Colt? Braids?"

"Hey, there are no rules against it," I point out. And I checked. Carefully.

"Such a cheater," he mutters, lips in a smile.

"It's all right, King. I know losing is hard, but there'll always be next year."

He crosses his arms, doing his best not to look happy about that. I take the opportunity to appreciate the view. Massive biceps, honed muscles, colorful ink trailing down to his wrists. The horseshoe peeking out from the collar of his shirt. He's wearing his favorite white hat today, but underneath is an artful mess of dark hair, the sides still shaved close in a way I refuse to find sexy. His belt buckle flashes, and his damn jeans mold to him like a well-worn-in glove. Full lips. Dark eyebrows. Eyes the color of flames flickering in a forge.

He's smokin'. Undeniably.

But that's not what has my pulse tripping in my chest every time I look at him. It's the curve of his smile and how freely he offers it. It's how I know what those arms can do. Toss me around a bit, sure. But hold me. Comfort me, when that's not something that's ever been easy for me to ask for. It's how every flicker in his eyes tells me exactly what he sees when he looks at me.

Being coveted by a man like Noah King is potent, to say the least.

"All right, everyone," Mr. Yadav calls, the judges returning to their table. "We're ready to announce the results."

Turns out, everybody loved the ribbons.

Noah groans when I win this year's Shoein', but he holds out his hand and gives me a hearty shake. I grin the entire time, basking in the congratulations from our families and the townsfolk who attended the event.

When we finally get home, Noah, Walter, and I enjoy a dinner of venison stew before Walter retires for the night. I watch him shuffle down the hall with a pinch in my gut.

"He has another appointment on Monday," Noah reminds me, giving the back of my neck a squeeze. "He'll be okay."

"I know," I mutter. Walter is strong. And his physiotherapy appointments have been a big help in managing his ongoing arthritis and scoliosis symptoms. But still. It's not easy seeing the people we love hurt.

Noah tugs me close, pressing his lips to my temple as he breathes me in. "Such a tender heart," he mutters, sounding fond.

"Am not," I grumble, shoving at his stomach. I get a little distracted by the feel of his abs, so the push is halfhearted at best.

Noah huffs a gentle laugh. "It's a good thing, Colt. Are you ready to go?"

"Yeah," I tell him, disentangling from my boyfriend to put the last of our dishes in the washer. "Let's see the fam."

Noah and I take Daphne over to the ranch. Having my arms wrapped around the man as he drives is certainly no hardship, and the motorcycle seats two far easier than a saddle.

It's nearly dark by the time we arrive, parking outside Jackson and Ash's home. Remi has free rein of the ranch house now, the only one of us who hasn't yet moved out. My parents long ago relocated to their own individual cottages beside the main house, seeing as they're divorced for reasons no one quite understands. Jackson had his house built on the property well before Ash came along. I moved out a couple years back to be closer to Noah, our home the one we share with Walter. And Lawson... Well, my oldest brother still lives in Darling, just not at the ranch any longer.

I think Remi will always live here. He doesn't work the ranch in the same way as Jackson or the ranch hands do, but he's responsible for the well-being of nearly every workhorse and petting farm animal here. I'm glad they have him.

And Remi knows he'll always have me, too. I'm just a phone call away should he need me. Although, truth be told, I think I always needed him a little more than he ever needed me.

Funny the things we learn as we grow.

Like the fact that certain hated archnemeses aren't our enemies at all. That they're pretty great, in fact. And that love can be found in the most unexpected of places... If you're willing to fight for it.

As Noah and I round Jackson's house, the bonfire comes into view. It's already roaring, a bottle of Darling Whiskey sitting beside Jackson's Adirondack chair, Ash sipping from a tin cup while atop my brother's lap. Remi is tossing twigs into the fire.

"No Lawson?" I call.

"On the way," Remi says, picking up a bag of marshmallows and chucking it at my chest. I snag it with a grin.

Noah sits in the chair next to mine. It takes me a minute to realize everyone is being suspiciously quiet. The only sounds are the snaps and crackles of the fire.

I stop loading my stick with mallows and look around. "What is it?"

Jackson clears his throat, and Ash appears to be biting his tongue.

"What?" I repeat, looking to Remi next. "What's going on?"

"Did you, uh…happen to see the paper today?" my younger brother asks.

"No," I say slowly. I long ago stopped religiously checking Noah's ads. No need to once I realized the man isn't my competition.

Sure, we're still the only two farriers in town. But there's plenty of work for both of us, and we've stopped arguing about the clients who switch their services.

It doesn't do either of us any good.

"Why?" I ask, looking around again. "What's in the paper?"

Noah clears his throat, and I swing my gaze his way to find him holding out a newspaper.

The fuck?

I take it like it's a live grenade, everyone's silence ramping up my adrenaline. What the hell is going on? Did Noah take out some ad my family thinks will piss me off?

"I kind of expected you to find it earlier," Noah says, which doesn't really tell me anything. "But here we are. Go ahead. Look."

Pulse pounding, I flip the paper open. There's just enough light to see by, so when I find the section of local ads, Noah's jumps out immediately.

"What…the fuck," I whisper, starting to read aloud. "'Noah King of King Farrier Service formally announces his intent to win the…'" I cough roughly and try again. "'…the *hand* of Colton Darling in loving matrimony. After all, everybody knows… Once you go King, you never go back.'"

I laugh around a too-tight chest, the sound more than a little ragged.

"You fucking dick," I growl. "Of course you had to sneak that in there at the end. You're such a—"

My words choke off as Noah slips out of his chair and goes down on one knee in front of me.

"Oh, fuck."

"Colt," the man starts, looking up at me as if I hung the damn moon in the sky. "I've lived in this town for over twenty years. I spent the majority of those hating your guts."

I choke out another laugh, and he smiles ruefully.

"I spent a lot of time not knowing who you really are," he says, letting out the softest of sighs. "And I've spent the last few years loving you more than I ever thought possible. They say there's a fine line between love and hate. That passion of one kind is similar to that of the other. And considering how many times I've wanted to throttle you over the years, maybe there's something to that."

"This is the best proposal," Remi whispers.

I sign a quick, *'Zip it,'* his way.

"But here's the thing," Noah says in stride, taking my hand and rolling it gently between his. "I didn't like hating you one bit, Colton Darling. Loving you has been better in every single way. You asked me once...*why you*. And I've told you a hundred times over, but let me tell you again. I love your passion. Your fight. I love the way you care so deeply and how that's extended to me and mine. I love how soft you are in the mornings and the way your kiss feels like coming home. I've loved every moment of finding out who you are. I love you because, well...because you're you."

My exhale is loud, and Noah squeezes my hand tight.

"I'll keep on loving you regardless, but it would be my absolute honor to share this life as your husband. If you'll allow it, I'll spend the rest of our time on this earth showing you precisely why I fell. You own me, Colt. There's no other. No one else. Marry me?"

I let out a heavy breath as Noah pulls a ring from his pocket. It's metal, that much is clear. But it's not a smooth band like I would have expected. Instead, it's designed to look like rope. Like a twisting band of rope.

"Fuck," I mutter, brushing Noah's hair back, my gaze running over his lips and eyes and his patient, hopeful expression. "King... You couldn't have sprung for the extra ad words? I mean, *Christ*, that would have looked real nice in print."

His mouth curves into a smile, even as he shakes his head. "You shit."

"You love me for it," I say, snatching up the ring. I slip it on my finger, the design a near-perfect match for the rope Noah wears on his skin. "You have me, King. This is just a formality."

"Oh my *God*," Remi groans. "That was the worst yes in history."

"Is it a yes?" Noah checks, even though the man must know...

"Yeah, Noah. It's you for me. Since the moment you bit my lip, I've been yours. Maybe even before that. So yes, I'll goddamn marry you. I'll be your husband. And I'll be so fucking proud to call you my own."

Noah tugs me forward, the man catching me with his lips before I can fall out of my seat. He smells like the forest, the smokey overlay from the fire a perfect match for the person he is inside. His grip is sure, the familiar press of his mouth both soft and demanding. Damn intoxicating.

Maybe love is always like this. I don't know. All I do know is I love this man. That hasn't diminished once in the past three years, and, if anything, it's only grown. Like the garden behind our house and the metal Noah twists into beautiful creations, it's expanded and flourished with each passing day.

Noah King and I were never meant to be enemies. But hell if we weren't meant to be. And I'll fight anyone who tries to tell me otherwise.

Ash whoops as Noah smiles against my lips. Someone claps politely. Jackson, I'm guessing. Remi mumbles something about *still gross, no matter how many times I see it.* And a truck door shuts nearby. Lawson, I'd wager, with his new spouse. My parents will likely show up soon, once someone texts them the news. And Noah and I will tell Clementine and Hazel in the morning, although I'm sure neither of our horses will be surprised.

But for now?

For now, there's my fiancé's lips pressing again and again to mine.

There's his, "I love you, Colt," like a promise whispered strong and true.

There's the way my heart skips and mellows, as it does any time he's near.

And there's my own vow, my hand pressing Noah's palm to the front of my throat. Reins, freely given to the one person I trust never to lead me astray.

Noah fucking King.

Soon, my husband.

But always, forevermore, the man who toppled me brim over boot in love.

The End

About the Author

Information about Emmy Sanders and her complete list of works can be found on her website. Subscribe to her newsletter, join her Facebook reader group, Emmy's Enclave, and connect via email or social media:

www.emmysanders.com

Find online:
www.facebook.com/emmysandersmm
www.instagram.com/emmysandersmm